"You're a good man. You've always been a…"

Carter stopped her by lowering his head to stare at the floor. For one life-changing moment he considered what he was about to do, and then he cast aside his doubts. Her eyes met his, moist and bright, and he pressed his lips to hers. The years separating them melted away as he wrapped his arms around her and deepened the kiss. The contact seemed to last for a blissful eternity and yet was over in an instant.

He dropped his hands, backed away. He felt her breath on his mouth, still warm from their kiss.

"Oh, Carter…" she whispered. She splayed her palm against his chest, her lips parted. He was certain she could feel the racing of his heart.

He blinked hard, swallowed. "This is crazy, Miranda. We can't do this."

Dear Reader,

Places of the heart.

We all have them, and they are different for all of us. But they stir us, comfort us and always call us back. I have been returning every summer to my place of the heart, the high country of North Carolina, three counties of majestic beauty and unrivaled thrills in the highest mountains of the Blue Ridge Parkway.

It was only natural that I would set a trilogy of stories in this unequaled land of forests and mountaintops. This is the debut book of the series, The Cahills of North Carolina. The title is *High Country Cop*, and it is the story of Carter Cahill, chief of police in the small town of Holly River. I hope you enjoy reading about Carter's journey to true love, and I hope you take a moment to think of the place of your heart. Look for Jace Cahill's story next, and following that one, Ava Cahill's.

Happy reading,

Cynthia

PS: I love hearing from readers. You can contact me at cynthoma@aol.com.

HEARTWARMING

High Country Cop

——

Cynthia Thomason

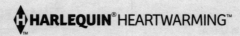

Recycling programs
for this product may
not exist in your area.

ISBN-13: 978-1-335-63350-7

High Country Cop

Copyright © 2018 by Cynthia Thomason

HARLEQUIN®
™ www.Harlequin.com

Printed in U.S.A.

Cynthia Thomason inherited her love of writing from her ancestors. Her father and grandmother both loved to write, and she aspired to continue the legacy. Cynthia studied English and journalism in college, and after a career as a high school English teacher, she began writing novels. She discovered ideas for stories while searching through antiques stores and flea markets and as an auctioneer and estate buyer. Cynthia says every cast-off item from someone's life can ignite the idea for a plot. She writes about small towns, big hearts and happy endings that are earned and not taken for granted. And as far as the legacy is concerned, just ask her son, the magazine journalist, if he believes.

Books by Cynthia Thomason

Harlequin Heartwarming

Rescued by Mr. Wrong
The Bridesmaid Wore Sneakers
A Boy to Remember
Firefly Nights
This Hero for Hire
A Soldier's Promise
Blue Ridge Autumn
Marriage for Keeps
Dilemma at Bayberry Cove

Harlequin Special Edition

His Most Important Win

Harlequin Superromance

The Men of Thorne Island
Your House or Mine?
An Unlikely Match
An Unlikely Father
An Unlikely Family
Deal Me In
Return of the Wild Son

This book is dedicated to all the small-town cops who do so much more for their communities than just enforce the law. And a special thank-you to the folks at Sugar Plum Farms in Plum Tree, North Carolina, for all their advice on growing those magnificent Fraser firs. Any mistakes are mine and not theirs.

CHAPTER ONE

CHIEF OF POLICE Carter Cahill was working the ten-to-six shift in Holly River, North Carolina, on this Friday. Since he had some extra time in the morning, he'd driven the patrol car out to Hidden Creek Road and stopped in to do some chores for his widowed mother. Carter or his younger brother, Jace, stopped by the family home at least once a week to help Cora with her to-do list.

Satisfied that the leaky pipe under the kitchen sink was fixed, Carter headed back to town, the place he'd called home his entire life. When his cell phone rang, and he recognized the number of the police station, he initiated the car speaker. "This is Carter. What is it, Betsy?" he asked his dispatcher.

"Just got a call from a witness who said he could shed some light on last night's break-in at the hardware store, Carter."

"What did he say?"

"That he saw Dale Jefferson's old Jeep in the alley behind the store at the approximate time of the robbery."

Carter wasn't surprised. Whenever a crime was committed in Holly River, Dale's name was usually suggested as the perpetrator, or at least as someone who could provide information. In all fairness, if Dale was guilty of even 20 percent of the crimes he'd been accused of, Carter didn't know when he'd have time to eat or sleep. Dale was adept at not getting caught. He'd served only a handful of short stints in the county lockup though he'd been accused of everything from public intoxication to stealing grapes from the supermarket.

"Who is the witness?" Carter asked Betsy.

"Mitch Calloway."

"Great, another call from Mitch. Maybe someday he'll get over the fact that Dale stole a few chickens from his coop and quit associating the guy with every minor crime in Holly River."

Betsy chuckled. "It's no secret that Mitch, and most everybody else in town, would like to see Dale locked up for good, but you're going to investigate anyway, aren't you?"

"Of course. Since I'm so close to the station, I'll stop on my way and see who's on duty today. I doubt I'll have any trouble at the Jefferson place, but it never hurts to know who my backup is."

He drove the last few blocks of downtown Holly River, an area that was familiar and comforting to Carter. The town consisted of quaint streets, a few mom-and-pop restaurants and shops, churches and a small college. There was one traffic light in the middle of everything, which was conveniently located between the police station and his brother's mountain adventure business, High Mountain Rafting. Carter noticed Jace's SUV in the parking lot of High Mountain and figured Jace was preparing for the day's first white-water trip. In view was Sawtooth Mountain, the highest peak in the Blue Ridge Mountains.

Once he determined that Sam McCall, the department's newest rookie and Carter's friend, was his backup, Carter left the station and headed out in the direction of Laurel Hollow Road, where the Jefferson clan had lived for decades. The fifteen-minute drive to Liggett Mountain would take Cart/

from the charming ambiance of sleepy Holly River to the run-down shabbiness of the cabins outside town. This was the part of the county the tourists never saw and the part where few residents ever managed to escape their poverty.

He smiled when he remembered Betsy's warning when he'd left. "You take care, Carter," she'd said. She was almost like a favorite aunt and never failed to issue similar warnings to all of Holly River's eight officers.

Soon the terraced, manicured lawns of Holly River's more prosperous residents gave way to the scrub and unkempt forested areas of the folks who couldn't afford gardeners, HOA bills or even ride-on lawnmowers. Some of the lawns, if a guy could even call them that, hadn't been tended in years and had been taken over by rocks and dry, sandy soil.

An old tire with a weary-looking mailbox post sprouting from its center marked the Jefferson cabin, the one Dale's parents had left to their oldest son—the one where the younger brother, Lawton, lived now after getting out of prison. Lawton hadn't been as lucky as his older brother. He'd been caught red-handed spray painting the mayor's BMW. That might not have landed him in the state penitentiary, but the twenty pounds of freshly manufactured methamphetamine next to the illegal firearm in the trunk of his old Buick did—for eight years.

As he pulled up the gravel drive to the house, Carter couldn't help noticing how worn out this place was. He didn't know why the battered chimney, looking like a mouth of missing teeth, was still standing. And surely the dozen patches on the shingle roof didn't keep the rain out. Carter figured there wasn't much extra cash for repairs. Dale's part-time jobs barely kept the electricity on and oil heat burning in the winter.

Carter climbed the three steps leading to the narrow porch, careful to avoid the holes in the rotting wood. He knocked on the front door and waited.

After a minute, Dale answered, wearing flannel pants and a T-shirt with the sleeves cut off. He scowled at Carter. "What is it this time, Carter? What're the folks in town accusing me of now?"

As usual Dale appeared unkempt ar

soiled. His dark hair hung in limp strands to his shoulders. His face was gaunt. But strangely he didn't look particularly tired, like he wasn't out at one o'clock in the morning when the robbery supposedly took place. Dale grabbed the loose hair around his shoulders, pulled it all back to his nape and let it fall again. A tall man, he seemed thinner, more wiry than he had in recent years. His eyes were lined in the corners. His cheeks seemed high and hollow. If Dale was practicing a life of thievery again, Carter wondered why he didn't target the supermarket in town. At least his thievery would benefit his health.

"Where were you last night, Dale?" Carter asked. "About one in the morning."

"Just leaving the Muddy Duck," he said. "Came home right after."

"Can anyone verify that?"

"Sure. Sheila was there all night. She'll tell you she and I were the only ones in the bar that late."

Carter nodded. Great. Dale's on-again, off-again girlfriend who tended bar at the Duck would vouch for Dale anytime.

"We have a witness who says your vehicle was parked behind the hardware store on County Road 17."

"That's right," Dale said. "I didn't know there was a law against parking on a county road."

"There's not," Carter said. "But the hardware store is more than a block from the tavern, so why did you park there?"

"I had a good reason. There's a particular lady I didn't want to see the Jeep in the area." He grinned in a conspiratorial man-bonding way that meant nothing to Carter. "You know how it is, Carter. We can't let all our lady friends know what we're up to, now, can we?"

"Did you see any unusual activity along the road when you left?" Carter asked. "Maybe anyone sneaking around the hardware store?"

"Nope. The whole area was as quiet as a church."

Carter took his phone from his pocket and reread an email he'd received that morning from the officer on duty. It contained a list of items gone missing from the store. Only twenty bucks had been left in the cash register by the owner. The full amount had bee stolen, but the store owner, Carl Harker, was moaning as if he'd lost a fortune. One item caught Carter's eye. He looked up at Dale. "You planning to start a garden anytime soon, Dale?"

"That's an odd question, Carter. You know most of my food comes from the Baptist Food Bank. Why would I grow my own?"

"Just curious," Carter said. Hoping Dale would slip up and mention some of the stolen property, Carter wasn't about to tell Dale that a dozen irrigation hoses were taken, along with several pole-type sprinklers. He evaded by saying, "Seems like whoever took this stuff is planning to cultivate a crop in a major way."

"Wouldn't be me, Carter. I got enough work on my hands with my chickens and them goats out back."

"Mind if I have a look around your place just the same?"

"You have a warrant, Carter?"

He didn't, and by the time he requested one from the county judge, if Dale was the proud owner of a new sprinkling system, the evidence would be nowhere to be found. "I'll come back with a warrant if I need one, but for now I'll just keep my eyes open for any new crops going in," he said.

Dale leaned against his door frame. "You know how it is...folks around here are always cultivating one thing or another, always waiting for a bumper crop." He gave Carter another grin. "Is there anything else?"

"I think I'll have a word with Lawton. Is he here?"

Dale jutted his thumb toward the back of the house. "He just got some company. The two of them are in the backyard discussing something, but I don't suppose it will bother them if you interrupt. Besides, you know the person who showed up this morning out of the blue."

Carter carefully maneuvered the steps to the ground. "I'll just go around back, then. And Dale..."

"Yeah?"

"I'm not forgetting that you were within a block of the robbery last night. So if you remember anything, even the smallest detail that might help us out, you give me a call."

"You know I would, Carter..."

When hell freezes over... Carter thought.

Anything else Dale might have said was muffled by the closing of the door.

Now, who could be visiting Lawton? Carter wondered as he walked around the cabin. He'd been released from prison just two weeks ago, and Carter hadn't heard that he'd made any friends or renewed acquaintances in town. In fact, Lawton hadn't even been seen in town, except for a visit to the grocery store. Maybe his parole officer was here. Or someone from one of the church groups. Or maybe...

He stopped dead at the corner of the rear exterior wall of the cabin. Lawton sat on a rickety old bench beside a young woman—a woman whose posture and size and shape were so familiar to Carter that the breath was trapped in his lungs.

It couldn't be Miranda. She didn't have a reason to come back to Holly River. Her daddy was dead. Her mother had moved to a condo in Hickory. True, she'd been raised a Jefferson. Her family had lived for a few generations in these hills just like her cousins Dale and Lawton and their parents had. But Miranda hadn't been able to wait to get away and make a life for herself. No matter whom she hurt in the process.

Her family had lived for years here on Liggett Mountain in a cabin slightly better than her cousins'. Still the more fortunate Jeffersons had struggled on one income brought in by Miranda's father, Warren. Carter couldn't take his eyes off the woman on the bench. Finally he released the breath he'd been holding. No, it wasn't Miranda Jefferson, or Miranda Larson now. His Miranda…funny how that phrase popped back into his mind after so many years…had light brown hair. This woman's shoulder-length waves had streaks of blond. He blinked hard. A successful woman could afford to change her hair color, couldn't she?

Rooted to the ground, Carter continued to stare at the back of the woman's head. Surely he would know if he was anywhere near Miranda, even today after fourteen years. Back then, when they'd graduated from high school, the electricity had seemed to buzz around them. Their connection had been that strong, that heated.

"Are you a real policeman?"

The question came from Carter's left. He

hadn't even been aware that another person was in the yard, an obvious mistake for a cop who was investigating a crime. He should have known. His head snapped to the left where he saw a little girl sitting on a tree stump, an electronic device of some kind in her hands. She had large round eyes, like Donny Larson's, and sandy-colored curly hair like Donny's. She was a miniature, feminine version of the man Carter once called his best friend.

"Ah, yeah, I'm real," he said.

"Is someone in trouble?" the child asked.

"No, nothing like that." Carter now knew without turning back to stare at the woman that Miranda Jefferson was sitting next to Lawton. Where else would this little girl look-alike of Donny Larson have come from?

But he did turn back and found Miranda's gaze locked on his, her fathomless blue eyes just like always—slightly wary, questioning everything but now with a mother's natural protectiveness.

"Carter…" The word fell from her lips without thought, seemingly without effort.

He moved toward her, his legs wooden,

his heart pounding. *Get a grip, Cahill*, he said to himself. *It's not like you didn't know this could happen. It's not like you haven't dreamed about it. Miranda still has kin in this area.*

"Miranda…how? When did you get back? What are you doing here?" Stupid questions, but maybe the fact that he was a cop would make him look less stunned, more in control.

If anything, she was more beautiful than when she was a teenager. This new, mature woman, a few pounds heavier than the thin, athletic cheerleader who'd made the sun come up every morning for Carter, had filled out, toned up as if she worked out. Gone was the long hair she always wore in a ponytail, replaced with a modern shoulder-length cut and color that framed her face in a loose, casual style that didn't look salon-made, but probably was.

Miranda stood. He quickly appraised her white blouse, dark-colored slacks and sensible black pumps. No, this woman was not the mountain girl he fell in love with years ago. This woman was sophisticated, confident and, he'd heard, really good at her job. Her bottom lip quivered slightly. Well, maybe not so confident after all.

"Who is this, Mommy?"

The little girl had walked over and now stood next to her mother.

"This is an old friend of mine," Miranda said. "Carter Cahill. Carter, this is my daughter, Emily."

"Hi, Emily," Carter said to the child, whose glitter-covered sneakers twinkled in the sunlight. She looked to be about nine or ten, perfect timing for her to be Donny Larson's.

"Did you come to see cousin Lawton?" Emily asked. "He didn't do anything wrong. He's out of jail now."

"I know that, and I don't think he did anything wrong. I'm just here to ask a few questions."

Lawton came around the bench and stood next to Miranda. In jeans and a T-shirt, he showed the effects of incarceration. Pale skin, slightly sunken eyes, a general demeanor of insecurity. His hair, the same brown as his brother's, had been cut recently. Carter heard the prison system did that for soon-to-be ex-cons.

"What kind of questions?" Lawton asked.

Carter explained about the robbery and the fact that Dale's Jeep had been in the vicinity.

"Then you should talk to Dale," Miranda said defensively.

"I did, but I've got to cover all the bases."

Miranda straightened her back. "You can't think that Lawton, released just two weeks ago, would commit a crime? He learned his lesson, Carter. And he doesn't even have a driver's license, so why would he be driving Dale's vehicle?"

"I hope that's true," Carter said. "But Carl Harker is missing some inventory and a bit of cash. Somebody took those things." He turned to look at Lawton. "Just to satisfy my curiosity, where were you at one o'clock this morning?"

"In bed, sleeping." Lawton frowned. "Unfortunately I don't have a witness, so you'll have to take my word for it." He glanced at his cousin as if expecting her to vouch for him.

"I see things haven't changed a bit around here," Miranda said. "A crime is committed and the cops immediately run out here to question the Jefferson boys."

"I told you," Carter said. "Dale's Jeep…"

"I heard you. *Dale's* Jeep. Not Lawton's. Law doesn't even own a vehicle."

"Mommy, why are you mad?"

Miranda took a deep breath, looked down at her daughter. "I'm not mad, honey. You know we came here to help cousin Lawton." She switched a stern gaze to Carter. "And it looks like he needs our help already on our first day in town."

"I haven't accused anyone, Miranda," Carter said.

"It's just a matter of time, like always," she responded.

Carter flinched. She wasn't being fair.

"Lawton paid his debt to this town," she said. "Now he's trying to make a clean start, and I'm here to see that he gets all the support he needs." She reached in her purse and drew out a business card. "I'm not here just as his cousin." Handing the card to Carter, she said, "I'm an official representative of the North Carolina social services department. We help ex-convicts start over, providing them with housing if necessary, assisting in finding a job, offering moral support."

"That's fine," Carter said. "I hope Lawton is completely rehabilitated." Turning to Lawton, Carter added, "I wish you the best, Lawton." He stuck out his hand. After a moment Lawton shook it and mumbled a half-hearted thank-you.

"How long are you staying?" Carter asked Miranda.

"As long as I need to before getting Emily back to Durham in time for school in the fall. I'm on paid leave."

"I'm sure Lawton appreciates your help." There being nothing left to say and certainly no evidence upon which to accuse either Jefferson man, Carter turned to leave.

He was almost to his patrol car when Miranda caught up to him. "Carter, wait."

He stopped, crossed his arms over his chest. When he turned back to Miranda, she looked more like the girl he'd known. Young and hopeful, and ready to stand up for anyone who needed it. He steeled himself to accept more criticism from her. "You don't have to caution me about Lawton, Miranda. I realize I was the one who arrested him eight years ago, but that doesn't mean I'm out to get him now."

She nodded. "I know that. I'm sorry if I seemed defensive back there, but Lawton's having a hard time."

Carter sighed with relief. At least Miranda wasn't going to continue her attack on his motives for coming out here.

"The people in this town don't want him here, and they've made that perfectly clear," she added. "But he has no place else to go. This is his home…" She paused and stared forlornly at the run-down cabin. "…such as it is."

"He'll be fine," Carter said. "As long as he stays out of trouble. But it might be a good idea if he kept a low profile for a while. People in this town don't easily forget."

"I know that's true," she said, giving him a look that was suddenly sad and somehow personal at the same time. "You've got to understand, Carter, I can't forget what Law and I were to each other growing up. Sometimes I felt he was the only friend I had… until high school anyway. And I know he felt the same about me. He's my cousin, but back then he was more like a brother to me."

The sadness left her eyes, replaced by the same determination he'd seen in the backyard. "I'm going to do all I can for him. I owe him, Carter."

"That's fine, Miranda," Carter said. "You help him all you can, but take one word of advice. Keep your distance from Dale."

"I'm not afraid of Dale," she said. "He's family. I know he's crossed the line a few times, but he's also had some bad luck."

Carter didn't want to argue, although he didn't blame Dale's choices on bad luck. Dale's life now was a result of bad decisions, greed and resentment. He touched the brim of his hat. "Whatever you say. I suppose we might run into each other while you're here. Small town, you know."

"Yeah, we probably will." She looked down at the gravel under her shoes, then raised her gaze to meet his and said, "I heard about your wife, the miscarriages she had, Carter. I'm so sorry. I wanted to reach out to you, but, you understand…"

"Sure. She left me five years ago. I like to think of it as history." He attempted a smile but knew he failed at the effort. "I've got to go, Miranda. There's somebody around here who has a shed full of items that should go back to the hardware store outside of town, and I've got to find him." He got into the car, but before rolling up the window, he said, "Nice seeing you again." He left the Jefferson property without even glancing in his rearview mirror. Seeing Miranda again had been like a knife slicing into his gut. He'd do well to think about the day ahead of him, not the years in his past.

CHAPTER TWO

DRIVING THE NARROW roads of Liggett Mountain was difficult anytime but seemed especially more so when Miranda left her cousin's place. Her hands, tight on the steering wheel, still trembled. Her head felt dizzy, her senses alert to any unusual stimuli. Was it the elevation? Five thousand feet into the clouds could alter anyone's well-being, but Miranda was a mountain girl, so she knew the height wasn't to blame for how she was feeling.

Seeing Carter had unnerved her. The road twisted and curved, and Miranda followed it, mindful of the rocky shoulder that didn't do much to prevent an unwary motorist from going off the road and plunging straight down. Still, sharp in her mind was the image of Carter's face, now even stronger and more self-assured than when he'd played fullback on the high school football team. Then his boyish face and mussed brown hair had turned lots of heads. His shoulders were still as broad, his back still straight. He'd been a hero back then to the folks who followed high school football. As a police officer, he probably was now, too.

"Does Daddy know that Carter man?"

Miranda pulled her thoughts into the present moment and turned toward her daughter. "What? Yes, Daddy knew Carter. We were all friends in high school."

"Daddy thinks he's dead."

Miranda narrowed her eyes at Emily. "No, honey, he couldn't think that." But she knew her daughter well enough to understand that when she said something, even something that didn't seem to make sense, the idea came from a place deep in her overactive and clever brain. "Why would you say that, Em?"

Emily slid her finger across the screen of her smartphone, looking at pictures she'd taken at Lawton's cabin. "We were at Grandma June's one time and Daddy said that you guys would still be married if it hadn't been for the ghost of Carter Cahill." She looked over at Miranda. "I don't believe in ghosts, but I guess Daddy does. Anyway, I'll tell him that Carter isn't dead."

Miranda's first inclination was to be angry with Donny for speaking so carelessly, but then she remembered Emily's recent habit of listening at keyholes. "Did Daddy say that when you were in the room with him and Grandma?"

"No, I just heard it, that's all." She returned to staring at the pictures, enlarging each one on the screen. "He'll be happy that Carter isn't dead, won't he?"

"What you heard about the ghost is an expression that people use sometimes to talk about another person. Daddy didn't think Carter was dead. He was just making a point."

"What point? Does he think Carter is scary? I didn't think he was very friendly, but he's not scary."

"No, Daddy didn't think that either." Miranda sighed. "I told you we were all good friends at one time. It's complicated, honey."

"I get it. You're not going to tell me."

"Not right now. All you need to know is that Daddy and Carter used to be on the football team together, but they had a falling-out. You know what that means?"

Emily nodded. "Like LeeAnn and me do sometimes."

"Exactly."

"Was it over you?"

Oh, boy. "It was over several different things," Miranda evaded. "Men argue just like everyone else, like you and I do sometimes. But deep down I think they could be friends again."

"They should have a sit-down like you and I do when we argue. Then it would all be over."

Nearing the bottom of the mountain, Miranda changed the subject. "Did you get any good pictures?"

"Yes. One I want to print out and put in a frame. There's a bunny in it. I wish you had brought our printer."

Thank goodness they were back to minor complaints and a world of bunnies. "We can go to Boone and stop at the office supply store. They can print the photo for you."

Satisfied for the moment, Emily put her head back and watched the town out her window. Miranda wondered what she thought of the quaint beauty of the mostly century-old buildings, the green area where concerts were held in the summer, the vibrant green holly that dripped from nearly every hanging pot on the sidewalk lights.

Though she'd been glad to get away from Liggett Mountain, Miranda missed the town, the security of it, the sameness, the way a teenage girl could walk among the large oaks and maple trees and imagine a better life for herself. And while she walked, she pictured herself in love for the rest of her life with the hero of the football team.

But so much had happened. Miranda's father, who, like many men in the area, worked at the Cahill paper mill, had died as a result of it. Carter's father, Raymond Cahill, had influenced everyone's lives. Miranda had used a sudden influx of guilt money from Raymond's payout to enroll in a university. Now she'd been gone fourteen years and the town belonged to those who'd stayed behind, like Carter. This was his town. He protected it and guarded it, but even amid the soothing comfort of home, tragedy had found him, not once but three times with a series of miscarriages, and he'd suffered. In their own ways, they all had.

BETSY GREETED CARTER when he walked into police headquarters. "Did you find the missing stuff from the hardware store?" she asked. "And did Dale Jefferson behave himself?"

"No, I didn't find it, and considering it's Dale we're talking about, I'd say he was mostly civil."

"Carl Harker has called three times this morning to see how you're coming with the case."

Carter strode by the counter where Betsy acted as receptionist and dispatcher for the department, picked up his messages and said, "Tell Carl not to call again. We'll call him when we know anything."

She snickered. "Like he'll pay attention to that… Did you see Lawton?"

"He was there. He claimed he didn't know anything about the break-in, and I believe him." Carter debated telling Betsy about the other person who was at the Jefferson cabin. Mentioning Miranda might cause a stir in town, but he had to tell someone, and Betsy had known Miranda when she lived here. "You'll never guess who was at the Jefferson place when I got there," he said, thinking he sounded casual enough.

Betsy shuffled some papers that probably didn't need shuffling. "Miranda Jefferson, now Larson, is my guess," she said.

So much for remaining casual. "How did you know that? Miranda just got to town this morning."

"I ran into Lucy Dillingham at the grocery store. As you know, she runs the new B&B. She told me that this nice young lady and her daughter had checked in and then took off to go somewhere. When she said the lady's name was Miranda, I assumed her destination was Liggett Mountain."

Carter tucked his messages into his shirt pocket. "Well, you're right. It was Miranda. She works for the department of social services, and I suppose now she's helping to acclimate our town's latest ex-con."

"You can't say Lawton doesn't need the help," Betsy said. "It's not like anybody welcomed him back with open arms." She shook her head. "I always say we have the nicest people in Holly River, and it's basically true, but you throw one poor soul into the mix that folks don't want here, and their claim to kindness seems to fly out the window."

"Lawton went to prison because he deserved to," Carter said, sounding a bit too defensive. "I caught him destroying property at the mayor's office. Good grief, Betsy, he burned down the wooden sculpture of the river elk that had been in front of city hall for fifty years. And that doesn't even take into account the illegal rifle and twenty pounds of methamphetamine in his trunk— drugs he manufactured in his own shed."

"I know all that," Betsy said. "But I still have a soft spot in my heart for that boy." Betsy had known many of the young folks in town back then, and Carter suspected she had a soft spot for most of them. "I don't think he would have turned out so bad if he hadn't been under Dale's influence. When their momma and daddy up and left them, Lawton was just a lost soul. He had no one to follow besides Dale."

"A lost soul who was going to sell meth to our high school kids." Carter sighed. "And who knows what he'd planned to do with that weapon. I agree with you about one thing, Betsy. Dale was always the instigator. You know I've investigated him several times, but he's always managed to weasel out of every jam...*weasel* being the operative word."

Betsy smiled, tapped a pencil on her desk blotter. "I see you managed to change the subject, Chief."

"What subject? We were talking about the Jeffersons."

"True enough, but we started out talking about Miranda Jefferson and we got sidetracked."

"Miranda Larson, remember?" Carter said, disliking the bitterness in his voice.

"How was it seeing her again?"

There weren't many relationships in Holly River that Betsy Moynahan didn't know about. Before she became dispatcher for the police department, she worked as a secretary in the high school's administrative office. She knew when anyone was absent and why, when anyone skipped school and what kids were on a path to matrimony. She always said she believed Carter Cahill and

Miranda Jefferson were on a fast track to a wedding march.

"It was fine," Carter said. "No problem." He paused, knowing he couldn't lie to Betsy. "It was strange, actually. She's changed. More sophisticated, sure of herself. I guess life with Donny is working out for her."

Betsy peered up at him over her glasses. "Don't you keep up with the goings-on in people's lives, Carter?"

"Not if I don't have to."

"Miranda and Donny are divorced."

"They are?" Carter grabbed hold of the edge of the counter to steady himself against what seemed like a tilting office floor.

"About three years now. I thought I told you."

"Well, you didn't."

"Wouldn't have mattered anyway. You've said often enough that you don't like gossip in the office, and you especially don't want to hear about a certain high school sweetheart."

"How come you know this and my mother doesn't?" Carter asked.

"Oh, Cora knows. I suppose she kept it to

herself because she didn't want to bring up old hurts. But now that Miranda's back…"

"She's not back," Carter said more forcefully than he'd intended. "She's here to help Lawton, and then I figure she'll go home to Durham. There's no reason to get all riled up."

"I'm not riled up. I was just doing some simple math. You're single. Miranda's single. Why, anyone can put one and one together."

"Don't you have some work to do?" He nodded at the papers on her counter. "Shouldn't those be filed or something?" He started to walk away but stopped and turned back to her. "And where's Sam McCall?"

"He's out on patrol," Betsy said with a grin. "I'll get him for you if you want."

"I'll get him myself." Carter went into his office and called Sam's cell phone number. He just might need a beer tonight with his newest friend—the rookie cop who didn't know anything about his history with Miranda Jefferson.

CARTER HAD WORKED long and hard to forget Miranda, to never again think of her ready natural smile—a smile that warmed a room in the dead of winter. He steeled himself over the years to never think of her glossy brown hair and the ponytail that trailed down her back. And he tried most of all to forget the way he felt when she touched him, the way she made his senses tingle, his heartbeat race. Sure, he'd been just a kid, but what they'd had seemed so real. Until the day everything changed. Carter lay his head back against his office chair and closed his eyes. There was no fighting it today. He was going to remember all of it.

Fourteen years earlier...

"CARTER, I NEED TO talk to you."

Miranda hadn't even come to the front door of his house. She'd stood outside in the yard until someone noticed her and told Carter she was there. He'd come out right away, reminded her that they were going to a movie later, but sure, if she wanted to talk now, that was okay with him.

They'd sat on a bench in his mother's yellow daisy garden. He'd taken her hand as he'd done since their second date, two years before. "You didn't need to come all the way out here," he said. "You could have called."

"No. This can't be said over the phone."

That was the first inkling he'd had that something was wrong, that his life might be about to change forever. The summer sun was bright and warm, and their future had seemed so perfect that day. Carter was going off to college on a full football scholarship. Miranda was getting a job and staying home, waiting for him to return for vacations. He'd promised her that if she wanted to go to college when he graduated and they were married, they'd find a way. She wasn't overjoyed with the decision but had agreed to wait.

"I've made a decision," she said.

"Okay, but why so serious?"

"I'm using part of the money from the paper mill to enroll in NC State. I requested a fast admission report, and I got it. I'm accepted for the fall term."

That damn money. From the moment his father had issued the check to the Jefferson family, it had felt like a barrier between him and Miranda. Not that Miranda's mother didn't deserve it. Warren Jefferson *had died six months ago from a lung disease associated with his work around the chloride tanks at the paper mill Carter's father owned. Warren had known the risks, signed a release of liability and taken the position because it paid more. Other men had done the same thing with no ill effects. But Warren had gotten sick, could no longer work, and the family had lived on disability for years. Raymond Cahill's "blood money," as Miranda called it, had avoided a long and costly lawsuit—and probably helped Raymond sleep at night.*

Carter tried to remain calm as Miranda gathered her thoughts for what she was about to say. This didn't have to be bad news. He'd known Miranda wanted to go to college. Why shouldn't she use some of the money to accomplish her goal? They could still make it work.

"My mother is moving to Hickory to be near her sister," Miranda said. "We've found her a condominium there where she'll be comfortable."

"You're moving?" Carter had said. It was only a couple of hours away, but the barrier kept growing.

"Mama wants to leave Holly River," Miranda said. *"And the truth is, I do, too. It was okay when Daddy was still alive, but now... Both Mama and I need a fresh start away from the memories."* Her voice shook. *"There has been so much grieving, and Mama doesn't seem to be snapping out of it. She sits in a chair all day long just looking out a window. I think in some part of her mind she believes Daddy is coming home.*

"In her lucid moments, she's bitter, Carter. She blames your father even though Daddy signed that release form. Legal papers don't take away my mama's sadness. She hates the Cahills. I know it doesn't make sense..."

Carter released her hand. He'd stared for long moments at the tree line at the perimeter of his mother's garden where the apple orchard started. *"I guess I understand that,"* he'd finally said. *"But Miranda, you know I'm not my father."* How many times had he said that over the years? He was so sick of apologizing for Raymond. *"I suffered with you when your father died."*

"I know that, but it's not just Mama's feelings about your family. Your father doesn't

approve of me, of us. You know it's true. I'm a Jefferson from Liggett Mountain. You're a Cahill. Your ancestors built this town."

Carter couldn't deny the differences between them, but to him, the differences didn't matter. "Do you think I give a darn about my father's narrow-minded prejudice?"

"I know you don't, but the animosity is there, thick as mountain fog. It's only going to get worse. What kind of a future could you and I build together if your daddy was constantly sabotaging us?"

"I wouldn't let him do that," Carter had said.

"I know you would try, but Carter, your father is a strong and determined man." She paused, and he tried to think of something to counter what he'd known to be true. After a moment she said, "And Carter, this is a chance for me. I didn't want to take money from your father from the beginning, but that check is giving my mama and me a new start. I need to get away from Holly River, the memories of my daddy's illness. It's so connected with your family, with...you. I can't see any better use for it than as an investment in my future."

"Funny," he'd snapped at her. *"I thought I was your future."* She hadn't said anything to that.

"So, what are you saying, Miranda? You want us to break up?"

"I think we need some time away from each other to let the feelings heal. I love you, but every time I look at you, I remember the way my family was torn apart. Maybe sometime if we want to try to make a go of it again..."

"No." He'd been hurting, and the hurt was quickly turning to anger. *"I'm not going away to college hanging on to the memory of a girl who* might *want to see me again. This is it, Miranda. It's either over or it isn't, from this moment."* He'd taken a chance that day by calling her bluff, but he wasn't going to give her an escape.

She'd stood, moved away from the bench. *"I'm sorry, Carter, but we're not kids anymore. We have to face the reality of who we are, the responsibilities we have. I'm so grateful for everything you've meant to me, but..."*

"I get it, Miranda. It's fine. Just go."

She'd gotten in her car and driven away.

Carter remembered not eating or sleeping for days, but then he took an accounting of his life and made some changes. Two months after the breakup, he met Lainey Roberts at college. She was sweet and understanding, and he'd fallen hard for her. Maybe he wasn't emotionally ready for that kind of commitment again, but he committed himself to Lainey anyway because that's the kind of guy he'd always been—steady, faithful, needing to be needed by someone he could love. They made plans, decided to marry and have children. For a while his future seemed bright.

And then he lost her, too, and Carter had to take another accounting of his life. This time he accepted that he wasn't going to dive into another relationship again. He wouldn't risk that kind of hurt a third time. He would dedicate himself to his work and living down the unsavory reputation Raymond Cahill had left in the town of Holly River when he died. It was enough for Carter.

CHAPTER THREE

BY THE TIME Miranda pulled into the parking lot for the Hummingbird Inn, she had
calmed enough to think about the duties that
lay ahead of her. She had to unpack two suitcases, prepare a lunch for her and Emily and
talk to Mrs. Dillingham about a reasonable
rate for renting the guest cottage behind the
bed-and-breakfast, rather than just a room.

Miranda had learned a great deal about
the inn in just the few minutes she'd taken
to register. The bed-and-breakfast had been
open only a year. The Dillinghams had purchased an old wooden dormitory once used
by a local college and turned it into a cozy
and warm space for Holly River tourists.
The cottage where Miranda was staying was
a separate building that had recently been
renovated from the original gardening shed.
The colors of the cottage matched the crisp
white-and-black exterior of the main build-

ing. Emily had fallen in love with the small porch with a swing hanging from the ceiling.

"I want to stay here, Mom," Emily had said when she first saw the cottage.

Miranda found Mrs. Dillingham in the living room arranging a bouquet of fresh flowers.

"Hello, dear," Mrs. Dillingham said. "How was your morning?"

"Fine, thanks. I'm going to be staying in Holly River for as much as a few weeks," she said. "I like your cottage, and I'm wondering what weekly rate we might agree upon."

"Let's see." Mrs. Dillingham smiled down at Emily. "How do you like it here?"

"It's really nice," Emily said.

"Okay, then." Lifting her gaze to Miranda, Mrs. Dillingham said, "How does two hundred per week sound?"

"Like a very generous offer," Miranda quickly agreed. "Thank you so much. I can start putting our things in there. Afterward, I'll make a trip to the grocery to stock the kitchenette. I really appreciate this, Mrs. Dillingham."

"Call me Lucy," the woman said. "After all, we'll practically be family living so closely together."

Miranda reached for her credit card. "Let me go ahead and pay for the first week now, Lucy."

The innkeeper set down her pruning shears and walked to the registration counter. She concluded the payment by writing the name *Larson* in the guest book, and thanked Miranda for paying in advance. "By the way, dear, I know you used to live in Holly River. It must be nice to return to such a charming town and visit with old friends."

Knowing it was quite probable that Lucy Dillingham had never driven into the hills and hollows of Liggett Mountain, Miranda kept her response vague. "I doubt many of my friends from high school still live here. I've been gone for fourteen years, and unfortunately I didn't keep in touch with my girlfriends from back then."

"What about family?" Lucy asked.

Miranda explained that her mother lived in Hickory and her father was deceased. Lucy reacted with customary expressions of sympathy.

"Then what brings you back here? Business perhaps?"

Durham was certainly different from Holly River, Miranda thought. In Durham no one would think to ask her why she was staying in one location for any length of time. But it appeared that Holly River curiosity had infected Lucy Dillingham as it had everyone else in town for as long as Miranda could remember. "In a way," she answered. "I do have a family member in the area who needs my help."

"Oh, my. Anyone I might know?"

"I don't think so…"

"It's our cousin, Lawton Jefferson," Emily said. "Do you know Lawton?"

Lucy's expression changed from one of mild curiosity to something bordering shock and disgust. "You're a Jefferson?" she asked.

"I used to be," Miranda said. "Larson is my married name, though I'm divorced now."

"Is Lawton related to Dale Jefferson?"

Obviously Dale's reputation had traveled even to this insulated place of charm and gentility in the middle of Holly River. "Yes, they're brothers."

"I see. I've never personally met either

one of the men. I understand Dale lives on Liggett Mountain."

"So does cousin Lawton," Emily said. "He just got out of prison and moved in with cousin Dale."

Lucy slowly shook her head and mumbled, "Hmm…"

Miranda patted the top of Emily's head. "That's enough for now, Em. We've interrupted Mrs. Dillingham's chores enough, and we've got our own chores to do."

They started for the exit, but Lucy stopped them with one last question. "Will you be going to Liggett Mountain to help out or will your cousin be coming here?"

Miranda understood the deeper meaning of the question. *Please don't allow your cousin to come on this property.* "I doubt he'll come here," she said. "I've already been to the mountain today. It's like going home to me. Liggett Mountain is where I grew up."

Lucy picked up a feather duster and flicked it over the top of her counter. "Have a nice day," she said with cold indifference. Miranda figured she was probably regretting the two-hundred-dollar deal she'd made.

When all their chores had been accomplished and the cottage was stocked with food, Miranda felt too lazy to fix dinner. "How would you like to go to the River Café, Em?" she asked her daughter. "If I remember correctly, there's an ice-cream store right next door."

"I want to," Emily said, reaching for her hairbrush. "I'm going to look nice in case we run into someone we know."

"We only know a handful of people, Em, so I wouldn't count on it."

Emily began enumerating Holly River citizens on her fingers. "We know lots of people. Lucy, Lawton and Dale, and that policeman who talked about Daddy. We might see one of them."

Miranda marveled at her daughter's enthusiasm. There was one person on that list who brought an old familiar tremble to Miranda's chest, and she certainly couldn't admit to the rush of complicated feelings, even to herself.

THE RIVER CAFÉ was crowded this Friday evening. Tourists occupied the outside seating area, where they could enjoy the live entertainment. Tonight Carter's younger brother, Jace, was strumming his guitar for Diana Melton, who could carry a sweet tune about as well as anyone in town. Tourists who wanted a quieter environment sat at the interior dining room tables. Holly River locals gathered at pub tables in the bar, where Carter had agreed to meet his friend Sam McCall after work. Carter glanced at his watch. Sam was late, so he ordered a beer and waited.

Sam came striding in a little after seven and settled on the other of the bar-height stools across from Carter. "Been waiting long?"

"Only as long as it takes to down one beer," Carter said.

"You're one ahead of me," Sam said. He raised a finger to get the waitress's attention and indicated he'd like two more brews brought to the table. Then he leaned across the table and said, "You see that waitress?"

"Yeah," Carter said. "I ordered my first beer from her. Don't think I've seen her in the café before, though."

"She's cute, don't you think?"

"Sure. She's cute."

"Her name's Allie and she's new in town. She waited on me Wednesday night."

Carter studied the waitress as she lingered at the bar for the bartender to fill the order. Pretty brown hair, a cute figure that showed to its full advantage in the River Café T-shirt. "So that's why you wanted to come to this place," Carter said.

"Good deduction. That's why you're the chief, Chief."

Allie brought the drinks and set them on the table. "Hey, I remember you," she said to Sam. "Wednesday night, right?"

Sam grinned in that easy, redheaded way a lot of Irish guys seemed blessed with at birth. Sam was the hottest bachelor in town. He attracted many local girls, but this was the first time Carter could remember his seriously returning the attention.

Sam leaned back, kept the grin in place and said, "Say, that's a pretty ring you're wearing."

Allie held up both hands. "I'm not wearing a ring."

Sam laughed. "I know you're not. Works every time. It's an old cop trick."

She returned his smile with her own flirty

grin. "Somehow you don't seem like an old cop."

Allie sauntered off to another table, and Carter just stared at his friend. "Could you be more obvious, Sam?"

"Sure could. Watch and learn, my friend. By the end of the night I'll have her phone number and a few other vital statistics."

Despite the troubling day Carter was having, he smiled. "I don't doubt it."

"What's with the glum expression you were wearing when I got to the table, Carter? You seem down even for you. Something bothering you?"

Carter didn't appreciate the unwarranted critique of his personality. He didn't think he was a downer. He was just a guy who'd loved and lost not one woman, but two, and was working his way back up the emotional ladder. And despite that ladder appearing to reach into the clouds sometimes, Carter thought he was doing darn well. "Not especially," he said.

"Then my guess is, this has something to do with an old girlfriend coming to town," Sam said.

Carter settled back on his stool and shook

his head. "Oh, for heaven's sake. Who told you about that?"

"Betsy. She was practically bursting with the news. Says she remembers you and this Miranda gal from when you were both in high school." Sam took a long sip of beer. "Kinda romantic if you ask me—two sweethearts meeting up again. Bet you were prom king and queen."

Carter wasn't about to admit that Sam was only half-right. Miranda had been beaten for the crown by a Winchester Ridge debutante. Carter's dance with the queen had seemed like the longest of his life while Miranda stood on the side and watched.

"Who cares about all that high school stuff?" he said. "It's all history."

"Got it. And it's apparent you want to change the subject."

Sam opened his menu, though like most of the locals he probably had it memorized by now. "What do you feel like eating, Carter?"

"Fried chicken," Carter said. "Won't be as good as Mom's, but it won't be bad either."

"Make that two." Sam called Allie to the table, shamelessly flirted with her again and ordered. Then his gaze wandered to the door, and Carter's soon followed—and lingered. Miranda and her daughter had obviously picked the River Café for their supper. What were the odds of that since the tourist guide showed at least ten restaurants in town?

Sam chuckled. "I see you noticed her, too, Carter. Tells me your cold heart is at least still beating."

"That's her," Carter said in a hoarse whisper. "That's Miranda and her kid."

"She has a kid?" Sam looked genuinely disappointed. "Is she married?"

"Didn't Betsy tell you that, as well? She was married, but she's divorced now."

"Oh, that's cool, then. You want them to join us?" Sam started to raise his hand.

"No. That's the last thing I want. I'm already wishing I was at any other restaurant in town but this one."

A restaurant employee led Miranda and Emily to a table in the bar. They were almost seated when Emily noticed Carter. "What did I tell you, Mom? There's the policeman, so we did see someone we know." She scurried over to Carter's table. "Hello, what's your name again?"

Carter told her.

"Hi, Mr. Cahill. Mom told me to call you by your last name. She said it's respectful."

"Hello." Carter fumbled for words. He didn't know how to talk to little girls, especially Donny Larson's kid. "Your name's Emily, right?" Of course he knew, but asking filled in a short block of time.

"Emily Larson," she said.

Carter introduced her to Sam, who complimented her Minions T-shirt. There was no female too young for Sam to charm.

Carter thought she'd go back to her table, but she stood there with her little hands gripping the side of his table. For a moment, Carter had a flashback of other small hands that might have reached out for him if Fate had dealt him a better future. "Is there something else you wanted, Emily?"

She hunched one shoulder. "No."

Miranda ambled over to the table. "Come on, Em. We have our own table and you're bothering Officer Cahill and his friend."

True enough. Carter was bothered plenty by this whole situation, not the least of which was trying to make conversation with this miniature mirror image of Donny Larson.

It didn't help that seeing Miranda with her child only brought back memories of his own losses.

And then there was the way Miranda looked. A bit tired perhaps, but that didn't detract from her put-together style. She'd changed from her business attire when they'd met at the Jefferson cabin. Her hair was casual, pulled back in a short ponytail reminding him of...well, reminding him of lots of things. She had on a pair of jeans that fit just right and a pink blouse tucked in to flatter her figure. Her thick bangs fell just short of her eyes, drawing attention to their unforgettable blue color.

"Imagine this," Miranda said. "Running into you twice in one day, and me only arriving in town this morning." Her voice quavered slightly as if the coincidence was not one she relished.

Carter introduced her to Sam, who thankfully kept his limited knowledge of their past to himself. "How did things go after I left Liggett Mountain?" Carter asked.

"Okay, I guess," she said. "Lawton needs so much help. Because of your profession, you probably know that a lot of men released from prison are incarcerated again within three years."

Sure he knew that. It was his business to know.

"Readjusting to life is difficult for many of the released," she added.

Yeah, and Lawton would no doubt experience the most trouble with trying to settle back into the town he'd violated so badly. "You'll have to excuse me for saying this," Carter said. "But maybe Lawton would have been better off to move to another location instead of back in with his brother. That combination spelled trouble before, and it could again."

Miranda started to respond, but Sam cut in. "I thought you said Lawton before. You're talking about Lawton Jefferson?"

Miranda stood a little straighter, as if she was used to hearing negative reactions to the mention of her cousin's name. "He's my cousin," she said. "I've come to town to help him get settled."

Sam looked at Carter. "Lawton's not in trouble already, is he?"

"No, he's not."

"Then why did you go visit the Jefferson boys today?"

"You know why." Carter was becoming irritated and aware that anything he said might set Miranda off again. "Dale's vehicle was seen in the alley behind the hardware store. I went up to Liggett to get some answers from him. My visit had nothing to do with Lawton."

"Lawton didn't do anything wrong," Emily said in defense of her cousin.

Miranda put a hand on Emily's shoulder. "Carter knows that, honey." Addressing Sam, she said, "It's my opinion that Lawton's biggest obstacle to finding success after release might be the way the people in this town have selective memories. They remember why Lawton was arrested, but conveniently forget that he served his time."

Sam gave Carter a look that said he was aware that this was a prickly situation.

Feeling the need to smooth things over, Carter said, "If there's anything my guys or I can do to help…"

Miranda's shoulders relaxed. "Thank you, Carter. I know we got off on the wrong foot this morning, but I truly believe you mean that."

Did he? Was he willing to help Lawton adapt to life in Holly River? Not really. He'd more likely help him move to the next town over in the county.

Allie delivered two chicken dinners to the table, and Miranda started to lead Emily away.

"Nice meeting you," Sam called. When they were out of hearing range, he said, "She might have a hard time convincing folks in this town that Lawton is completely rehabilitated. I've only been here a couple of years, and even I know that Dale Jefferson's name comes up every time we have a crime. And it's common knowledge that Lawton was his sidekick for a number of years."

Carter nodded. "I know, but the Miranda I remember is a determined female, so unless she's changed, she'll do everything she can to make Lawton's transition an easy one."

Sam had already dug into his chicken dinner. Watching Miranda across the room, Carter didn't know how the greasy Southern meal would settle in his knotted stomach.

CARTER TOOK TWO days off every week, Wednesday and Sunday, a luxury not afforded to many small-town police chiefs. He took Sunday because things were usually quiet in town with tourists leaving the High Country mountains at the end of their weekends. He took Wednesday because the tourists hadn't yet started to invade the mountains for cooling weekend trips. Normally Carter went out to Snowy Mountain Farm on Wednesdays to see if he could help out.

Carter's maternal grandfather had started Snowy Mountain five decades earlier, and it was still a small but thriving business. The Cahill family grew five thousand Fraser fir trees every year, selling most of the crop to North Carolina residents who came back year after year to pick out their holiday trees. Christmas-tree choosing and cutting had become longtime traditions to the folks who kept coming back, and Carter's mother, Cora, who'd inherited the farm from her father, always welcomed families with hot cocoa, a visit with Santa himself and a full gift shop of ornaments and trinkets.

In truth, it took a lot of work and effort

to have five thousand trees ready every November. Trees had to be shaped and sheared several times during the year, and a new crop had to be planted from seeds, fertilized and watched over until the trees were full grown in seven years' time. When a family picked out a tree, few realized that the Cahill family had been nurturing the heavenly scented beauty for almost a decade.

Holding the gasoline-powered shears, Carter turned to his brother, Jace, who had shown up today to help. Carter took sound-deafening headphones from over his ears. "How many part-time guys do we have working today, Jace?" Carter asked.

"Five. I could use a couple more hands, but if we keep on schedule, we should have a hundred trees pruned by the end of the day."

"That will be a good start to the summer cuts." He turned his attention to a lone figure winding her way up the hillside between stands of trees. "Here comes Mama. Hope she's got coffee in that thermos."

"Me, too," Jace said.

When Cora Cahill reached her boys, she sat on a block of wood the men used to trim the highest tree levels and took a deep breath. "That climb up the hill gets harder every time." Smiling, she added, "But I've brought coffee, so I'm sure you boys will think that my nearly killing myself was worth it."

"Why don't you use the golf cart?" Carter asked, taking the cup she offered.

"And admit I can't make it up here?" Cora said. "Never. Put down the shears for a minute, fellas, so I can catch up with you."

"We're coming to dinner tonight, Mama. You can catch up then."

"Yeah, but some topics can't wait."

Using this opening to mention a subject that had been on his mind, Carter said, "Yeah, like why you aren't going with Aunt Dolly to Hawaii."

Cora frowned. "Did she tell you that? Dolly's always had loose lips."

"She told me you canceled on her. But she said you didn't tell her why. What's going on?"

"I did so tell her. I said it just wasn't a good time for a vacation, that's all. A woman's allowed to change her mind."

Carter narrowed his eyes. "You were looking forward to this vacation, so why don't you reschedule? Pick a winter month when you'll really enjoy the sunshine."

"I have my reasons for making this decision," Cora said. "So enough about this trip. I want to ask you some questions, Carter."

Carter and Jace sipped their coffees, knowing the futility of stopping Cora once she wanted to be heard.

"Okay, since neither of you will ask, I'll tell you." Staring at Carter, she said, "Miranda Jefferson is back in town, but I'll bet you already knew that."

Carter sighed. *Here we go.* "I knew. I ran into her at Dale Jefferson's place. She's doing some social work for Lawton, trying to make his leaving prison easier."

"How did that go?" Cora asked.

Trying to steer the conversation away from his mother's obvious interest, Carter said, "How did Lawton's integration go? Don't know, Mama. He just got back to town."

"That's not what I mean, and you know it," Cora snapped. "How did it go between you and Miranda?"

"Fine. Why wouldn't it? Miranda and I called it quits years ago. A lot has happened since then."

"Most definitely has," Cora said. "But now you're both single, and you never know…"

"Mama, stop it. I'm not interested in Miranda. You know that, and I'd appreciate it if the gossip in this town turned to other subjects. Miranda and I might end up friends after all this time, but I even have my doubts about that."

Cora looked at a spot halfway down the hillside. "I'm not so sure," she said.

Carter turned his attention to the narrow path his mother had just taken up the hill. Sure enough, another woman was coming up to join them. The blond streaks in her brown hair glinted in the sunlight as she progressed up the incline slowly and carefully. "What the heck is she doing here?" Carter asked. "And why would she attempt this trip in those stupid sandals? She probably hasn't climbed a mountain in years."

CHAPTER FOUR

CARTER NEVER HAD a chance to satisfy his curiosity about Miranda's arrival on Snowy Mountain. His mother had shot up from her wood block seat and was rushing down the path to meet her. "Miranda, oh, honey, it's so good to see you."

Carter could hear the squeals from several hundred feet away.

Cora was a profusion of questions and smiles. Apparently she was determined to get Miranda to open up since her son had refused. Well, she likely wouldn't get any more information than her son had given her. Miranda was here on business to take care of her cousin. That was that.

"How have you been?" Cora asked. "Why haven't you come home before now? I hear you have a daughter. I want to hear all about her."

Unfortunately Carter couldn't hear Miranda's answers. Her enthusiasm at seeing Cora again seemed genuine but underwhelming next to Cora's boisterous greeting. Although Miranda and Cora had always gotten along, which was a victory in itself considering Raymond Cahill's constant attempts to keep Miranda away from his family.

Arm in arm, like two long-lost friends, the two women joined up with the men.

"Hi, Carter," Miranda said.

"Morning."

"I stopped at your office, but the dispatcher told me this was your day off. And by the way, I was so happy to see Mrs. Moynahan again. She was always so nice to us in high school."

"She's a peach," Carter said. "Why did you go to the office?"

"I wanted to see you. Mrs. Moynahan said you'd probably be here at the tree farm."

"Same as most every Wednesday," he said. "You're here without your daughter?"

"I hired a girl from the college to watch Emily today. They're going to the animal rescue center. An injured hawk came in last night, and the vet is going to repair the bird's wing. That's right up Em's alley."

She looked around at the trees nearest her. "The crop looks good this year."

She would notice that, and she was right. Back in high school Carter and Miranda had driven the golf cart up this hill many nights, though back then, their purpose had been, among other things, to watch the moon, not the growing firs.

"It's coming along," he said.

"We're trying something new this year," Cora said. "We're offering trees in large planters so when the season is over, folks can plant the evergreen in their yards. After nurturing these firs for years, it seemed a shame to just cut and decorate them. Now, if folks choose to, they can have their tree near their homes for years to come."

"I think that's a wonderful idea," Miranda said. Turning to Jace, who had thus far remained silent, she added, "You're looking good, Jace. Have you taken over full-time management of Snowy Mountain?"

Jace's involvement with the tree farm had been an ongoing issue between him and Cora for years. Cora wanted him at the farm full time, but Jace wasn't ready to give up his laid-back lifestyle of playing his guitar and delegating rafting trips to his help. Occasionally Jace conducted the trips, but mostly he assigned the younger, more enthusiastic guys.

Jace made it clear that he wasn't ready for a permanent gig yet. The tree farm would tie him down with responsibilities, and he valued his free-spirited way of living too much. He liked having to answer only to himself and his scruffy mountain dog.

"Not yet." Jace smoothed a thick strand of nut-brown hair off his forehead and responded to Miranda's open arms with a quick, indifferent hug. Carter figured that's all the welcome Miranda was going to get from his loyal brother, who had helped him through their breakup. Jace was one individual who could carry a grudge to the grave. Since their father died a little over a year ago, he was only now coming to terms with the bitter feelings he'd had for Raymond.

Carter had gotten along with their father better than Jace had, but still, he hadn't shed a tear when the old man died. Jace, though, the third born, the one his father always viewed as weak and incorrigible, he'd practically smiled through the entire graveside service. Their older sister, Ava, was the only one who'd never seemed to raise their father's dander. But then, she was pretty, smart and successful.

Carter cleared his throat. It was time to get down to business. "So what brings you up here, Miranda?" he asked. "I assume this visit and the difficult trek up the hill is about more than you visiting a few Christmas trees."

"You're right," she said. "I have a proposition for you."

"Yeah? What is it?"

She glanced quickly at his two family members until Carter took the hint. "Can you guys give us a minute?" he said.

"Let's check on the fellas up the hill," Cora said to Jace. "I'll bet they want some coffee, too."

"Don't be a stranger, Miranda. Bring that daughter of yours out to the house and we'll have some girl talk," Cora said as she and Jace wandered away.

"I'll do that, Cora. Thanks."

Once they were out of sight, Carter said, "I can offer you a wood block to sit on. That's about the fanciest accommodation we have around here. But when you're ready to leave I'll have one of the men come up with the golf cart and take you down." He attempted a smile. "I couldn't help noticing your shoes aren't quite appropriate for hill climbing."

Miranda sank onto the block, slipped her sandals off and rubbed her feet. Carter used to massage her feet after cheerleading practice, but best not to think about that now. "Thanks," she said. "I'll take you up on that. I'd forgotten how steep the hills are."

Carter folded his arms across his chest. "You mentioned a proposition you wanted to discuss."

"Yes, that's right." She looked up at him with the clear, beautiful eyes that had once made him do anything she wanted. He reminded himself not to be taken in again. Those days were over.

"It concerns Lawton," she said. "I've decided that he needs a bit more help than I can provide."

"Have you tried the churches?" Carter asked. "We might even have a support group in town for guys like Lawton."

"You don't," Miranda replied. "I'm will-

ing to look into any solution for Law's dif-
ficulties, but first, I hope you meant it the
other night when you said you'd be willing
to help."

Whoa. Had he said that? He recalled the
words, but now he wondered at the wisdom
of the promise. "What does he need?"

"He needs a mentor, Carter. Someone
from Holly River preferably. Someone who
is respected in this town, whose opinion
matters."

Carter held his breath.

Miranda lightly touched his arm. "I'm
hoping that mentor will be you."

CARTER'S FACE PALED to nearly ashen. He took
a deep breath. "You're kidding, right?"

Miranda had expected him to be surprised
and probably reluctant, but a stiffening of
his spine told her this was not going to be
an easy sell. "I'm not kidding at all. Lawton needs a strong male figure in his life,
certainly not Dale, but someone with good
moral values to help him acclimate."

"I don't doubt that it would be helpful,
Miranda, but not me. I'm the cop who put
him in jail."

"He doesn't resent you for that," Miranda said. "What else could you have done after you searched his car? He knows you were only doing your job. He got caught with an illegal substance, which he manufactured himself, and an unregistered weapon. He knows he deserved to be arrested."

Miranda was attributing a generous, forgiving trait to Lawton, and she figured Carter would question her opinion. How many ex-cons were willing to forgive the cop who arrested them? She just hoped he would listen and not refuse her request until he'd heard her out.

"Don't forget his public vandalism," Carter added.

Miranda frowned. "I haven't forgotten anything, Carter, but it's history. For Lawton's sake, everyone needs to move forward."

Carter rubbed his jaw. "Moving forward is one thing, but you'll have to admit, Miranda, this whole idea is at best impractical and at worst inconceivable."

"Why is it so impractical?"

"I have a job. I'm busy."

"This won't take much of your time." Miranda was so certain that this was the proper course of action that she wasn't going to let Carter talk himself out of helping.

"That's only part of the problem," he said. "You may think Lawton doesn't resent me, but I guarantee that on some level, and maybe not so deep a level at that, he does. I was responsible for him losing eight years of his life…"

"He was responsible for that," Miranda pointed out. "And he knows it."

"Maybe so, but he's hardly going to want me giving him advice now."

"I think you're just the person he does need," Miranda insisted. "He can look up to you. You both come from Holly River. Your upbringings were different, and your lives are certainly different now, but you're a figure of authority around here, someone Lawton would listen to."

Carter held up both hands and slowly shook his head. "I'm sorry, Miranda. This idea would never work. Wasn't it just a few days ago that you pointed out to me that I went immediately to Liggett Mountain when a crime had been committed? I hadn't gone up there to catch Lawton at something, but

Dale is always a strong suspect, and that's not going to change."

"This isn't about Dale." Carter had brought up an argument that Miranda had considered before coming to Snowy Mountain. "And that's my point. You drove up Liggett to investigate Dale because you know he's a troublemaker, always has been. This fact alone makes it all the more important that Law has positive influences. How healthy can it be for Lawton to have his older brother as a role model now? And I'm afraid that's what will happen if he doesn't have anyone else to guide him. I have faith in Lawton, but old habits are hard to break."

Carter scraped his index finger across his chin. Miranda couldn't help noticing that he hadn't shaved this morning. Just like she couldn't help noticing that he had on work boots, worn dungarees and a green Snowy Mountain T-shirt that molded to his upper body. He'd looked official in his police uniform on Monday. Today he looked more like the boy she'd ridden in the golf cart with. She'd immediately thought of those nights when he mentioned the cart a few minutes ago.

"Lawton and I were never that close," Carter said. "I know you and he had a special bond, but that didn't extend to your…" He hesitated as if searching for a word. "…friends," he finally finished. "Lawton didn't even finish high school, so I didn't know much about his life after the tenth grade."

"You know what I told you," she said. "You know I loved him. He protected me and supported me, and listened to me for hours on end. Lawton was the main reason I was able to get by after my daddy died. Momma was always so depressed. I couldn't talk to her. Lawton…and you…were the ones I depended on."

He didn't look convinced, but at least he gave her idea a few moments of quiet thought. Finally he said, "It won't work, Miranda. There's too much history between the cops in Holly River and the Jefferson boys." He paused as an intuitive light suddenly appeared in his eyes. "You can't think that if I acted as a mentor to Lawton, or maybe because of the past relationship you and I shared, that I'd ignore the Jeffersons when a crime was committed."

His veiled accusation hurt. Did he really think she was suggesting this arrangement to keep Lawton and her worthless other cousin out of trouble? She'd thought he knew her better than that.

Her expression must have clued him into her thoughts. "I shouldn't have said that. I know you don't have an ulterior motive other than Lawton's well-being," he said.

She tried another line of reasoning, hoping to engage Carter's sense of fairness and community. "Did you know that when Dale picked Lawton up at prison, Lawton had the clothes on his back and twenty-five dollars in cash? That was it, and the money was spent immediately on food because there was hardly a bite of anything in the cabin."

"That's not much of a start…"

"And you said yourself…he has no family but Dale. Their parents moved away and never contact their boys. And even if they did, it would be an extremely dysfunctional relationship. And Lawton has a limited education, and no job opportunities, not without someone vouching for him anyway."

"So I would be putting my reputation on the line to help Lawton get a job?" Carter said. "It's asking a lot, Miranda, and I don't know if I'm willing to do that."

For the first time Miranda had doubts about her plan. She'd heard stories about Carter's involvement with the community, the blind eye he often cast to minor traffic violations, the raccoons he'd chased from garbage cans. But she'd never expected Carter to worry about the consequences of his job over someone's well-being. Still, she knew in her heart that Carter would be the perfect person to help Lawton. "I guess supporting Law might have an effect on your position here," she admitted. "But at least talk to him. That's not too much to ask is it? You said you'd help."

He expelled a long breath. Maybe she was wearing him down. "Give this a try, Carter. I'm sure you'll see that Lawton has changed. You could make the difference in him becoming successful on the outside or becoming a statistic who ends up back in prison.

"Just think for a minute about the life skills that you and I take for granted. Lawton doesn't even know what a smartphone is. He doesn't know how to work a computer. He's never heard of Uber and apps.

He has no idea how to act at a job interview. Heck, Carter, he doesn't even have a photo ID anymore."

"You could introduce him to all these things," Carter said.

"I'll do what I can, but he needs a strong male influence, someone who has a strict code of ethics. I'm just the little cousin he used to push over Holly River on a tire. You could give him hope for making something of himself." She stopped, took a deep breath. "I know you, Carter. You may think I've forgotten that at one time I knew almost everything about you…"

His eyes clouded. She hoped she hadn't gone too far.

"I don't think much has fundamentally changed," she said. "You were a good, honest, hardworking boy, and you're the same now. I'd stake my life on it."

He stared at her for a long moment. In those deep green eyes that once were a window to every feeling he'd had, she couldn't read his answer today.

"Who else have you asked?" he said. "Maybe a minister in town, someone who's more familiar with this type of volunteer work?"

She managed a slight smile. "Only you, Carter. I want you. And Lawton needs you."

His eyes widened, perhaps at the frankness of her statement, perhaps at the wording she'd used. "Give me a couple of days to think about it," he said. "Where are you staying?"

She told him.

"I'll stop by the Hummingbird Inn on Friday and give you my decision."

"You have my number on my business card, if you kept it," she said.

"I've got it somewhere. And Miranda, my decision will only be to talk to Lawton. I won't be agreeing to anything else at this time."

"That's fine. Thank you, Carter. You can't know how much this means…"

He took his cell phone out of his pocket. "Don't let's get ahead of ourselves," he said, punching in a number. "Hey, Richie, would you bring the golf cart up here?"

Miranda was relieved to be getting a ride back down. She was suddenly tired and drained, and a large blister was forming on her big toe. But still, it had been a good day so far.

When the golf cart arrived, Carter surprised her by handing Richie the shearing tool and getting behind the wheel of the cart. "Take over, Rich. I'll be right back." To Miranda he said, "Hop in."

She did. They started down the pathway. "I suppose I could have gone down on my own," she said.

"Yeah, and I suppose you could have gone dancing with that blister on your foot."

She smiled, deciding that smiling with Carter felt so natural, so good. They rode silently for a while until Miranda said, "I have to admit, Carter, your choice of profession isn't what I would have imagined for you. I don't recall you ever mentioning you wanted to be in law enforcement."

"I didn't, especially, but then I sat in front of that college catalog, and 'criminal justice' just seemed to fly off the page at me. And here I am, years later, right back where I started."

"Well, the fact that you settled in Holly River doesn't surprise me," Miranda said. "You always loved this place."

"And you always wanted to get out."

She twisted her hands in her lap. "Not always."

Another silence followed until Miranda asked if he enjoyed police work.

"I suppose I do. I've always felt it was a way to give back to a community that gave so much to me."

"Do you have much serious crime here?"

"No. Haven't had a murder, well, not that I know about. Few burglaries. We do get some auto thefts, and that's a problem when the car belongs to a wealthy tourist from Atlanta. Those people always seem to think that locking a car in quiet Holly River is a precaution they don't need to take." He glanced at her as he drove. "I'd say our biggest criminals are bears and raccoons."

"Do you wear a gun?" she asked, remembering that she hadn't bothered to look when he was in uniform on Liggett Mountain.

"Yes, ma'am. I've had to draw it a few times. Once I even fired a round in the air when a bunch of tourists from Florida forgot they'd come here to ski, not just drink. But if you're wondering if I ever aimed at a real person, no, I haven't. Hope I don't have to either. Our latest crime involves sprinklers and garden hoses, and I'll be content to track those down and leave the major crime to the big cities."

"I'll bet you get some strange calls from people wanting you to do things that aren't in line with crime busting."

"I've pulled my share of snakes out of sheds and investigated a number of UFO sightings. It's all part of the job, I guess."

"But you enjoy it?"

"Yeah. As I said, it gives me a chance to be a valued member of the community. That's important to me because my ancestors weren't always such good citizens." He cut a sharp glance her way. "I guess I don't have to tell you that. My dad, his father and his father before him were only interested in making money. It didn't matter who got hurt."

Like my father did, Miranda thought, remembering the stench of the paper mill Raymond Cahill owned. The factory was just far enough away that the smell never reached Holly River, but on hot summer nights, when the windows were open, folks on Liggett Mountain used to complain. Not that Raymond cared. Until the chemicals used killed her dad and left Miranda and her mother without a father and husband.

She'd never imagined that Carter would bear the burden of what his ancestors did. She'd known he didn't get along with Raymond, but his mother, Cora, was always so sweet and caring. She mediated many arguments between the men in her family. "You told me once that you aren't your father. Remember that?"

He nodded.

"Well, it's true."

He smiled. "If I have anything to say about it, I never will be a clone of Raymond Cahill. I'm probably the nicest cop in North Carolina, but there's a lot of past regret to make up for."

They'd reached the bottom of the hill, and Miranda got out of the cart. "I promise to abide by all laws while I'm here," she said.

"You don't know what you're saying. Some of our statutes are pretty quirky, and you could break a law without even knowing it. But, heck, Miranda, you're one out-of-towner I'm not worried about."

She leaned under the top of the cart.

"Thanks for the lift. I'll see you Friday. And Carter, don't overthink this whole thing with Lawton. You'll be a great mentor if you decide to do it."

He drove off, heading back toward the hill path, and Miranda walked to her car. She felt strangely sad when she thought back to Carter's comment about her being an "out-of-towner."

CHAPTER FIVE

THE DRIVE FROM Snowy Mountain to the veterinary rehab center where Miranda had left her daughter was almost a half hour—time enough for Miranda to think about Holly River, the sadness she experienced here and the regrets she had upon leaving. One day in particular she would never forget.

Fourteen years earlier...

"I'M SORRY, MRS. JEFFERSON, but there just isn't anything else we can do. This day has been coming for quite a while."

Miranda stared up at their family doctor from the uncomfortable seat in the Bolton County Hospital waiting room. She and her mother had been at the hospital around the clock since Warren Jefferson had been brought in by ambulance three days before. All thoughts of graduation parties and spending time with Carter had been forgotten as Miranda waited for word on her father.

"There must be something you can do," Miranda said. *"You can't just give up."*

Loreen Jefferson had covered her daughter's arm with her hand, trying to comfort her. "Let Dr. Jackson talk, honey."

"The cancer in Warren's lungs has spread to his colon and his liver. Even if we could control the lung cancer, his other organs would shut down. In a way, it's a blessing that he was brought in when he was. He's been able to receive medication that alleviates his pain."

A blessing! Miranda had wanted to scream. She'd found her father in his favorite recliner, the TV blaring loudly and blood gurgling from his lips and his ruined lungs. It had seemed to take hours for the ambulance to arrive.

"How long does he have?" Loreen asked.

Dr. Jackson's face reflected the difficulty of what he had to say. "I think you ladies should use this time to say your goodbyes."

Five years! For five long years, Loreen and Miranda had watched the man they loved struggle with every breath until finally he could no longer speak and his appetite had dwindled to practically nothing. Thank goodness the family had health insurance and no mortgage on the Liggett Mountain cabin. There was no way they could have survived on the little disability Warren received from the state of North Carolina and the small paychecks Miranda earned at the hot dog stand outside of town.

As her father was being wheeled into the ambulance on a stretcher, Miranda had walked beside him, holding his hand. "Be strong, Daddy. Don't leave us. I'll make Raymond Cahill pay for what he did to you."

And what had Raymond done exactly? He'd offered Warren a substantial raise if he would work in the boiler plant of the paper mill, a position that carried some degree of risk due to the asbestos lining used in the pulp boilers. The last man who'd held the job had retired with no ill effects, and to give his family a better life, Warren had decided the benefits outweighed the risks.

Only he hadn't been as lucky as the man before him. After ten years working next to those boilers, asbestos dust and tiny filings settled in his lungs and finally ended his job at the mill and now his life. And there wasn't really anything Miranda could do in the way of retaliation. The personnel manager at the plant showed her a letter her father had signed agreeing to the terms of his higher-paying job and acknowledging the risks.

"Is there anything else you'd like to ask me, Loreen, Miranda?" Dr. Jackson said. "If you're wondering if Warren is comfortable, I can assure you he is. And there should be relief in knowing he won't be struggling much longer."

Miranda had stood, placed her hand under her mother's elbow and helped her to her feet. "Let's go sit with him, Mama."

Like a wooden statue, Loreen had managed to slide one foot in front of the other, her practical shoes scraping on the polished linoleum of the hospital floor. They'd gone only a few steps when Miranda saw a man coming toward them. Not just any man. No, this was Raymond Cahill, the man she hated most in the world. Raymond was approaching them with a purposeful stride, and he had an envelope in his hand. What was inside that envelope changed everything.

"Hi, Mom!" Emily bounded into the car, her natural energy seeming to fill the entire space.

"How was your afternoon?" Miranda asked. She reached into her wallet, handed the young woman she'd hired to watch Emily a few five dollar bills, and thanked her.

"Anytime, Mrs. Larson," the girl said. "Emily is such a bright, curious child."

"It was so neat," Emily began as soon as Miranda turned around in the facility parking lot. "You knew about the bird, right? Well, the doctor fixed him. I mean he can't fly yet, but he will. Right now he's in a cage and his wing is bandaged, but he'll be fine soon. I got to watch the whole thing."

Miranda headed onto the road that led to the Hummingbird Inn. "I would say you had a great afternoon, Em."

"I did. Now I know for sure that I want to be a veterinarian when I grow up. Veterinarians are so smart. They are the only doctors whose patients can't tell them what's wrong. They just have to know."

"I suppose that's true. I think you would make a wonderful vet, honey."

"Are we going back to our cottage now?" Emily asked.

"Yes. I picked up something for supper, and I thought we'd stay in tonight."

"That's okay. We can watch a movie."

Miranda's cell phone rang, and she checked the car's digital screen for the name of the caller. *Don't do it, Miranda*, she said to herself. *Don't show your impatience in front of Emily.* Unfortunately the last person she wanted to talk to was her ex-husband, Donny.

"It's Daddy," Emily squealed. "I want to talk to him."

"Just a minute," Miranda said. "Let me see what he wants first." She took Donny off speaker and pressed the connect button on her cell. "Hi, Donny."

"Hello, 'Randa. I was grateful to get the text you sent me informing me that you and Emily had arrived safely in Holly River. I must say, though, I would have preferred a phone call."

Never a compliment without an accompanying dig. "We were busy unpacking, Donny. I meant to call you later, but…"

"Never mind. The important thing is that you're there. Have you seen your cousin?"

"Yes. He's got more than a few challenges to face. I'm going to do all I can for him."

"That's commendable, really."

Miranda looked for a hint of sarcasm in Donny's tone. He hadn't approved of Miranda's bringing Emily to Holly River. Donny had never thought much of Lawton, and like most people, he'd thought even less of Dale. He'd warned Miranda to keep a sharp eye on their daughter when she was around those "good-for-nothings."

"I'll be with her at all times, Donny," Miranda had told him, though she never once doubted that she could trust Emily with Lawton. After all, there had been a time or two when Miranda entrusted her own safety to her cousin, and he never failed her.

"How did you find the old hometown?" Donny asked.

"The same as when I left it." In fourteen years, she'd been back only a couple of times. Once was when she helped her mother pack up her belongings for the move to her condo in Hickory, and the second was when the sale of the Liggett cabin went through. Both times Miranda did what she had to do and left as soon as possible. She hadn't been ready to face her grief yet, or the decision she'd made with regard to Carter. "There is still a warm feeling here..." she started to say.

"Wouldn't be for me," Donny said. "I was glad to leave that town in my rearview. Have you seen anyone you know? Old friends maybe?"

She knew he wanted her to tell him if she'd seen Carter, but she refused to take the bait. Though Donny had never brought up Carter until the divorce, Miranda knew he always kept track of his boyhood friend, the one adult male he resented every day of his life now. During the divorce proceedings, he'd accused Miranda of still having a "thing" for her old boyfriend. Miranda had adamantly denied the accusation, though in her heart, she had to accept that perhaps it was true.

"It's strange, I guess," she responded, "but I don't see many faces I recognize. I suppose that, like we did, most of the people we knew moved on."

"How long are you going to stay?"

This was at least the third time he'd asked that question, and her answer hadn't changed. "I don't know, Donny. Lawton was my best friend growing up, and besides that, you seem to forget that helping him is my job. I have to see him settled now. The last eight years have taken a toll on him. You would hardly recognize him, and he needs some assistance."

"What he needs is to stay out of trouble and as far away from Dale as he can get," Donny said.

"He isn't in any trouble, Donny. At least not the kind you're thinking of. And as far as Dale is concerned, I'm working on that. Finding housing for an ex-con isn't easy. He needs a job first, some social interaction with the town. You can't imagine what life is like for him now. It's so difficult..."

If Miranda thought she might instill some sympathy in Donny, she realized that was a futile effort.

"He brought it all on himself. You really can't keep making excuses for him, 'Randa."

Miranda bit her lip to keep from snapping back. "Is there anything else, Donny? Emily really wants to talk to you."

"I guess not. Put her on."

Miranda handed the phone to her daughter and only halfheartedly listened to the excited chatter. Her mind had already wandered to the man she wanted as a mentor for her cousin, someone she believed would be fair and compassionate, as different from those who would continue to condemn Lawton as anyone could be.

THE NEXT DAY was a difficult one for Miranda. After stopping at a large supermarket and stocking up on supplies for Lawton, she and Emily headed to Liggett Mountain. She had to pass her old cabin on the way to the Jeffersons. On her last trip, Miranda had purposefully avoided looking at the cabin, but this day she slowed the car and pointed the property out to her daughter.

"This is where you used to live, Mommy?" Emily said.

"This is it." Surprisingly the cabin had undergone some renovations, thanks to the folks who'd bought it. "My room was in the back right behind the kitchen. Grandma's bedroom was behind the living room."

"I wish we could go inside. Maybe some of your stuff is still in there."

"I don't think so. An older couple bought the property, and something tells me that if I'd forgotten anything, they wouldn't keep stuffed animals and high school cheerleading pictures around the house."

"No, probably not." The house passed from view, and after a few moments Emily said, "What did you do there, Mommy? Did you even have electricity?"

Miranda chuckled. "Yes, we did. It's a small house, but we had everything we needed." Unfortunately, any time Miranda and her mother had a few dollars to spare, something always came up. "And my father and I kept a really great garden in back," Miranda said. "We grew most of our own vegetables, and your grandma canned them for the winter months. It was fun."

Emily didn't look convinced. "I don't know if I would like to live on this mountain and grow my own food," she said. "But I'm glad you liked it."

Miranda patted her daughter's knee. "Well, when the summer's over, we can go back to Durham to our nice house, and you won't have to think about living on Liggett Mountain again if you don't want to."

"Okay."

They reached the Jefferson house, and Miranda pulled into the rough gravel driveway. She was relieved to see that Dale's car was not there. She hoped he was out working somewhere to provide income to the household. There had to be a few people in town who still hired him to manicure their lawns.

"You can help me carry the bags, Em," she said. Together they carted four full sacks into the house.

"What's all this?" Lawton asked, coming in the back way. He gave each of the females a hug, a sign that perhaps his former emotional security was returning.

"We brought you some things," Emily said.

Miranda unpacked the first bag. "These are all cleaning supplies," she explained. "I noticed you didn't have any products under your sink, and these are all good for the environment and will make cleaning easy and fast." She figured Lawton would be the one using the supplies, since it had been obvious on the first visit that Dale never had.

"Thanks, 'Randa," Lawton said. "I guess the place could use some sprucing up."

"Yeah," Emily said. She approached them holding her index finger in the air. "Look at the dust I found on one table only!"

Miranda held her breath, hoping Lawton hadn't taken offense. His eyes widened and then he smiled. "Did I ever tell you that it's nice to have a couple of neat-freak gals around the house?"

She and Lawton emptied the other three bags, setting the items on the kitchen counter. Miranda had purchased vegetables, fruit, a few good cuts of meat and healthy cereals. She'd even included a couple of desserts. Lawton needed to put on a few pounds.

"This is great," Lawton said, picking up a sweet potato. "Now all I need is a cookbook."

"When in doubt, roast everything." Miranda showed him a bottle of olive oil. "Just a little drizzle of this and a moderate oven is all you need for most of this food." She hoped the oven was working.

"I really appreciate this, peanut," Lawton said, using the pet name he'd had for

Miranda when they were kids. He pushed a lock of sandy-brown hair from his forehead. "Dale eats most of his meals in town, so we don't keep a lot of food around here except for what the Baptist group brings." He opened the refrigerator door. "We have a lot of cheese and bread."

"Well, there's no need for you to go hungry. Soon you'll be able to buy your own supplies." She sat on a kitchen chair. "So how are you today, Law? How's everything going with Dale?"

He didn't get a chance to answer because at that moment Dale came in the front door. He pounded a few clods of dirt from his boots, took off his ball cap and hung it on a nail by the front door. His dark hair was tied back in a leather strap, and the hatband had left a film of dirty sweat on his forehead. "Well, howdy, cousin Miranda," he said and then looked at Emily, "And little missy."

"Hello, Dale," Miranda said. Emily gave him an offhand wave.

"Cut two lawns today," Dale said. "Got a fat fifty bucks from some generous people over in your old boyfriend's neighborhood. Salt of the earth, those rich folks." He slapped a twenty on the table. "That's what's left after I gassed up the Jeep and had a couple of beers."

Finally he noticed the groceries and cleaning supplies on the counter. "What's going on? This all from you, Miranda?"

"I thought you guys could use a few things," she said.

He strolled over to the purchases and began picking each one up and staring at the labels. "Are we on some sort of health food kick around here?" Laughing, he looked at his brother. "I hope you're hungry, Lawton, 'cause I'm sure not going to eat any of this…"

Miranda stood, scraping the wooden chair across the plank floor to cover the word she suspected would come from Dale's mouth. "Come on, Em. We have to go now."

Emily came close to her mother and whispered, "I think Dale was going to say a bad word."

Miranda pushed her toward the door. Lawton followed them outside.

"I'm sorry, 'Randa," he said, walking her

to her car. "Dale probably forgot that Emily was in the room."

"Yes, I'm sure that's it," Miranda said. She waited until Emily was in the car and then asked her cousin, "So how are things really going, Law? Are you getting on with Dale?"

"Oh, sure," he said. "Dale's okay. Like always he complains about his situation. You know his rant—life hasn't been fair, the cops are always out to get him, but I think he's glad to have me back."

"Just so you don't buy into what he's saying and he doesn't try to bring you down with him," Miranda said.

Lawton scratched the back of his neck. "That's a funny one, 'Randa. I'm the one just out of prison and you don't want Dale to bring *me* down."

"Keep thinking positive thoughts, Lawton," she said. "I'm working on some things that should help you out."

"You've already done so much, peanut. I know I've got to rely on myself and find a job. It'll all work out."

She leaned up and kissed his cheek, grateful that she inhaled the strong scent of soap. He was trying.

As she drove back down the mountain, Miranda thought of Carter, and realized that much of her plan for Lawton depended on Carter's answer. Well, she'd know tomorrow.

CHAPTER SIX

AFTER A RESTLESS NIGHT, Carter left his comfortable log home on Cross Junction Road and headed for the police station. At 7:30 a.m., he had a good hour and a half until he could tell Betsy he'd be in the office.

He passed High Mountain Rafting and was surprised to see his brother Jace's truck in the parking lot. Jace was not an early riser if he could help it. And he was a confirmed bachelor who could sleep as late as he wanted to. Carter was a bachelor, too, but for different reasons. Still, the result was the same. Both men had probably left their homes with no breakfast and only a pint of coffee to fuel their day.

Carter pulled into the parking lot for the River Café, just a half block from High Mountain, and walked into the restaurant. He would order two pancake breakfasts to go and see what was up with Jace.

Sam McCall was seated at the restaurant counter. Carter spoke to a few other morning people as he walked to Sam. "Not that I need to ask, but why are you here so early?"

Sam nodded toward Allie, who was balancing three full platters of eggs and sausage on her arm. "She's got the breakfast shift this morning."

"You keeping track of her schedule now?" Carter teased.

"As much as I can. All I really care about is her schedule tomorrow night. She's going out with me." Sam grinned. "I finally won her over."

Carter settled on the stool beside Sam. "Yep. She looks very excited. Congrats on convincing her into a date."

Sam stared at Allie. "Just don't ask me to take an extra shift tomorrow night."

Allie delivered meals to other customers and returned to the counter. She refilled Sam's coffee cup and said good-morning to Carter. "What can I get you, Chief?"

"Two pancake breakfasts in to-go boxes," he said. "And your promise that you'll keep a sharp eye on this guy tomorrow night."

She laughed. "Hey, if a girl can't trust a cop, who can she trust?"

She went to the cook's window to place Carter's order.

"Speaking of tired," Sam said, "you look pretty beat yourself. Not much sleep last night?"

"No, not much. I have to make a decision today, and I haven't come to a conclusion yet."

"Something I can help you with? My advice is gold around here."

Carter thought a moment. Telling Sam seemed like a good idea. He already knew he could trust the rookie to keep a confidence, and Sam had good instincts. Besides, Carter knew without asking what Jace would say. He would warn his older brother against doing anything for the woman who'd broken his heart. Sam didn't have a prejudiced mind on the subject, so Carter told his friend the basics of Miranda's plan.

"So, she wants you to mentor Lawton?" he repeated when Carter was finished. "That's a tough one."

"Should it be?" Carter said. "At one time I would have done anything for Miranda, and truth to tell, those feelings haven't exactly gone away over the years."

Carter shook his head. He'd intended to tell Sam only about the mentoring proposition, and here he'd bluntly stated feelings he hadn't even admitted to himself.

"Those first loves are sometimes hard to shake," Sam said. "I suppose your instinct is to say yes."

Carter nodded.

"But there's more to consider here. You've worked years to build a darn good reputation in this town. People respect you. They look up to you. Do you want to tarnish all that good work by hooking up with the guy who vandalized the statue of the sainted elk on the town square?"

"Among other things," Carter said. "But truly, folks around here probably only look up to me because I'm the second-chance cop. I believe everyone deserves one."

"Don't sell yourself short. You're fair. You treat people right."

To erase my ancestors' greed and opportunism, Carter thought. But yes, he'd managed to earn the reputation as the fairest cop around. "So you're saying my helping Lawton could ruin my reputation?"

"Maybe not ruin, but certainly affect it. The Jefferson boys are a breed to themselves. Either they find trouble or it finds them. Quite a few people have come to me in private asking me if there is a way to get the boys to move. There isn't, I know that. It's a free country, but I wonder what folks will think if you stick your neck so far out for one of them. If you're going to be a good mentor, as well as an advocate for Lawton, you won't be able to hide your role in his life."

"No. I expect I'll have to help him in many public ways."

"And what if Lawton ends up disappointing you? How will you rationalize helping him if he slips up again? And what will you do if you have to arrest him and send him back to prison? Will Miranda blame you and might you make a lifelong enemy of her?"

Carter had thought of all this during the long nighttime hours. They were all good points, and still, Carter had gotten up this morning thinking he would say yes to Miranda. He simply couldn't imagine himself saying no to her.

"Honestly, I don't think Miranda would think less of me if I had to arrest her cousin again," Carter said. "She's realistic about Lawton's past mistakes and about his chances for success in this town."

"Sounds like you've made up your mind," Sam said.

Allie returned and set two boxes in front of Carter. "Here's your order, Chief."

He left a few bills on the counter, told Sam he'd see him in an hour and walked out of the café. When he entered the door to High Mountain Rafting, he found his brother alone, behind the counter. Papers were spread out in front of him, and Jace was frowning.

"Not open yet," he said, and then looked up. "Oh, it's you. What smells so good?"

"Pancakes. Enough for two, but I can eat them both if you're too grumpy to appreciate the gesture."

Jace grabbed a box. "You, my brother, are a man among men."

"It's just pancakes, Jace."

"Don't make light of my rumbling stomach that suddenly finds you very attractive," Jace said.

"Never mind." Carter removed the lid from his box, took his plastic silverware out of the wrapper and started to eat. "What's with the paperwork? You figuring out how much money you make sending folks down the Wyoga River?"

"Already know that, and it's not much. No, I'm filling out forms for licenses, checking our supplies to make sure we meet the latest safety requirements." He took a sip of coffee. "It's kind of ridiculous, Carter, that I'm in the business of giving people thrills, and because of all these safety precautions, I end up having to explain why they didn't have any."

"Didn't you tell me once that you lose a couple of people a week from one of the rafts?" Carter asked.

"You make it sound like those folks drowned when in fact all that happened was that they got a good dowsing."

"Okay, so isn't that enough of a thrill for the ones who fall in?"

"Yeah, I suppose, but accidents happen mostly because a customer has been jumping around when he shouldn't have been. The Wyoga is a pretty tame river unless the rain has been heavy." He took a bite of pancake. "Why are you here with that glum look on your face? Something little bro can help you with?"

"Maybe."

Jace looked surprised. Carter rarely asked him for advice. And Jace never asked Carter for any. "Okay, I'm listening."

"Miranda wants me to be a mentor for Lawton until he gets settled."

Jace stopped chewing and stared at Carter. "Bad idea, bro. You sure you want to be associated with either of those two boys?"

"No, I'm not sure, but I don't want to disappoint Miranda."

"You don't want to disappoint the girl who dumped you with no warning and, to my way of thinking, no decent reason?"

"She had her reasons." Carter wanted to argue, to tell his brother again that Miranda had been grieving over her father's death, that she blamed Raymond for the loss and she needed to get her mother and herself away from Holly River. But Carter truly couldn't make a good case for what Miranda did. He'd spent too many hours in the past thinking about her words the day they broke up. No warning and no reason he could believe in about summed it up. "I suppose I shouldn't feel any obligation to her..."

"Darn straight."

"But I think I can help Lawton."

"You think you can help everyone, Carter. And maybe you ought to realize that your job is not just to help people. It's to remind them that we all live according to the law, and if they mess up, they will pay." Biting off a piece of sausage, Jace added, "Sometimes, brother, you can be too moral. People take advantage of you, and the last person you should let do that is Miranda Jefferson."

Jace washed down his food with a sip of coffee. "My advice, since you asked, is to put your darned integrity, not to mention long-lost feelings for a girl who dumped you, on the back burner and realize what a relationship with Lawton could cost you in this town."

"You make it sound like I'm a pushover."

"At least you're a good, honest pushover, and you like it that way."

That last remark rankled. "You know why

I tend to be lenient with folks around here, especially those who lived here during our father's reign of terror. Too many people had to smell the stench from the paper mill, and too many worked for minimum wage when they should have been earning more."

"I know that, and your motives are understandable, though I don't feel the need to erase any of the stuff our father did. If people in this town want to condemn me for what that old buzzard is responsible for, I can't stop them, and I won't try. But that's just the difference between you and me. The bottom line is, Carter, you could be tackling too much with Lawton. You're the good brother, you know, and you've spent years earning that title."

The pancakes were beginning to sit like lead in Carter's stomach. Sometimes his brother made good sense. "I've got to go to work. Thanks for listening, Jace."

"No problem. By the way, I gotta say that Miranda is even better looking now than I remember. Mom told me she has a kid. Have you seen her?"

"The daughter? Sure. Her name is Emily."

"She look like her mother...or Donny?"

Jace asked the question without a sign that he was twisting the knife in Carter's pancake-laden gut.

"I don't know," Carter lied. "I didn't pay that much attention to her. She looks like all kids—short, cute."

Carter tossed his food box into the nearest trash can, stood up to leave and then stopped. "One more thing, Jace. Have you noticed anything going on with Ma?"

"Like what?"

"I don't know. She seems to be avoiding certain topics. Like why she won't go with Aunt Dolly to Hawaii. She's always wanted to go there. Now's her chance, and she tells me she's suddenly lost interest. That make any sense to you?"

"No, it doesn't." Jace shook his head.

"And she seems to be avoiding hiring help to keep the house up," Carter added.

"Can't be money," Jace said. "A trip to Hawaii could run two grand or more, but Ma is getting regular checks from the mill, isn't she? Dad may have been a louse, but he did leave her set financially with that profit sharing plan."

"I haven't watched the mill books as

closely as I could," Carter admitted. "Ava's the one with the mathematical brain, but our dear sister doesn't come home that often. I have asked Ma, and she says she's getting her share of the profits from Uncle Rudy."

"Dad's brother may not be an angel, but he's not as bad as Dad was," Jace said. "I don't think he'd cheat Ma."

"Well, then, if the problem isn't money, do you think she's afraid to travel?"

"No, at least not if she's going with Aunt Dolly."

Carter headed for the exit. "Just keep your ears open, Jace. Don't pressure her too hard to give you a reason, but if she tells you anything, let me know. I hate to see her miss this opportunity. I can just see her and Dolly dancing the hula when we're stuck in Holly River in three feet of snow!"

"Good luck with your decision," Jace called as Carter left the shop. Carter returned to his car and drove the few blocks to the police station.

He would work until five and then call Miranda and go over to the Hummingbird Inn. He hoped he would have a busy day. At this point he was just darned tired of thinking about all the Jefferson cousins. Maybe the answer would come to him when he was chasing a nuisance bear from someone's bird feeder.

At five o'clock Carter phoned Miranda and told her he was coming to the Hummingbird Inn. She sounded happy, hopeful. Carter hated to spoil that feeling, but he'd pretty much decided not to mentor Lawton. The two guys he'd gone to for advice had made good sense. The folks in Holly River wouldn't understand why he was helping an ex-con, and truly, what did Carter owe Miranda anyway? Nothing.

Miranda had told him she and Emily were staying in the cottage behind the inn, so Carter pulled up the long, tree-lined drive and passed the main house. The cottage was small and cozy-looking. Carter hoped it wasn't so cozy that he'd have to tell Miranda his decision in front of the kid.

Though he'd seen Emily a couple of times, Carter couldn't get comfortable with her. Emily reminded him too much of Donny, and then there was the history. Back then, Carter had been the one who wanted to have kids with Miranda. Now, thanks to a couple of tragic twists of fate, Miranda had ended up with his best friend, and Carter had lost what was possibly his last chance at happiness. He'd accepted that fact and didn't need to develop confusing feelings for Donny Larson's daughter.

Miranda stepped out the front door when Carter turned off the engine to the patrol car. He got out of the car still wearing his uniform. He'd brought casual clothes with him this morning but decided it would be better to keep this meeting as professional as he could.

"Thanks for coming by, Carter," Miranda said.

She had on a dress, a cute sleeveless above-the-knee thing with tiny yellow flowers all over it. The dress showed off her figure and reminded him that she'd always had great legs—and he'd always liked her in a dress. She looked like she belonged in Mrs. Dillingham's colorful garden, and in Holly River.

Don't get sidetracked, he told himself. *Miranda works for the government in Durham.*

She'd made the decision long ago that Holly River wasn't for her.

"No problem," he said. "I told you I'd stop by this evening."

"Emily's in the house working on a project." She pointed to a swing a few yards away. "The weather's nice. We can sit out here and have a private conversation."

Thank goodness. "That's fine." He waited for her to walk ahead of him. The swing was one of those sturdy wooden-framed ones that could easily hold two people who together weighed five hundred pounds. Carter clocked in at 180 and Miranda couldn't have topped 120. They each settled on the flowery cushion. Miranda's feet didn't touch the ground, but Carter glided the swing back and forth just slightly with his toe. For a moment he couldn't take his gaze away from the breeze lifting her hair from her shoulders.

"So have you made a decision?" she asked.

"I have. There were a number of factors to consider, and I thought long and hard about this."

Her face fell. "You're not going to do it."

"Let me explain…"

"It's all right." She stared straight into his eyes and seemed to reach his heart. "I'd so hoped, but… I'm sure you have your reasons."

"I just don't think it would work, Miranda. I'm on one side of the law and Lawton's…well, he and Dale have notoriously been on the other."

"That's not a fair statement, Carter, not anymore. Law is reformed, and I want to make sure he stays that way." She shook her head. "There are so many things working against him now that he's out. He's having to adjust to new feelings. Prison life is regimented and dehumanizing. The attitude he took in prison won't work on the outside. In there he was tough, withdrawn and antisocial. Those mind-sets won't help him in Holly River."

Carter couldn't look away from the disappointment in Miranda's eyes. She'd accepted his answer, but now she seemed hell-bent on changing his mind. She was nothing if not determined. Lawton was lucky to have her on his side.

"Why did Lawton come back here?" Carter asked.

"I told you before. He had twenty-five dollars when he left prison. The only place he had to go was Liggett Mountain. The only family he has is Dale. I hoped, I *prayed* that Dale would have changed and would encourage Law to stay crime-free. But you know Dale, Carter. He's the same as always—uncaring, unfeeling and just out for himself."

Carter couldn't argue. Heck, he didn't even like to think of Miranda and Emily in the company of Dale Jefferson, even if he was kin.

"All that's true," Carter said, "but there's another reason. I didn't see what I could offer Lawton. I mean, I'm not a psychologist, and that's probably the kind of help that he needs."

"He doesn't need a psychologist. He has me to talk to, and I'm trained to help people like him. He needs a friend, Carter, someone who can guide him in the right direction, someone who can help him to feel like a man again, not a number."

Carter felt his resolve weakening. "And you think I'm the one who can do that?"

She smiled. And then she did something entirely unexpected. She reached across that cushion and wrapped her hand around Carter's arm. He felt her touch all the way to his shoulder. The swing stopped as he drew in a quick breath. "I know you, and I know you are," she said.

He released the breath he'd been holding. "What exactly do you want me to do, Miranda?"

"Help him to assume responsibility for his future. Look what you've done with your life. Lawton can't help but be impressed with all you've accomplished. Work with him on finding a job. He'll take almost anything at this point. Maybe you can go with him on interviews. A show of confidence from Holly River's chief of police will go a long way."

Yeah, maybe, but what would Lawton's appearance with the chief of police do to Carter? "Does he even know how to fill out a job application, how to prepare for an interview?"

"I can help him with the paperwork," Miranda said. "And maybe you can get him in the doors around here for interviews. But most importantly, here's where you can be especially helpful... Lawton needs to learn constructive, peaceful ways to deal with conflicts between him and Dale. And he needs to work well with authority figures, like his future boss. In prison, the inmates mostly resent anyone in authority, and that attitude has to change if he's going to be successful on the outside.

"I can help him with things like getting health insurance, saving money, budgeting," she added. "But I won't be effective in getting him a place to live. I may be wrong, but I've sensed some resentment toward me since I've been back. The people in this town might just give Law a chance if he's got you on his side." She took a breath. "The truth is, Carter, if Lawton is going to succeed, he needs both of us. And maybe you can talk him into getting his GED and even going on to take some college courses."

One of the Jefferson boys in college? Carter shook his head. He admired Miranda's spunk and determination, but maybe she wasn't being realistic. But as he looked at her with her bottom lip between her teeth, her blue eyes so hopeful, as if he alone could make everything right, he suddenly wanted to help her. At least he didn't want her to fail because he'd turned his back on her.

"Tell you what, Miranda. I'll talk to Lawton on Sunday. That's my day off. If I come away from the conversation believing that Lawton and I could work together, that our differences wouldn't keep us from accomplishing what you're hoping for, then I'll give it a try. But if not…"

"Oh, Carter, I just knew you'd help us!" She was suddenly leaning across that flowered cushion and wrapping him in a fierce hug, her face buried against his neck. The swing went slightly off-kilter, as did every major organ in Carter's body. His heart pounded. His head spun. And he panicked.

"Miranda, don't do that," he said, gently pulling her arms to her sides.

She sat back. "What's wrong?"

"What's wrong?" He couldn't believe she'd asked the question. Did she honestly think that enough time had passed that she could give him a friendly hug as if they were nothing more than old buddies? The feeling of her body pressed against his brought back memories he'd taken years to forget. He stood.

"I'm sorry, Carter," she said. "I didn't mean to make you uncomfortable. But I'm so grateful to you."

With his feet firmly on the ground, he managed to recover his bearings. "It's okay. You caught me off guard. I overreacted." *And started thinking about all I'd lost and all you meant to me at one time.*

"Do you want to go up to Liggett with me on Sunday?" he asked.

"I would really like to. I'll hire that girl from the college to watch Emily again. Just tell me what time to be ready."

"Around ten works for me," he said. "I promised my mother I'd help out at her place in the afternoon."

"I'll be waiting," she said. And he knew that he would be, too.

CHAPTER SEVEN

Sam stood in front of his bathroom mirror to give himself one last look. He smoothed a thick strand of coppery-colored hair off his forehead. Funny, but girls had always liked his hair. One had even called it the color of a hot chili pepper. It hadn't been so much the words that had gotten to him, but the husky timbre of her voice when she'd said it. For the first time since his embarrassing freckles had been replaced by a healthy, ruddy complexion, he hadn't wished he'd been born with any hair color other than red.

He adjusted the collar on the forest-green sports shirt he'd picked to go with long, lean, dark brown jeans. And then he brushed his teeth one more time just in case some of the spice of his Mexican lunch lingered on his tongue. He was taking Allie to Brickstone's tonight for steak and a really good bottle of wine. Holly River didn't offer a better restaurant. One more deep breath and he left his apartment. Sam hadn't been nervous about a date in a long time, but going out with Allie seemed like a milestone in his life.

He drove to the address she had given him, surprised that a place just beyond the borders of his town was unfamiliar to him. He thought he'd seen every country road and gravel path in Bolton County. At least he'd never arrested anyone from this location.

Well-manicured, quiet neighborhoods within Holly River boundaries gave way to large lots with small clapboard houses and areas of struggling vegetable growth. Most of the houses looked tired, as if they'd been standing for a century or more. Following Allie's directions, he turned off the paved road onto a dirt lane and progressed half a mile until he came to a boxy-looking frame house painted a washed-out white. He parked and got out of the car.

"Hi, Sam," Allie called from the tiny front porch. She shut the door behind her and hurried down two steps and across a dusty patch of dirt that didn't look like it had supported flowers or even grass for many years.

Sam wasn't about to draw any conclusions about Allie's home. After all, she was a waitress and had to get by mostly on tips. And she looked so darn good and seemed so sweet that she could have lived anywhere and he wouldn't have cared. He'd seen her only in black pants and a white T-shirt with the River Café's logo on it, an artist's interpretation of the Wyoga River. He'd thought she was pretty then, but in tight-fitting blue jeans and a pink sweater, she was a knockout.

"You look great," he said.

She brushed a strand of brown hair from her shoulder and smiled. "You, too."

"Is Brickstone's all right with you?"

"Are you kidding? I've wanted to go to that place since I got to Holly River."

Pleased with the choice he'd made, Sam headed toward town. He told Allie about the tourist who'd gotten bit by a cottonmouth and how Sam had driven him to the hospital. Allie confessed to dropping a tray of food this afternoon. He found himself laughing and smiling a lot—and wanting to reach across the console to take her hand.

The restaurant was crowded, mostly with

tourists. The few locals who recognized Sam greeted him when he and Allie walked by their tables. Sam figured his date with the River Café waitress would be all over town by Monday morning.

Sam ordered the wine, and they set their menus aside while they enjoyed a first glass. "How long have you been in this part of the state?" Sam asked. "I know you've only been at the café for a week or so."

"That's about how long I've been around. Got the job a few days after moving in."

"You like it here so far?"

"It's nice. I've only lived in cities, so this is quite a change for me."

"I guess it seems too quiet for a city girl," Sam remarked.

"Quiet is what I was looking for," she said.

"What brought you to the High Country?"

She looked into her glass as if the rich red color held some sort of fascination. "I guess I can tell you," she finally said.

"Sure you can, if you want to."

"I was in an abusive relationship in Charlotte, and I had to get out. I'd stayed with this guy for over two years. Kept thinking it would work if I could just figure out what didn't set him off." She chuckled, but it wasn't a happy sound. "Problem is, *everything* set him off, and I got to the point where I knew I'd have to leave or die trying to fix the relationship."

Sam clenched a fist under the table. His sister had been in a similar situation, and he'd forced her to recognize what a threat her boyfriend had been. Lila had hated him for a while. Like Allie, Lila thought she'd marry the creep and make a decent man of him. But Sam knew it was no use. Now Lila thanked him every time they talked. Sam had no tolerance for men who mistreated women.

"Did the guy try to get you to stay?" Sam asked.

She frowned. "Let's just say he was very persuasive. I actually left in the middle of the night with nothing but a suitcase and my cat. Bart came running out of the house as I pulled out of the drive. I don't know if he got in his car to chase me, but I'm glad a cop wasn't clocking me as I drove away."

She reached across the table and placed her hand over Sam's. "I really don't like to talk about this. I got out in time, so now it's history and I'm fine. I'm happy to change the subject."

"Okay. But one last question. Does he know where you are?" Yes, this was his cop's mind working, but he felt he had to know.

"I don't see how he could. I'm on the other side of the state, on the outskirts of a small town. I'm using my mother's maiden name, Shroeder, which I plan to make my own soon. Since Bart never asked many questions about my family, I'm sure he has no idea what my mom's name was. And everyone at the café just knows me as Allie anyway." She smiled. "And admit it, Sam, it takes more than a good GPS to find my house."

He turned his hand over and entwined his fingers with hers. "That's for sure. You own that place?"

"No. I'm just renting a room. The lady who owns it used to babysit me when I was a child. She's known my family for years. When I left Charlotte, I called her to see if she had a place I could stay for a while. Luckily she did."

He squeezed her hand. "And lucky for me."

She seemed pleased by his statement. "I haven't accepted any dates since I've been here, but you seemed so different. It's not just that you're a cop. I mean you can't tell everything about a person from his job. For heaven's sake, I work in a restaurant, and I can't boil water. But I instinctively trusted you from the first time you came in the café."

She gave him a warm smile. "I guess I shouldn't have admitted to my lack of cooking skills. That's not something most country men want to hear."

He returned the smile. "Ma'am, if you boil water for me, I promise to praise it to the sky."

He poured an inch more of wine into her glass, liking the way her hazel eyes reflected in the mahogany color and the low restaurant light. Sam used to tease his friends—men and ladies—that he was no choirboy, but heck, that wasn't true. He'd come from a good Irish Catholic family and he had actually been a choirboy. So yeah, he could be trusted, but once a woman indicated in that special way women had that she was ready for more than a kiss, he was always anxious to please. He would wait for when Allie was ready. She was worth waiting for.

"So anything besides the snake scare happen today?" she asked him. "You and the chief solve any big crimes?"

Sam chuckled. "We don't have too many big crimes in Holly River. Right now we're trying to locate a dozen hoses and pole sprinklers stolen from the hardware store." Carter had given the okay to mention the stolen items, or Sam would have been more vague. Maybe someone would provide a clue, Carter reasoned, and besides, Carl Harker had told everyone anyway.

"This may not sound like Charlotte-level crime, but here it's a big deal. The guy who owns the store said the total value of the items taken is over three hundred dollars." He paused, thinking about the hours Carter had put in today looking for the missing goods. "It's not the money. It's the violation that really counts."

"Of course. Where are you looking?"

"Outlying farms," Sam said, pleased that she showed an interest in his job. "We've been in a drought, so watering systems are needed almost countywide. Carter has a list of people he suspects, and if one of them suddenly has a bumper crop, he'll probably find his thief."

"Seems to me that farming would be difficult in the mountains," Allie said.

"Why? Because of the uneven land?"

She nodded.

"I need to take you to our vineyard. When you see what those guys did with their terraced land, you probably will change your opinion of mountain farming. The valleys around here are rich with minerals. As a matter of fact, the River Café buys its produce locally. It's some of the best around."

She gave him a subtle smile. "I'd like to see it—the vineyard I mean. Did you have a day in mind?"

This date was going well. Now Sam had a second date to look forward to, and he sure as heck planned on getting a good-night kiss.

Sam collected that kiss in his car when he brought Allie home. He might have tried for a second one, but a woman waited by the door of the house. Allie got out of his car and practically ran to the porch. Sam figured the woman was the family friend Allie had spoken of, the one who owned the house. He rolled down his window to listen to the exchange between the women. Everything seemed normal until he heard the older woman say, "I know that man. He's a Holly River cop, isn't he?"

Sam tried to identify her, but she ducked inside the door out of the glare of the porch light. He wasn't sure if she was glad Allie was dating a cop, but he figured she was. A cop was certainly a better choice than the guy Allie had left behind.

SUNDAY MORNING CARTER SHOWERED, shaved and slipped into a pair of worn jeans and a T-shirt. He had his coffee on his front porch, listening to the sounds of the creek running along the edge of his property. He'd searched long and hard for this perfect piece of property just outside Holly River. He and Lainey went over several house plans until they decided on a three-bedroom, two-bath log home model.

Lainey had just announced she was pregnant for the third time when ground was broken for the new house. And then, two months later, after the sturdy framing had been accomplished, disaster struck again. Carter could almost never sit outside his house in the shade of the great old oak trees and not remember the day Lainey called him at work and said she was having some pain and driving herself to the hospital.

Five years earlier...

CARTER BROUGHT LAINEY *home from the hospital after learning that her third pregnancy had resulted in another miscarriage. The car they were riding in was deathly quiet, neither of them speaking. When they pulled into the parking lot of their apartment, Carter took Lainey's hand. "We'll try again," he said. "Next time..."*

Lainey looked at him with devastatingly sad eyes. "There won't be a next time, Carter."

"You don't want to try again? The fourth time may be..."

"No, Carter, I don't," she interrupted. "I can't do this again. It's too hard. It's hopeless."

"You don't know that," he argued. "Lots

of women have several miscarriages before they carry to term."

"We've failed," she said. "It's not working for us. I want to start over." She let several tense moments pass before saying, "Away from Holly River."

"Okay, we'll move. Maybe a new environment will make a difference."

"No, Carter. I'm sorry this is such bad timing, but I'm leaving. I'm leaving Holly River, and I'm leaving you. If I don't, the heartbreak will kill me."

Soon after, Carter changed the plans for his house. He eliminated the third bedroom since there would be no children. In a way, he understood what Lainey had tried to tell him. Like her, he couldn't go through this again. He enlarged the master bedroom and added a garage. And now he had a 1,500-square-foot home with four huge rooms, two nice bathrooms, a double garage and one lonely man rattling around inside.

The house, with its wide front porch, sloping burnt-orange roof and sturdy chimney, was as cold and empty as a greenhouse when the plants had all died. His mother and sister, Ava, had bought furniture, and curtains and bedding—all the things he'd imagined Lainey buying. They'd tried to make the house welcoming and comfortable. To Carter, it was a place to live.

Carter remembered his father putting his arm around his shoulders at the only show of affection Raymond had ever given him. The day Carter moved into the house, Raymond came to him, leaned in close and said in a voice almost cool and certainly collected, "I'm sorry, son. This has been a really tough break." Carter had clenched his fists to keep from striking his father's face. Raymond Cahill had fathered three children. Carter had failed three times. Oh, it was a "tough break," all right. And then Raymond had walked to his car while the rest of the family tried to make the housewarming a celebration.

The "tough break" had nearly broken the man who'd lost everything. Carter decided he would never marry again either. He had two reasons for reaching this decision. One, he knew he could never survive such losses a second time. And while he wasn't the type to anticipate tragedy in his life, he figured it could happen. It had happened once…

And two, going back three generations, the men in the Cahill family had basically been heartless and didn't seem capable of empathizing with anyone's grief or loss. In fact, some of the Cahill ancestors had actually benefited from other people's misfortunes. Great-grandfather Vernon Cahill had wrested the land for the paper mill from a grieving family. Carter's grandfather had employed men at less than the minimum wage and scoffed at the idea of unions that might have improved their lives. Raymond had allowed Warren Jefferson to work in the boiler room, where asbestos poisoning eventually killed him.

Carter had been thrilled when Lainey announced each of her pregnancies. He put the fear of the "Cahill curse" from his mind. Each time he believed in the future, and each time he'd been forced to accept failure. So now Carter was resigned to not having children, to not loving so completely ever again. He spent his days in the town he loved, doing work he thought mattered. Some people believed he was too fair, too lenient with folks who broke the law. Maybe he was, but he had a lot of bad karma to make up for.

Finished with his coffee, Carter stood and went into the house for the keys to the patrol car. He was early, but he'd stop at High Mountain Rafting and see if Jace was around before going to the Hummingbird Inn to pick up Miranda.

Miranda...another victim of Cahill greed. And the one woman in the whole darn county who could make him want to feel again. But he wouldn't. The cost was too great. But he would do one more good deed for someone who had suffered at the hands of the Cahill family. Maybe he could save Lawton, and to Miranda, it might begin to make up for what she lost.

CHAPTER EIGHT

"YOU LISTEN TO Becky, Emily," Miranda said, with her hand under Emily's chin and her eyes locked on her little girl's soft blue ones.

"I will, Mom," Emily said.

"We'll be fine, Mrs. Larson," Becky said. "I've brought some art projects from the college. When you get back, we'll have some beautiful things to show you."

Thank goodness for Becky, Miranda thought. The girl was solid and sweet, and focused on her education. Miranda supposed she'd become an overly protective mother, but, like many parents who'd chosen divorce, she suffered from enormous guilt when it came to Em. Emily loved her father. She was only just now coming to a nine-year-old's terms with her parents' splitting up.

A car coming up the gravel drive to the main house alerted Miranda to Carter's arrival. She checked her appearance, satisfied with the jeans and plaid shirt she was wearing. "I've got to go. There are sandwiches in the fridge and chips in the cupboard. You two have fun."

They were already doing exactly that when Miranda left the cottage and headed toward the main house. Seeing the patrol car ahead, Miranda hurried her pace so Carter wouldn't have to wait long for her. She'd just reached the corner of the inn when she heard voices—Carter's and Lucy Dillingham's. She stopped and listened.

"So nice to see you, Chief Cahill," Lucy said. "What brings you out this way?"

"I've come to see one of your guests, Mrs. Dillingham."

"Can't imagine who would need our police chief," the woman said. "The Wyndemeres are off hiking, and the Rolston family went to Tweetsie Railroad for the day. That leaves only..." She drew in a quick breath. "You're here to see Miranda Jeffer... I mean Larson, aren't you? Is there trouble I should know about?"

Miranda's stomach clinched. How would Carter answer such a blunt question?

"No, ma'am. I'm just taking Mrs. Larson

out for some sightseeing. We went to high school together, and I figured she'd enjoy seeing some of the changes around here."

Mrs. Dillingham released a deep breath. "I'm glad to hear that, Carter. I was afraid your trip here had something to do with that cousin of hers, Lawton—the one that just got out of prison. I believe everyone deserves a second chance, but those Jefferson boys— they've used up more than two chances, as far as I can see. Frankly I wouldn't trust either one of them to water my flowers."

"Lawton served his time, Mrs. Dillingham," Carter said. "So far he's been a model citizen. I don't think you need to worry that he'll cause trouble for you."

Miranda said a silent prayer of thanks to Carter.

"I don't personally know those boys," Mrs. Dillingham said. "But of course I've heard things. You can't live in a small town without hearing things."

"I understand, but you're fine here in Holly River. You have a competent police department that keeps you safe."

After a pause Carter said, "I'll just go to the cottage if there's nothing else."

"Enjoy your day, Chief," Lucy said. "Miranda seems like a sweet enough girl. But just be aware. You know what they say about blood being thicker than water."

"I do. You have a nice day, too."

Miranda backed up a few steps in case Lucy followed Carter around the side of house. She didn't, and Miranda quickly caught up to Carter. "That old hen!" she said in a hoarse whisper.

"Don't worry about her," Carter said. "If you started fretting over everyone in Holly River who had a strong opinion on a subject, you'd have little time for anything else."

They got in Carter's car, and he pulled into the road and headed toward Liggett Mountain.

"Does Lawton know we're coming?" he asked.

"They don't have a phone in the cabin," Miranda explained. "And Lawton doesn't have a cell phone." She reminded herself to arrange for him to have one. "I did call Dale and told him I was coming out. He was out somewhere, but he assured me that Law was at home when he left. And since he doesn't have transportation, I assume he's still there."

Carter glanced over at her. His eyes suddenly went soft and as deep an emerald green as she'd ever seen them. His gaze warmed her to her toes just like the old days when one look from him could send her mind tumbling. She clasped her hands. "Something wrong?"

He smiled, focused on the road again. "I guess I'm just wondering how I got myself into this."

He hadn't said the words with any malice intended. In fact, his attempt at a complaint reminded her of the time when she spent nearly every day with him. So many thoughts lately were taking her back to when she was a teenager in love. She recalled sitting in a movie theater and Carter grumbling, "Why did I agree to see this girlie movie?" And then he'd take her hand in his and offer her more popcorn.

Or he'd promised to take her to the mall, and while there, he shuffled his feet and pretended disinterest, all the while telling her he hated shopping. But they'd end up in the food court enjoying milk shakes and the supreme satisfaction of being young and in love. She always paid him back by helping out at the Christmas tree farm on Saturdays or tutoring him in French.

Miranda sighed. She'd never been as close to anyone in her life as she had been to Carter in those days. Not her parents, not even Donny when she accepted his proposal. But Raymond Cahill's obvious disapproval of the Jefferson clan, and finally her father's death, had seemed to suck all the air from the balloon of their young lives. And Miranda hadn't known how to fix it.

"So did you hear about it, when my father died last year?" Carter asked. "I suppose it wouldn't surprise me that the news reached you in Durham."

"I did hear," Miranda said, slightly shocked that Carter had brought up Raymond just when she'd been thinking of him. That kind of a connection used to happen to them years ago. Maybe some bonds were never broken completely. "My mother knew and she told me. I should have sent a card to your mother…your family, but, well… I didn't know if my condolences would be of any help."

Carter made the sharp turn that led up Liggett Mountain. "My mom was always fond of you, Miranda. You know that. And from the way she reacted to seeing you the other day on Snowy Mountain, apparently her feelings haven't changed."

"Yes, your *mother* was always kind to me."

Carter smiled again. "I get what you're saying. But remember, my father suffered from a lack of social graces. Unfortunately none of us knew the cure."

"That's how you would describe his blatant prejudice against the Jeffersons and everyone like them?" Miranda regretted her words. This was Carter's father after all. "I'm sorry. That was sharp."

"Maybe, but also true. I'll admit he did have a deep-seated opinion of folks on Liggett. He seemed to have forgotten that we Cahills rose from nothing and only achieved success by swindling others and watching our backs like our heads were on the wrong way. Raymond Cahill was a man who always carried a knife and looked for someone's back to put it in."

"Still, he was your father... He loved you."

"He loved Ava," Carter said with bitterness in his voice. "He tolerated me, and he practically hated Jace. He couldn't accept that a son of his was born with a heart defect. Even when surgery corrected Jace's problem, Dad still looked at him like he was the weak link." He stared over at Miranda. She felt the force of his gaze in a slow throbbing of her temple.

"I didn't celebrate his passing like Jace did, but I admit I never grieved for the old man. I never missed him, not one day." Carter's upper lip curled at the corner. "I suppose that's a terrible thing to say. I've never admitted it to anyone before."

Miranda resisted the very strong urge to touch Carter, perhaps lay her hand on his knee or feel the tendons in his upper arms flex through the tips of her fingers. Despite his comments, Miranda knew Carter wasn't a cold man. Far from it. But he'd suffered a great loss. How had he adjusted to losing three babies and his wife? In fact, even now, did he ever experience the life-affirming compassion everyone needs once in a while? Did he seek comfort from family and friends? Did he go out on dates? Did he share his emotions with anyone? But she clenched her hands into fists and knew she was probably the last person from whom he would seek pity.

"You know, Carter," she said, "we feel what we feel. And our feelings are real. They combine to make us who we are. You have nothing to be ashamed of."

They rode in silence for a moment, following the faded yellow line that led to the summit of Liggett Mountain. Carter drove slowly, almost mechanically, as if lost in his thoughts. They still had a mile to go before reaching Lawton's cabin. After a minute he said, "Did Dad ever say anything to you, Miranda? I mean, did he ever try to belittle you in any way? If he did…"

"No, Carter, nothing so obvious as that." It wasn't true. There had been times when she'd felt about as significant as a clod of dirt under Raymond's boot. Like when she'd appear at the door and he would say, "Oh, it's you again." Or he'd pass the kids in the living room, speak a curt hello to Carter, usually followed by a stern reminder that he still had chores to finish, and ignore Miranda as if she didn't exist in a Cahill world.

Or the worst time, when he gave her the envelope in the hospital right before her father died and announced with twisted pride that he felt bad about what happened to her father. "This is more money than you'll see in three years of working at some menial job in this town," he'd said. "But I owe it to you and your mama."

Thirty thousand dollars. Enough to provide her mother with the down payment for a cute little condo in Hickory that she could manage with Warren's Social Security checks. And there was enough left over to see Miranda through four years of college if she applied for some local financial aid. She'd always thought she would end up waiting for Carter and working a job in Holly River, just like Raymond said. But that day she determined that she would make something of herself, and the Raymond Cahills of the world wouldn't make her feel as if her contributions to society were less important than anyone else's.

That was the same day she decided she would leave Liggett Mountain. Her mother needed to get away, and Miranda could no longer see a happy future for herself in Holly

River, where somewhere, deep inside, she would always blame a Cahill for her father's death. If she told Carter her feelings, she knew he would try to talk her out of her decision. But she couldn't stand between Carter and his family, and she wouldn't be looked down upon by anyone just because she came from Liggett Mountain.

A minute later, Carter pulled his SUV onto the gravel patch in front of Lawton's cabin. There was no other vehicle there, and Miranda was thankful Dale hadn't returned. This conversation was going to be difficult enough without Dale lending his opinion. Oddly, between the three of them—herself, Carter and Dale—the only one who didn't seem interested in helping Lawton was his own brother.

Lawton came out the front door wearing the same clothes he'd had on the last time she'd been here, jeans and a T-shirt. The clothes were clean, thanks to the old washing machine on the cabin's back porch, which obviously still worked. She'd have to take Law on a shopping trip as soon as possible. She'd "lend" him enough money to purchase some clothes. Perhaps that way he'd accept the money without hurting his pride.

Lawton walked out to the car, a guarded look on his face. "Carter, Miranda…" he said. "What are you all doing up here today?"

"We came to see you, Law," Miranda said, getting out of Carter's car and giving Lawton a quick hug. "How's everything going?"

"Okay, I guess." Law answered Miranda's question though his gaze never left Carter's face, almost as if he expected Carter to arrest him at any moment.

"I'm not here on business," Carter said. "This is a social call, Lawton. Can we go up to the porch and sit a minute?"

Lawton shrugged, glanced at Miranda, and she nodded her okay. "I don't have any lemonade to offer," Lawton said. "I can give you a glass of water."

Carter headed toward the porch. "That'll be fine."

After Lawton went in the house to get the water, Carter tried to turn the decrepit porch into a comfortable area for talking. He turned over an old crockery pot and shoved it next to the only chair, a rocker that had seen better days. An upside-down galvanized bucket would serve as the third chair. Carter smiled at Miranda. "Ladies' choice," he said. "But I'd advise you to take the rocker."

Lawton returned with the water and took the crockery jug for himself, leaving Carter to settle on the bucket. "What's this 'social call' about, Miranda?" he asked his cousin.

"We want to talk to you about making some strides toward re-entering society," she said. "I think you need to get out of this cabin. It can't be good for you to stay here day after day without having direction. Your life needs a purpose."

"I'm managing," Lawton said. "Besides, I don't really have anywhere else to go."

"I know that, but perhaps we can change that. After eight years of incarceration, I know you must be facing some difficult challenges."

"I've just been lying low," Lawton said. "I figure the less people see of me the better. I'm not comfortable going into town."

"What about earning a living?" Carter asked. "You and Dale can't be doing too well on what he makes at lawn work. Don't you want your own money?"

"Well, sure, but I don't think anyone around here will hire me. And I don't even know what jobs are available."

"That's why we're here, Law," Miranda said. "Carter and I both want to help you."

"Right…" He drew the word out as an expression of his doubt. "You've already helped me, Miranda."

"Yes, and I'm glad I can help you, but it's more important that you help yourself, and I think Carter can make that easier for you. You can't stay up here on this mountain with nothing constructive to do. You need to interact with other people."

"What are you suggesting?" Lawton narrowed his eyes at Carter. "What does Carter have to do with any of this?"

Carter cleared his throat. "Here's the thing, Law. Miranda thought…and I agreed, that you might benefit from a mentor. Someone who could guide you into assuming responsibility for your future. Someone who could support and encourage you, help you to get over the culture shock of being on the outside again."

"And that mentor would be you, Carter?"

"Maybe. I'm thinking about it."

Lawton stared at his hands clasped between his knees. His mouth moved as if he were talking to himself. His eyes, in his gaunt face, blinked hard. "Are you forgetting that you're the one who put me in prison, Carter?"

Miranda started to say something, to warn Lawton not to draw conclusions about Carter's feelings. But Carter raised his hand to stop her.

"I haven't forgotten," Carter said. "And I'm not going to apologize for it. You broke the law, destroyed public property and threatened the well-being of our young folks with drug sales. But that's in the past." He waited until Lawton raised his face and stared at him. "What you do from this day forward is what matters now, and I'll help you if you want me to."

"What can you do for me, Carter?" It wasn't a serious question, more a challenge for Carter to prove his sincerity.

"You need a place to live, a job. You need to take care of the details that enable you to live a productive life. You might need counseling. Heck, Law, you might even want to get your high school diploma."

"I had my fill of counseling on the inside," Lawton said.

"I know you had many counseling sessions in prison," Miranda agreed. "But that was so you'd understand what you did wrong and how you could prepare to leave prison. Now I think you need counseling to help you with the day-to-day struggles of meeting challenges on the outside. Because it is a struggle, Law. Carter and I recognize that."

Miranda reached over the arm of the rocker and placed her hand on Lawton's knee. "But you have to want this, Law. You can't go into an arrangement like this, take up Carter's time, if you resent him for what happened in the past. You have to let that go."

Lawton nodded slowly. "I never had anything against you personally, Carter," he said. "Dale told me I should have. He said you're so goody-goody with everyone else in town but you throw the book at a Jefferson anytime you can."

"And you think Dale's right, that I've been unfair to you and your brother?"

A few moments passed until Lawton shook his head. "No, not to me. I deserved what I got."

Miranda released a breath of relief. "That's another thing, Law," she said. "You can't believe what Dale tells you, and we need to get you out of this house, into your own place. I know Dale's your brother, but I don't think he is interested in helping you succeed. You should get away from him."

Lawton huffed a disbelieving chuckle. "Like I have the money to do that."

"I have a place in mind," Carter said.

Miranda stopped the rocker from moving. Carter knew of a place for Lawton to stay and was willing to suggest it?

"It's nothing fancy," Carter continued, "but it's near the bottom of the mountain where you can catch a bus into town. I think I can talk the owner of the cabin into letting you in without any up-front money."

"You'd do that?"

"I'd try as a start to this whole mentoring idea," Carter said. "But you've got to agree to listen to me, Law. Sure, we can talk things out. Sometimes our decisions will go your way, but most often they'll go mine. And you have to accept that. This is going to be hard work for you, and you have to be determined."

"And Law," Miranda said. "You can't harbor ugly feelings toward Carter. I have to believe that you'll listen to Carter and give him a chance. He knows this town, the people. And he knows you."

Carter stood, put his hand out to Lawton. "Do you need time to think about this, or do we have an agreement?"

Please, please, *Lawton*, Miranda thought as she stared at Carter's hand. *Do the right thing*.

Lawton rose, took Carter's hand. "Thank you, Carter."

And Miranda's heart melted a little bit more for both men.

ON THE WAY down the mountain, Miranda kept up a cheerful, chatty conversation. She was pleased that the meeting had gone well. She was thankful to Carter for participating. She was hopeful for Lawton's future.

"This means so much to me, Carter," she said, expressing the same thought for the umpteenth time.

"You can quit thanking me, Miranda. We'll give it a shot. That's all I'm promising."

"But you see that Law has potential, right? I mean, you didn't know him like I did, but he was always my protector. He stood up to the bullies on the mountain, threatening to come after anyone who hurt his little cousin. Until Law quit school in the tenth grade, I never worried that someone would steal my lunch money or take my book bag."

Carter smiled. "Come on, Miranda. You may have had to search the couch cushions for loose change once in a while, but you make it sound like you were this pathetic, lost soul who couldn't stand up for herself." He chuckled. "That's not the Miranda I remember."

He had a point. Once Miranda got in high school, she learned how to fit in. She shopped the stores that offered the best buys in junior-size clothing and took meticulous care of everything she owned. She managed to get braces and have her hair cut every couple of months, and she made friends with kids from all the different neighborhoods. And she attracted the attention of the nicest, cutest guy at Bolton County High School. By the time she entered her senior year, she was captain of the cheerleading squad, and though far from being a scholar, she was in the top half of her class academically. And she was Carter Cahill's longtime girlfriend.

But during those formative years of grade school and middle school she'd been an awkward, struggling kid whose safest place was next to her best friend, Lawton. She was secure with Lawton, happy to be with him. She told him everything and knew her secrets were safe. And then he quit school and she was on her own. Looking back, maybe Lawton's decision was the turning point in her life, the act that made her stand up for herself. But she owed him for so much.

Carter took a turn onto the last road before the bottom of the mountain.

"Where are we going?" she asked.

"I thought you might like to see the cabin I have in mind for Lawton. Knowing how women are—" he chuckled "—I figured you'd want to start thinking of ways to pretty it up."

"I'd love to see it," she said.

About a quarter of a mile farther, they

pulled up to a small cabin that seemed like a relic of pioneer days. But it had a porch, wide, cheery windows, parking for one car in front and a sturdy chimney.

"It's only two rooms and a bath," Carter said, putting his car into Park.

"Who owns it? Anyone I know?"

"You remember Mr. McNulty who taught civics at BCHS?"

"Yes. I always liked him. He owns this place?"

"He does. His mother lived here until she died twenty-some years ago. I guess McNulty didn't have the heart to sell it. He's living in a retirement place in Boone now but comes into the station once in a while to see what's happening in Holly River."

"So you've stayed close to him?"

"As close as a former student can be to his teacher I guess."

Miranda was charmed by the log structure, the wood-slat shutters at the windows, the small and welcoming porch. "And you think he'll rent this to Lawton?"

"I think he might be persuaded."

Miranda grinned at him. "Do I know how to pick mentors or what?"

He gave her a teasing look. "You know how to make it impossible for one to say no to you."

Carter reached above the lintel, ran his hands over the rough wood until he found a key. "Let's go check it out."

She took hold of his elbow and felt him flinch. He obviously still did not want her to touch him, even as a friend. "There's one thing I probably should tell you…"

"Okay." He paused with the key in the door. "What is it?"

"Lawton cornered me right before we left and told me about an idea he had."

Carter's eyes narrowed. "Why am I suddenly worried about this idea?"

"You have good instincts," she said, and let a pause settle between them for a moment. "Here's the thing, Carter… Lawton wondered if he might get a temporary job at the Christmas tree farm."

CHAPTER NINE

"AT OUR FARM? Snowy Mountain?" Carter felt the need to clarify since the announcement had left him staring at Miranda as if she'd just announced she were an alien. Secretly he hoped she'd meant any of the other dozen tree farms in the area.

"Yes. And it's really not such a bad idea…"

He interrupted her. "It's a terrible idea. First of all, we don't need any help. We have five guys who will stay the weeks during shearing, and then…"

"They're just temporary help, though, right? I mean those guys come and go. If a better job opens up, they'll take off. The way I remember it, you and Jace were always looking to fill vacancies when your help wandered off."

Carter could only shake his head. Miranda had an awfully good memory.

"Still, it would only be for a few weeks at most, even if I could find a spot for him."

"It's a start," she said. "And he won't walk out on you in the middle of shearing unless he gets a permanent job, and that's what we're all hoping for, right? Maybe someone in town will hear good things about Law's performance at Snowy and hire him for a different position, a permanent one."

"Are you even thinking about the fact that Jace has a lot more interaction with that farm than I do? And I can state with good authority that Lawton isn't Jace's favorite person."

Miranda frowned. "He still believes that the Jefferson boys stole his truck in high school?"

"When truck parts showed up in a Boone chop shop owned by an acquaintance of Dale's, it was a pretty good bet."

"That's all circumstantial. No one *proved* that Dale and Lawton stole that truck."

"No, it wasn't proven, but only because Dale was always clever about covering his tracks." He scowled, remembering the uproar when the truck was stolen. It had taken all of Carter's powers of persuasion to keep

Jace from hightailing it to Liggett and confronting the Jeffersons. "And Lawton just lucked out on that one. The theft may have happened years ago, but I guarantee Jace still harbors a grudge, not to mention the one he has against you."

He regretted saying that last part as soon as the words were out of his mouth. Yes, Jace had been upset that Miranda dumped his brother, but his feelings for Miranda should have changed by now. After the curt greeting Jace gave her at the farm the other day, obviously Jace still wanted nothing to do with Miranda.

"Against me?" Miranda said.

Carter knew she wouldn't let that one slide.

"Because we broke up?" she asked.

"No, because you dumped me. There's a difference." At the time Jace had almost become annoying in his concern for his big brother. While Carter had just wanted to be left alone, Jace kept asking him how he was, following up with suggestions of things they could do together. Carter had felt smothered by brotherly love.

Miranda straightened her spine. "Well,

that's just ridiculous, don't you think? I mean people break up all the time and family members don't carry hate in their hearts for all these years. Besides, maybe Jace was upset for you, but I guarantee your father was dancing the Texas two-step."

"I couldn't have cared less about my father's reaction back then, Miranda," Carter said. "And neither did Jace."

Her lips turned down. "I know. I'm sorry. But let's not allow old feelings to affect this opportunity now. Maybe if you talk to Jace, tell him how Law is trying to start over. Wouldn't he hire Lawton if you wanted him to?"

Yes, he would. Jace would grumble and complain and ask Carter if he'd forgotten the pain the Jeffersons had caused them. But in the end, if Carter wanted him to hire Lawton, he would. Refusing to give in so easily, Carter said, "I don't know what he'll do, Miranda. But it suddenly seems that this mentoring deal has more strings attached to it than a marionette."

Miranda wrinkled her nose, something she used to do when she feared she was taking a conversation too far. "But you could at least ask."

He sighed. "Come on inside the house. You don't need an answer right now."

"Okay."

He opened the front door and they went in. With one finger on her lower lip and her eyes taking in every square inch, Miranda was in decorating mode. "This is perfect, Carter. I can refresh the curtains and throw rugs, buy some pillows for the sofa and furnish new sheets and towels, and Law could live here quite comfortably."

She flitted into the small bedroom and bath and came back to the living room, where Carter had plopped onto the comfy old sofa. "When will you talk to Mr. McNulty?" she asked him.

"I'll ask him after I ask you a question, Miranda." This whole conversation about the past had brought up all the old doubts Carter had let simmer for years. He should just follow his grandmother's advice to "let sleeping dogs lie," but that wasn't his way. His need to understand the truth hadn't faded much with time, and there was one question that had burned in his mind since

Betsy had mentioned a significant fact to him in the station the day Miranda arrived.

"Sure," she said. "Ask away."

He cleared his throat, leaned back on the sofa and crossed his legs. "Why did you divorce Donny?"

Obviously that was not the question Miranda thought he would ask. Her mouth opened, she took a deep breath. "Carter, why do you want to know that? People get divorced all the time…"

"Just like they break up all the time, right?"

"Yes, right, and usually the memories are bitter and sad."

"You don't have to tell me," he said. "I'm a member in good standing of the bitter divorce club."

"I can understand that, but I don't know why you're so curious about Donny and me."

He shrugged, an effort to appear casual, but he'd started this conversation, and he was going to finish it. "Gee, I wonder why. My two best friends from high school married at the drop of a hat…"

"It wasn't like that."

"Okay, dated a few months and married."

He sat forward, holding her gaze. "Let's simplify this and start at the beginning. Did you love Donny when you married him?"

"Of course I did. How can you even ask that question?" She turned away from him, stared at the floor.

"Maybe because you had so recently been in love with me, or so you said."

"I loved you. You can't doubt that." Her gaze remained fixed on the floorboards. "But we were kids, and it was a kids' kind of love. It was fun and exciting, but we didn't know what the future would hold for us."

"I knew. My future was you."

She closed her eyes, and he feared he'd gone too far. He hoped she wasn't crying, or maybe he hoped she was. "So, you loved Donny."

"I said I did."

"Why didn't it work out?"

She spun around to face him. Her eyes were moist, but she was under control. He doubted she ever lost control these days. "Irreconcilable differences," she said.

"Ah. The divorce catchphrase."

She took a step closer to the sofa. His hands trembled with the effort not to touch her. "What do you want me to say, Carter? That I divorced Donny because I still loved you?"

He hated to admit it, but some shallow, bitter part of him wanted her to say exactly that. "Did you?"

"Donny and I just grew apart. It happens."

He sighed. "Did Donny believe you two could reconcile your differences?"

"I don't know. Maybe." Her face softened. She crouched down in front of the sofa and took one of his hands. He felt the tingle of her fingers all the way to the nape of his neck. All those years of convincing himself that Miranda was out of his life and out of his mind. All that self-discipline, and one touch from her, one earnest, sad look in those beautiful blue eyes… He struggled to keep his hand in hers.

"So why did you leave Holly River?" he asked.

"I told you at the time."

"Yeah, you did. Tell me again."

Her thumb moved languorously over his knuckles. She remained silent for several moments. "My father had just died. Asbestos poisoning from that damn paper mill.

Your father came to the hospital and gave us his big check, his pitiful way of making it all okay for Mom and me."

"Money was always my dad's answer," he said.

"I didn't want to take it. In fact, accepting his guilt money made me feel dirty."

He shook his head. "Then why did you take it, Miranda?" A slight throbbing in his temple alerted him to a pain behind his eyes. "If you hadn't taken that money, you would never have left."

"Maybe not," she admitted. "I would have been trapped here on Liggett Mountain just like my mother had always been. The truth is, Carter, I hated your father, but I didn't hate his money. I wasn't smart like your sister, Ava, and I needed it. My mother was suddenly so alone and frail, wrapped up in her sad, grief-stricken world. I couldn't save my father, but I had to save her, get her off this wretched mountain. And the best way to do that was to go with her."

Her hand moved to his knee. "I couldn't let my feelings come between you and Raymond. Yes, I hated him, but he was your father. I wasn't welcome in your house. And after I took the money, I knew I could never look Raymond in the eyes again. It was guilt money from your father, but it seemed the guilt was mine for taking it." She trapped a sob in her throat. "I told myself it was going-away money for me, a chance to start over for what was left of my family. But I don't think I ever forgave myself for accepting that check. The truth is, the thirty thousand dollars made me resent the Cahills even while it saved my mom and me."

"But you broke up with me. Are you saying you resented *me* for the money my father gave you?"

"It wasn't fair. I know that now. But at the time I couldn't make the distinction. I was grasping for a way to get us off Liggett and ease the memories from my mother's mind."

She leaned close to him, cupped his cheek in her hand. "What you and I had in the protected, brilliant world of young love was forever tarnished. We couldn't make it better with a few kisses in the back of your car in your mother's apple orchard or a few stolen beers. At the end of the night, you still went back to your big house on Hidden Creek Road and I went back to my little cabin."

"But now you're back." The words sounded hopeful, almost desperate, and he hadn't intended that. He didn't want her back. She was right. There was too much history, too much lost trust.

"I'm back for a while," she said. "But truthfully, Carter, I didn't come back with any thought of seeing you." She smiled. "Silly, I guess. Holly River is a small town. Lawton needed me, and I had to come. I know you loved someone else. I know we can't get back what we once had, but I'm glad I did run into you right away. You've been such a help to me. I can't thank you enough…"

He stood. There it was, expressed in the simplest of terms. Gratitude to the most helpful cop in North Carolina.

Gratitude.

Well, isn't that what you wanted to hear? he asked himself. *Miranda came here only to help her cousin. She had no interest in seeing you again. Running into you was an act of cruel fate.* Just as well. He'd carved out a life for himself without Miranda, without Lainey. He didn't want to get married again. He didn't want children. *Just as well you cleared the air with her today. Now you can get on with things without having to concern yourself with Miranda's feelings.* She was simply grateful.

He rubbed his hand across his mouth, nodded his head slowly. Sometimes a person just needed to know where he stood, even if it hurt. He cleared his throat. "You ready to go?"

"Carter..." Her voice was low, intensely personal. "I didn't mean to minimize what we had when we were kids. It was wonderful, some of the best memories of my life."

"Pretty great, huh?" He walked to the door, opened it. "Let's go."

She walked out ahead of him. When they reached the car, he said, "Miranda, I'll talk to Jace."

"You will?"

"Yep. I can get him to hire Lawton." *And what the heck*, he said to himself. *Might as well spread that gratitude around.*

CHAPTER TEN

FOLLOWING HIS CHIEF'S instructions, Sam McCall was headed into Boone this Monday morning to check out a few second-hand stores that were known for carrying anything from antique china to old galvanized buckets. The folks of the High Country were skilled in turning junk into dollars, and merchandise of all kinds and conditions was found each weekend at impromptu garage sales and thrift stores. And in this case, "You want it? We got it" shops.

Sam was looking for anything on the list Carter had given him of objects stolen from the local winery last night. He had concrete descriptions of a tiller, fertilizer, weed whacker and numerous other gardening supplies. It seemed that Holly River's latest crime spree, the one initiated by the theft at the hardware store, was perpetrated by someone hoping for help with a green thumb.

Traffic was light on the main street at 8:00 a.m., but Sam took the alley behind Holly River's shops and restaurants just to check out early-morning activity. And he found some.

A couple of hundred yards down the alley, behind the River Café, he saw Allie. She and another woman were leaning against an old sedan that had been gathering rust spots for about twenty years. They were talking, and of course, interesting Sam.

As he got closer, he realized the other woman was most likely the lady he'd seen from a distance at Allie's house on Saturday night. And now that he saw her up close, he recognized her. Pulling alongside the two women, Sam rolled down his window. "Good morning, ladies."

The older woman, Sheila, nodded a quick hello and opened her car door. "I've got to be heading out, Allie," she said. She climbed into her car, started the engine and proceeded to back away from the patrol car. She did a quick about-face and headed down the alley, leaving a trail of dust behind her.

"What's her big hurry this morning?" Sam asked.

Allie smiled, leaned her arms on the open window. "Don't worry about Sheila. She's always got something going on. How are you, handsome?"

"Not bad at all…now." With one eye on the fleeing sedan, he said, "Taking a break?"

"Yep. But I'd be glad to get you a cup of coffee."

Sam grinned at her. "I'd take it, but there's something I want that I'd pick over coffee any day." He crooked his finger, drawing her head into the car.

She chuckled. "Happy to oblige."

She kissed him on the mouth, a quick, over-way-too-soon peck that made him long for the kisses they'd shared while parked at the shore of Sycamore Lake last night. He'd had just the right music playing on his iPod and a couple of tall, cool beers in the console. The weather had been perfect, the moon high and full. The kisses had been spectacular. In fact, everything about Allie filled that category.

"Where you off to?" she asked.

"Just checking out some possible leads on stolen property that Carter gave me."

"Another hardware store robbery?" she said.

He didn't know why, but he didn't admit that the merchandise on his list was related to the theft from last week. "No, this stuff is bigger and better," he said. And that was true. And worth about four times as much as the loss from the hardware store.

She stood straight. "I'll get you that coffee now. Can't have you trekking off into the wilds of Bolton County without the proper fuel."

He held her wrist. "I know your landlady. She works at the Muddy Duck Tavern. She's served me up a couple of drafts."

"Right. She does."

Sam recalled that Carter had told him that the bartender at the Duck had a connection to Dale Jefferson. More specifically, she was a longtime girlfriend, or as Carter intimated at the time, an accomplice.

"So you say Sheila is an old family friend?" Sam asked.

"From way back. She was about fifteen

when I was just a kid. That's why she baby-sat my brother and me."

"Where was that?"

"Small town by Wilmington. Why?"

"No reason." Sam gave her another of his winning smiles. "Can't blame me for wanting to know everything about you."

"Now, Officer," she said, "a woman's got to have some secrets, doesn't she?" She tapped Sam on his nose with her index finger. "You already know more than any other man around here." She backed up and grabbed the handle to the restaurant's back door. "I'll see you in a minute with that coffee."

Sam drummed his fingers on the steering wheel. Why should it bother him that Allie was living with Dale Jefferson's girlfriend? That didn't mean Sheila wasn't a good person. And even if she was bolder and more brazen than Allie, that didn't mean that Allie was like her.

Problem was, though, he liked Allie, way more than he'd liked any woman in a long time. He couldn't keep his protective instincts from surfacing. Allie was nice, a sweetheart really. She told him she was a one-man woman, and he'd hoped that he could be that man. Jumping to conclusions had gotten many a guy into trouble, ruined many promising relationships, and Sam wasn't about to get caught in that trap.

Allie came out the back door, a steaming foam cup in her hand. No one should be able to make a pair of black pants and a white restaurant T-shirt fit like a second skin. Her hair was bunched up in a messy bun kind of thing, with strands falling around her face. She was a beauty from head to toe, he thought.

"Here you go," she said. "Enjoy. And be careful out there."

He returned her smile and did exactly as she said.

BY WEDNESDAY MORNING, Miranda had accomplished a lot—on only ten hours of sleep in three nights. As soon as she heard from Carter Monday morning telling her the cabin was ready for Lawton, she and Emily drove up Liggett Mountain to pick up their cousin and take him to his new home.

Lawton had been quite satisfied with the arrangements and felt the cabin would suit his needs just fine. He and Miranda made a short list of items he would need until he was okay financially. After their shopping trip, they spent the rest of the afternoon tidying up the cabin and putting supplies away.

Along with news of the cabin, Carter had also told her that he'd spoken to Jace and his mom and they agreed to hire Lawton on a temporary basis. Miranda and Lawton had mapped out the route to Snowy Mountain and discovered public transportation was available most of the way. Lawton just had to walk down to the base of the mountain in the mornings and wait for the town shuttle, which would eventually drop him about a half mile from Snowy.

If it weren't for the way Carter's voice sounded on the phone, Miranda would have sworn that everything was working out beautifully. But Carter had seemed distant, even cold. The conversation was kept short and on point. Miranda barely had time to thank him again for all his efforts before he claimed work was piling up in his office and he had to go. She hoped he wasn't regretting his decision.

On Thursday, Miranda picked up Law and

drove him to the Christmas tree farm. She figured he could use a little extra support from his family on his first day of shearing. She dropped him at the foot of the mountain where a large Santa statue waved visitors up the road. Miranda watched her cousin a few moments as he trudged up to the growing areas.

"Just be yourself, Law," she'd whispered to his retreating figure. "People will learn to trust you when they see you're a changed man."

She wasn't certain if she were giving advice or saying a prayer.

Miranda spent the rest of Thursday trying to get Lawton's paperwork in order. He needed to fill out forms for health insurance and a driver's license and have utilities in the cabin transferred to his name. Luckily, his health records were in good order. At least the prison system had released a man who, except for the obvious weight loss, seemed to be in perfectly good health.

Now if she could just keep him away from Dale's influence.

And if she could just figure out what she could do for Carter to show her appreciation for his trust in her in this matter. This last problem had kept her awake, too. Why it should, she wasn't quite certain, and she wasn't ready to admit that her sleeplessness was more her confusing feelings for Carter and not just anxiety over thanking him properly.

And now, on a bright Friday morning, Miranda smiled across the breakfast table at her daughter and decided they both deserved a special kind of day. She recalled Cora's invitation to visit her at the Cahill home. What child wouldn't love a trip to a big old house? Cora's home was filled with pretty crockery and scenic paintings of local attractions. The house had a big back porch that opened onto a large farming area with giant sunflowers and healthy, ripe vegetables. And that wasn't even taking into account the barn with a docile cow that probably still lived there and numerous goats and chickens.

Miranda admitted that a trip to the Cahill home wasn't just for Emily. She wanted to see the house again for herself. So many of her memories were wrapped up in that property, both good and bad. "Hey, I've got an idea," she said.

The ringing of her cell phone interrupted her. She glanced at the screen. Donny. This was the third time he'd called in the two weeks they'd been in Holly River, and she couldn't just ignore him. He had a right to speak to his daughter whenever he wanted to.

"It's Daddy," she said to Emily. "Do you want to answer?"

"Yes." Emily enthusiastically took the phone. "Hi, Daddy. Are you coming to see us?"

Miranda watched Em's face for a sign of Donny's answer and was relieved when her little girl's lips turned down into a pout. "Okay, that's all right," Emily said.

They chatted another few minutes until Emily handed the phone to Miranda. "He wants to talk to you."

Miranda took a deep, calming breath. "Good morning, Donny. Is everything okay with you?"

"Oh, yeah, I guess. It's just that last weekend was supposed to be my time with the squirt and now I'm facing another lonely weekend without her."

Donny was a good father, and he and

Emily shared a special relationship. But he had agreed with Miranda's plan. "I understand that," she said. "But Donny, we talked about it. You knew I would have Em with me for a few weeks."

"Sure, I knew, but I bought her this baton. She said she wanted one, and I found a really cool one with those plastic strips on it that you see on bicycle handles. She's going to love it."

"She will. I won't tell her and spoil the surprise."

"So do you have a timeline yet? How long will you be there?"

"I've made some strides with Lawton, but there is still work to be done. And I'm committed to staying as long as necessary." There was a pause during which Miranda sensed Donny wanted to say more. Finally she asked, "Is that it?"

"No. I might as well just come out and say it. Have you seen Carter?"

Her stomach clinched. She had to make her contacts with Carter sound casual and friendly. Well, they were, weren't they? "Yes, Donny, I saw him."

"Did he mention… Did he say anything about me?"

"No, he didn't. Did you expect him to?"

"No. I've known how Carter felt about me for a long time."

"I didn't see any sign of animosity where you're concerned," she said. "Carter seemed perfectly fine. Besides, he's had so much sadness in his life that he doesn't have to dwell on what happened to all of us over a decade ago."

"Yeah, I remember hearing about the miscarriages. And how did you feel when you saw him? Any tingling going on you want to tell me about…?"

"Donny, stop it. I saw him. We chatted a bit." *My heart pounded, my palms sweat, my blood raced…* "He actually offered a good suggestion for Lawton, and I thanked him."

"Good old Carter," Donny said. "Always willing to help out. What did he do for you?"

She told him about the cabin, but neglected to mention he was mentoring Lawton. So far Donny was taking Emily's absence pretty well, and she didn't want to upset him. "I have to go, Donny…"

"Wait, just one more question. What are you girls doing today?"

Going out to the Cahill home? No, she couldn't say that. "We were just starting to plan our day when you called. I'm not sure what we're doing."

"Okay, tell Em I miss her."

"Do you want to tell her yourself?"

"I already did. And I'm a little tired of talking about all this right now."

All this what? Miranda wondered. Was he tired of hearing about Carter or tired of wondering when they'd be home?

He ended the call without saying anything else. Miranda sat at the table and looked out the window onto Mrs. Dillingham's lovely garden. She'd believed she loved Donny. She'd told herself she did. But no amount of persuasion worked. She did care for Donny, but her feelings for him simply had not run as strong as the ones she'd had for Carter. And now she'd damaged both of their lives.

Thirteen years earlier...

A LIGHT DUSTING *of snow covered the campus of North Carolina State University in Raleigh. Snow was rare in North Carolina, and when it came, the entire population seemed mesmerized by its beauty. Miranda had just returned to school after spending the Christmas holidays with her mother in Hickory. Her freshman year was going well so far.*

She entered the Liberal Arts administration building, took off her cap and brushed the snow away. And then she saw Donny Larson at the end of the hallway.

"Hey, Miranda!" he called. "I heard you were going to school here." He trotted toward her. "Funny we haven't run into each other before this."

Happy to see a familiar face from home, Miranda smiled at him. She'd wanted to ask if he'd seen Carter, but didn't. "Great to see you, Donny. How have you been?"

"Okay. College is the life, isn't it? Nobody screaming at you to do your homework or get to bed earlier."

"I suppose," she said. "What's your major? Have you decided yet?"

"Nah. I've got time. Now I'm just taking the regular freshmen courses the university recommends. How about you?"

She told him about her interest in social

work. They chatted for a while until she told him she had to get to class.

"Hey, wait. Want to go out for coffee sometime? Or a movie?"

She gave him a strong look. "You don't mean a date, do you? I mean you and Carter and I...?"

"Oh, no. Just a friendly thing. Two High Country kids getting together. That's all."

"Well, then, sure. That would be fine." She gave him her cell phone number and went on to class. He called her that night and asked her opinion of the movies being shown at the Cineplex.

They pseudo-dated for most of the freshman year while going out with others, as well. By the end of term, Donny told her he was serious about her and wanted more than a buddy relationship.

At first Miranda gently declined, explaining that there was too much history between them. She even confessed that she still had feelings for Carter. But Donny didn't give up. He said that they could continue seeing each other as friendly companions, exchanging simple kisses and occasionally holding hands. "But here's the deal,

'Randa," he said. "If by the time we graduate, and neither one have found the loves of our lives, then I'm going to ask you to marry me."

She'd almost laughed at the absurd suggestion, but realized in time that he was sincere.

"I mean it," he said. "I'll pop the question and you give it serious consideration." He smiled, took her hand and looked into her eyes. "That's the deal."

And she did give his offer serious consideration. By graduation she realized that she was very fond of Donny. She trusted him, felt comfortable and secure with him. He'd done well in school, and they shared the same goals. She'd never seen Carter again and even heard he'd married.

Miranda had accepted a job offer in Durham. So had Donny. They liked the same movies, laughed at the same jokes, enjoyed the same food. They'd been dating for four years, and marriage was the next logical step. So, without a lot of fuss, they married in the courthouse of Durham's government district with just their parents and a few *friends in attendance, and they started their lives together.*

And she never admitted that her feelings for him weren't quite as strong as the feelings she'd had for...

"Mom, what are you doing?"

"Oh, nothing, honey, just looking out the window." *Snap out of it, Miranda*, she said to herself.

"What was your idea?" Emily asked. "What should we do today? Do we have to help Lawton again?"

"No, I don't think so. Lawton is at the Christmas tree farm." *And Carter is working since this isn't his day off.* "I'm going to call an old friend, Em, a lady I used to know very well. She's Carter's mom. If she says it's okay, we're going out to her big house in the country and see her garden and her animals. How does that sound?"

"Like fun. I want to go."

Yes, it sounded like fun. And it also seemed safe. With Carter working, Miranda could indulge her memories of the past in leisurely walks around the property. Maybe she could feel as close to Carter as she once had without the specter of Raymond always hanging over her head. Maybe today the memories would only be sweet ones, and she could stop thinking about how Carter was affecting her life, her sleep, her rational thoughts now, fourteen years later.

"Hello, Cora? This is Miranda..."

The question was barely out of her mouth before Cora was urging her to come out to the farm and gushing that she couldn't wait to meet Emily.

CHAPTER ELEVEN

THE DRIVE OUT of town to Hidden Creek Road was cool, fragrant and lush with summer greenness. Many old-timers still lived on the large lots on Hidden Creek in big houses they'd bought or inherited from relatives. Many had moved into town, deciding the oversize properties were too much to maintain for couples in their golden years.

Miranda had driven Hidden Creek with Carter so many times she could name most of the families who lived in the homey farmhouses. "That's where the Sampsons lived," she said to Emily. "Mr. Sampson grew the state-fair-winning pumpkin one year. The Martindales lived there. Marty Martindale was on the cheerleading team with me. And that's where…"

"Jeesh, Mom, did you know everybody?"

Miranda laughed. "No, but probably most everybody. Now I don't even know if the original families still occupy those houses. Many people have probably moved on."

"Like you did, right?"

Miranda nodded.

"But these houses are really nice," Emily said. "Why would anyone want to leave places like this?"

Like they would the cabins on Liggett Mountain? Miranda finished the thought in her head. "Things just change," she said. "And people go away to find something else they're looking for."

"What were you looking for, Mom?" Emily asked.

"I was just looking for a good education, Em." A good answer, but considering her need to escape the overwhelming grief, a lie.

The Cahill home appeared around the next curve, looking large and stately, but more like a house from a Norman Rockwell picture than a Southern mansion. Cora Cahill had made a beautiful home out of this structure. Miranda had always wanted to feel welcome inside the cozy walls, but Raymond Cahill had prevented that from happening.

She pulled into the curving drive and

parked in front of the two-story white wooden house with its wraparound porch, subtle Victorian charm and sturdy brick foundation. Oddly, the home did not reflect the grandeur that Miranda remembered. The gingerbread trim over the porch was in need of paint. The porch floorboards were faded, and the cushions on the chairs worn. Funny, Miranda thought, how one's perceptions were often quite different from reality. Perhaps maintenance on the house had suffered since Raymond died. But it was still a welcoming property, and she was glad to be here.

Cora came out the front door wearing jeans, a T-shirt and an apron tied at her waist. She scurried down the steps to the drive and grabbed Emily's hand when she got out of the car. Miranda had noticed her mostly gray hair at the tree farm, but today the color seemed almost silver.

"Well, looky here," she said, staring at Emily with eyes filled with maple syrup warmth. "You must be Emily. You look just like your mommy."

"Emily, this is Mrs. Cahill," Miranda said.

"Nonsense. It's Cora, honey. Nobody calls

me Mrs. Cahill unless they're expecting a donation."

Emily passed a confused glance at her mother but then said, "Nice to meet you, Cora."

"I've got dough ready on the kitchen table," Cora said. "Just waiting to put in the chocolate chips. How would you like to help me? Then maybe your mom will let us cheat a bit and have cookies before lunch."

Emily waited for the encouragement her mother gave her and darted along behind Cora into the house.

"You come in when you're ready, Miranda," Cora said. "Or just take some time here on the porch. We'll be fine."

Standing on the worn red-stained planks of the wide porch, Miranda felt like time had stood still for her. The white railings were still smooth under her palm. The large ferns hanging from the ceiling still tickled her forehead and cheeks. The breeze was like no other—tinged with peat moss and the sweet scent of cut grass and new flowers from the garden.

When she heard the door open again, Miranda turned to see who had come onto the porch. Was Carter here after all? No, she hadn't seen his patrol car. Still, her heart beat a sudden rapid rhythm at the thought.

But it was Ava Cahill who appeared on the porch, Carter's sister and oldest of the three Cahill children. Tall, elegant, classic Ava, always the one to command respect even though she didn't need to command it. There had been times when poor Miranda Jefferson had hidden her jealousy of Ava, the girl who had everything. Good grades, lots of friends and nice to everyone, even the ones who envied her... Carter used to say that Raymond really had only one child—Ava. Jace and himself, the old man just tolerated.

Two years older than Carter, Ava was thirty-five, and she carried her years with confidence and style. No blue jeans for her, she had on creased black denims with a white, almost businesslike blouse. Her dark hair fell to her shoulders in a sleek turned-under do that seemed to have been artistically created for her prominent cheekbones and finely arched brows.

"Miranda Jefferson," she said, giving Miranda a hug. "Mama said you were coming out this morning."

Miranda smiled. "Hello, Ava. How have you been?"

"Busy, working too hard, always homesick."

"Really? You miss Holly River?"

Ava chuckled. "Who would have thought, huh? But yeah, I do. The corporate world isn't for me. In fact, I'm trying to get a position here in Holly River."

So Ava had left and she wanted to come back. Miranda wouldn't have been more surprised if she'd heard that a member of royalty wanted to become a peasant. "Where are you applying?" Miranda asked.

"At the Sawtooth Mountain Children's' Home," Ava said. "They have an opening for a director, and I think I could do the job." She indicated a pair of wicker chairs behind them and suggested they sit. "Mama's having fun with Emily, so we can talk a few minutes."

Remembering Ava's ability to get along with almost anyone and gently persuade others to her way of thinking, Miranda was certain that Ava could do any job she set her mind to. "That's great," she said. "Your mother must be thrilled that you're coming home."

"She is. She's already talking about letting me redecorate my old room, though I've told her often enough that I'll be living at the children's home. It's what I want. I'm just here for a few days now to have interviews and the like. And, if I get the job, I won't be starting until the fall." Ava leaned close. "I'm so thankful you brought your little girl here today, Miranda. Mama needs some female companionship once in a while—other than those old hens at the church."

Miranda smiled. "It must have been hard for Cora when you went off to Charlotte and left your two brothers behind."

Ava nodded. "It wasn't easy for her, the only woman among three males—especially considering that those three males couldn't get along for as much as ten minutes at a time." Patting Miranda's hand, she added, "You probably remember that my daddy, Raymond, wasn't the easiest man to please."

Did she ever. Not wanting to bring up unpleasant memories, Miranda simply nodded and stared over the green lawn that spread to the barn and said, "I always loved this place. It's so beautiful."

"It is," Ava agreed. "Daddy was always prideful about keeping the house in perfect condition, almost like it was a showplace and testament to his success." She chuckled, looked around the shabby porch. "Obviously, Mama has different priorities."

So it wasn't just Miranda's imagination. The old home had suffered from neglect recently.

"Since I got home, I've been after Mama to hire someone to make some needed repairs around here, but she doesn't seem bothered.

"You know, it's funny," Ava continued. "Since we were speaking of Daddy and how hard he was to get along with, I suppose you noticed that the boys had a more difficult time with him than I did. He was always on Carter's case about doing better on the football field, getting better grades. And Jace, well, that relationship seemed a nightmare from the beginning. And Jace never did anything to make it better."

Miranda had noticed, but she didn't respond to Ava's statement. She didn't know why Ava had brought up the subject or what Ava wanted her to say.

"I didn't ask to be the favorite child," Ava went on. "But Daddy didn't even try to hide it. Life was tough for Carter and Jace, but I know I don't have to tell you that."

Ah. So Ava was aware that Miranda had suffered under Raymond's disapproving watch.

Ava looked around the porch. "I guess that's the reason this place never felt much like a real home until he passed on."

She shook her head. "I can imagine how that sounds, like an ungrateful daughter speaking ill of the dead, but honestly, Miranda, this old house went from a war zone of sorts to a sanctuary in a matter of days after Daddy was buried. We all found a measure of peace with his passing. It's just a fact."

"I'm sorry to hear that, "Miranda finally mumbled. "Fathers are so important."

Ava gave her a sympathetic nod. "I know you felt that way about your own daddy, Miranda. Mama and I always felt awful about the circumstances of Warren's death."

"It wasn't your fault," Miranda said.

"No, but Daddy was mean. There's no way to sugarcoat it. He loved Mama, I know that for sure, and he liked me, and he accepted Carter, so long as he excelled as a fullback…" She paused, looked at Miranda. "I guess you heard about what happened to him."

"I did," Miranda said. "I was sorry to hear about Carter's losses and his divorce."

"It was hard on everybody, even Daddy. He was always a kinder, gentler man when Lainey was expecting."

"How about you, Ava? Do you have children?"

"Me? I never married. Just wasn't in the cards for me. Had a couple of serious relationships, but something always happened to tear us apart—either my job or his." She smiled. "But if I get this position at the Sawtooth Children's Home, I'm hoping to have eighty kids under my watchful eye when I move back to Holly River."

Miranda experienced a pang of sympathy for Ava. She obviously cared for children. She was willing to change her life to help them. But she'd never had one of her own. "I hope it goes well for you, Ava," Miranda said.

"Thanks…"

"What's going on around here? Whose car is…?"

The boisterous voice coming from the corner of the porch belonged to Jace Cahill. He stopped midstride, letting his sentence hang in the air, stared at his sister and her guest. "When did you get here?" he asked.

Not certain to whom he was speaking, Miranda kept silent. "Yesterday morning," Ava said. "Don't I even get a 'welcome home, sister'?"

"Obviously, you're welcome," Jace said. He looked like a workingman in his T-shirt, grubby jeans and high-top leather boots. His light brown hair was pulled back and held with a bit of sisal twine. He removed a bandanna from his neck and wiped his tanned brow. "Just didn't know you were coming."

"I believe in the element of surprise," Ava said. She glanced at Miranda. "You remember Miranda Jefferson?"

"Sure." Jace gave her an icy stare. "Saw her the other day at the tree farm."

"Hi again, Jace," Miranda said.

He shot a glance at the house. "There's a kid in the kitchen with Mama. Saw her through the window." Looking back at Miranda he said, "She yours?"

"That's my daughter, Emily," Miranda said.

"She's cute," Jace said, almost as if the words were difficult to get out. "Whatever they're baking smells good."

Miranda wanted to ask him how Lawton was working out at the tree farm, but maybe now wasn't such a good time, especially if Carter had had to persuade him to hire Law.

"Did you come for sandwiches?" Ava asked, standing up. "Mama made enough for all the workers. I'll go in and get them."

"I came for sandwiches, but I think I'll stay for cookies." When Ava headed into the house, Jace sat in the chair she left. The uncomfortable vibe Miranda had experienced since he came onto the porch was more pronounced now that Ava had gone. She resisted an urge to squirm under his intense gaze.

Jace leaned forward, rested his elbows on his knees. "So, last week I see you on Snowy

Mountain and today you're here on Mama's front porch."

The condemnation in his voice prickled the hairs on Miranda's arms. "Cora invited us for a visit, Jace," she said.

"I'm sure she did. Mama's like that, a true believer in Southern hospitality."

Miranda sat straight, refusing to be cowed by Jace's tone. "As opposed to someone who holds a grudge for more than a decade."

Jace smiled, but it wasn't a natural expression. "Has it been that long, Miranda? You should know that as far as grudges go, I can hold them longer than a decade or two."

She scowled. "I'm sure you can."

He leaned back, a gesture of relaxation that Miranda didn't believe for a second. "Your cousin Lawton is working up on Snowy today trimming trees. But I guess you knew that."

"Yes, I knew."

"You can still get my brother to do most anything you want, can't you? Including making me hire the delinquent who stole my truck and carted about twenty pounds of methamphetamine around in his car a few years ago."

The last thing Miranda wanted on this near-perfect day was to get into an argument with Jace, but she had to defend her cousin. "No one proved that Lawton stole your truck, Jace, and as far as the other is concerned, Law paid his debt. He's not dealing in any drugs now."

"Course not. Kinda hard to make contacts when you're locked up. But I'll bet he's still got a few numbers."

Miranda's cheeks flushed with anger. "Look, Jace, you didn't have to hire Lawton, and as far as I'm concerned you don't even have to speak to him while he's at the tree farm. You just have to pay him what he's worth shearing your trees. You don't have to be his best friend."

"Well said, Miranda, but I don't want to snipe with you. I just want you to recognize a solid truth."

"And what's that?"

"I'm not the only one who resents Lawton coming back here. Folks are starting to talk…"

"I couldn't care less," Miranda said. "Narrow-minded…"

"They're talking about you, too," Jace

said. "Folks don't much like that you've come back after so many years just so you can force this town to accept a criminal back into their midst."

"For heaven's sake, Jace, Lawton is a human being first. Can't you and all the other people in this town cut him some slack?"

"Sure, I did. He's working at Snowy right now. Doing an okay job, too. But you should know that the feelings for the Jefferson boys have only gotten worse over the years. And it isn't such a big surprise that the crime statistics in this town have risen since those boys got back together. We've had a couple of significant burglaries since Law got back."

Miranda stared straight ahead and took a deep breath. She didn't want this argument to ruin her and Emily's day. She was here to visit with Cora and give her daughter a happy memory of her time in Holly River. If Jace wanted to act like a jerk by jumping to ridiculous conclusions, fine, but she wasn't going to sink to his level.

"But this isn't just about Lawton, Miranda," Jace said. "It's mostly about Carter.

You hurt him bad, and I'm one Cahill who isn't so quick to forgive and forget."

"I noticed." She slanted him a narrow glance. "How noble of you to stick up for your brother, even when he doesn't need it. In case you haven't figured it out yet, he's a grown man who can take care of himself."

Jace almost smiled. "I know that. But he's been through a lot, and I guess he's settled into a kind of quiet life now that suits him. At least he seems content most of the time. I'd hate to see him upset and all mopey again. I'd really hate that."

"Mopey?" Miranda could only stare at Jace. "How can you refer to your brother, after what he's been through, as *mopey*?"

"I was referring to the way he moped around this house when you left him."

Miranda's hands were shaking so badly she clasped them tightly and shoved them between her knees. And then she looked down the drive and realized the exact person they were talking about had just driven in. Miranda's anxiety over seeing Carter's unexpected arrival was overshadowed by her relief at ending the discussion with Jace.

"I guess we'll find out how he is today," she said. "Isn't that his patrol car?"

Jace squinted into the sun. "Sure is. I'm going back inside. But just remember one thing, Miranda. I'm watching. Don't hurt him again."

He strode around the porch to the back of the house. Miranda's blood was throbbing in her temples. How dare Jace? As if she would ever hurt Carter again. She didn't mean to hurt him back then. In a way she'd been trying to save him—from alienating his father, from her own grief and growing animosity toward the Cahills. And she'd been trying to save herself and her mother. If Jace were truly such a family-first kind of guy that he wanted her to suddenly believe now, why couldn't he see that?

The sweetness of her high school romance with Carter had turned sour, and there had been no way to get it back again. But now... sitting on this porch again, the promise of a long walk around this comfortable fresh-smelling farm this morning, she'd considered a few times that maybe some of the sweetness was still there. Why was Jace warning her? Was he afraid that whatever had existed between her and Carter just needed a bit of encouragement to blossom into something really wonderful again? Miranda felt a shiver in her spine. What if it could? But one thing was certain. That encouragement wasn't going to come from Jace.

CARTER PULLED NEXT to the midsize automobile he'd seen parked at Mrs. Dillingham's bed-and-breakfast. Miranda's car. His breath caught in his lungs. He got out of his vehicle and strode slowly to the house.

"Hi, Carter," Miranda said.

"Hello, Miranda." He kept his voice low and calm so she wouldn't see that her unexpected presence here had unsettled him. "What brings you out here?"

"I talked to your mother this morning, and she invited us out. I thought Emily would enjoy seeing the garden and the animals." After a slight pause, she added, "It's nice to see you. I thought you would be working."

He glanced down at his uniform. "I am. Just on my way back from a minor traffic accident and thought I'd check on my mother."

Miranda smiled. "The ladies have been in the kitchen since I got here, making cookies."

"Who's that? Mama and your daughter?"

"And Ava."

"Ava's here?"

"Yes. It was so good seeing her again. She looks great."

Pieces of this puzzle began falling into place in Carter's brain, including the phone call he'd just received from his mother. He stepped up onto the porch. "How long ago did you talk to Mama?"

"This morning some time. I'd say two or three hours ago. Why? Did she tell you we were out here?"

"No, she didn't, and we talked very recently. She called me and asked, if I had a few minutes, if I would come out and get rid of a beehive by the back door."

Miranda's eyes widened. "I didn't notice any bees…" She covered her mouth with her hand. "Are you thinking what I'm thinking?"

"If you're thinking that the only pesky critter here isn't a bee, then yes."

Miranda took a step toward the porch

railing and wrapped her hands around the smooth wood. "Don't be upset with her, Carter. Your mama was the one Cahill who liked me, I mean really liked me."

He gave her a crooked smile. "And I didn't?"

"Yes, of course you did. But I think your mama always kind of hoped that..."

He stopped her midsentence. "Well, she was wrong, wasn't she?"

Miranda's expression withered. "She wasn't the only one. For a long time I thought you and I would be together forever."

"I suppose that's true enough." He positioned himself next to her at the porch railing and looked over the land surrounding the house. "How does the place look to you?" he asked. "Porch needs staining and the house could use a coat of paint."

"Still, it looks wonderful." She pointed to a copse of trees a few hundred yards from the house. "The apple orchard is lush and green. You'll probably have a good crop this year."

He nodded. "Yep. And then it's an endless stream of apple pies, apple butter, apple cobbler, you name it." He stepped aside, putting a few more inches between them when it suddenly occurred to him that years ago, he and Miranda had stood like this often on his parents' front porch, looking over the land, talking about their future. Then warm feelings had flooded his heart. Now he just wanted to keep the conversation impersonal.

A moment of silence passed between them until commotion coming from the side of the house caught their attention. Cora, Ava, Jace and Emily appeared beside them. Ava gave her brother a hug. "Guess who's home?" she said.

"Looks like we all are," Carter answered.

Emily held a tray of cookies. "Hi, Carter," she said.

"Ah, hello," he responded. His throat felt dry.

"We made cookies," she said. "Would you like one?"

He waved his hand in a dismissive gesture, not realizing until he'd done it that she might be hurt by his disinterest. "Not right now, kid," he said.

"Oh, okay." Emily sniffed, looked around for someone else to give a cookie to."

"I'd like one, Emily," Jace said. "In fact,

I'm so glad Carter didn't take one that I might take two."

After Jace took his cookie, Emily showed her mother the tray. "How about you, Mom?"

"Oh, absolutely," Miranda said. "I remember Miss Cora's cookies, and no one can turn down her chocolate chip."

"These are mostly Emily's doing," Cora said. "She put her own special love into each one."

Miranda took a large bite. "Heavenly," she said.

Carter looked away. He certainly hadn't intended on coming to his mother's today and ending up feeling like a heel. But the damage was done.

Jace praised his cookie to the sky. "Not only is this little lady cute as a chipmunk on a fence post, but she's a master chef."

Carter's temple began throbbing. He knew what Jace thought of Miranda, and yet his brother was pouring on all his charm. Well, sorry. The kid was Donny Larson's, through and through. Her eyes, her curly blond hair, that round face. Maybe Jace could ignore that, but Carter couldn't.

After a few uncomfortable moments,

Cora, Ava, Jace and Emily turned to go back to the kitchen. "I think that next batch is ready to come out of the oven," Cora said. From the corner of his eye, Carter could see, and feel, the look she gave him. Condemnation and disappointment all wrapped up in one scathing glare.

So here he was, standing like the schmuck he'd proved himself to be after disappointing his mother and knowing quite clearly why she was upset. And stuck with the other woman he'd probably left inconsolable. He risked a glance at Miranda. Bad idea. She was seething. In fact, she grabbed his arm and marched for the porch steps.

"Where are we going?" he asked, though he wouldn't have been surprised if she'd marched him to the property border after stopping for a shovel to dig his grave.

"Away from the house so no one can hear us."

Wow, had she always had that strong a grip? He dutifully followed her, the silence between them growing heavier with each step.

When they reached the apple orchard, she

positioned them behind a tree and whirled on him. "What is wrong with you?"

"Nothing. What are you talking about?" Surely he knew.

"Would it have killed you to take a cookie?"

"I didn't want a cookie. Is that a crime? If so, I'm the head of the police department and I've never heard about it."

"Shut up."

He did.

"You could have taken a cookie, nibbled a bite and given the rest to a squirrel for all I care. But, for God's sake, Carter, you take the cookie!"

"Well, excuse me, but I left mine for another lucky person. Jace was happy enough to take my share." Jeesh, he was sounding more petulant by the minute.

"Don't you know anything about children?" Miranda demanded. And then suddenly her face went soft, the glare of anger left her eyes. "I'm sorry. I shouldn't have said that. It was cruel, considering your history."

Finally he sensed he had the upper hand. "Don't let the tragedy of my past interrupt your tear, Miranda. Go ahead, give it to me good."

"Again I'm sorry, but you must have been around children. You know how important it is for a parent to recognize their kid's accomplishments. Emily contributed to those cookies. And now that we're on the subject…"

She drew a breath. He cringed inside.

"…you've barely said three words to Em in all the times you've seen her. Why is that, Carter? Because she's my child?"

Now she was really off base. "No. Absolutely not."

"Well, it can't be because she's Donny's child. You couldn't be that narrow, that… mean. She's just a little girl, Carter. She doesn't know about the animosity you feel toward her father, or the animosity you feel toward her mother. For Pete's sake, give her a break."

Silence hung heavy over the two of them. Carter knew it was his turn to speak, but all he could think to say was, "You're wrong on both counts."

"What? What does that mean?"

"I can't treat Emily like I would any other

child exactly because she is Donny's. Just like you were."

"That's ridiculous. Hate me if you want, but treat my child with the kindness and courtesy she deserves. She likes you. I don't know why, but..."

"That's the other thing."

"What other thing?"

"I said you were wrong on two counts. The second is that I hate you, or that I hold animosity toward you. I don't." He almost shouted the words. Then he lowered his voice to almost a whisper and said, "Good God, Miranda, I don't."

She raised her face to look at the clear blue sky before lowering her gaze to the ground. Then she stared directly into his eyes, and he felt his knees go weak. "So you don't hate me for marrying Donny?"

For a heart-stopping moment he remembered the exact second he'd heard that his girl had married another guy. Not just any guy, but his best friend. He'd just gotten home from college, with his degree in criminal technology under his belt. His parents threw a party for all his friends. One of them, Josh Lerner, walked up to him, an empty bottle of beer in his hands, and said, "So, how do you feel about Miranda marrying Donny Larson?"

He hadn't believed it. Donny wouldn't do that. But Josh was almost as good a friend as Donny was. He wouldn't lie.

There had followed some back-and-forth conversation.

"Doggone, buddy, you didn't know," Josh said.

"I didn't," Carter said. "But why should I care? What Miranda does with her life is her business."

The party was over in that instant for Carter. He hadn't seen Miranda in four years, but time and his heart had stopped when he'd heard the news. He'd always thought, hoped... At that moment he hated Donny, but he'd never been able to transfer those feelings to Miranda.

"I don't hate you for anything, Miranda," he said now. "I was hurt." A bitter chuckle exploded from his lips. "Yeah, that's an understatement. But..." He matched her gaze and held it. "I never hated you. How could you think...?"

She raised her hands and cupped his face,

her soft palms resting on his cheeks. "Oh, Carter, I'm so sorry for hurting you. I just couldn't go on the way we were, pretending everything would be okay. So much had changed. I couldn't ignore it. And I'm so sorry for what happened to you with Lainey. You're a good man. You've always been…"

He stopped her by lowering his face. For one life-changing moment he considered what he was about to do, and then he cast aside his doubts. Her eyes met his, moist and bright, and he pressed his lips to hers. A gentle brush became suddenly hard and hungry. This was Miranda, and she felt so good, so natural. The years melted away as he wrapped his arms around her and deepened the kiss. The contact lasted for a blissful eternity and yet was over in an instant.

He dropped his hands, backed away. He felt her breath on his mouth. She was breathing heavily, her lips parted, still moist from his kiss.

"Oh, my…" she whispered. She splayed her palm against his chest. He was certain she could feel the racing of his heart.

He blinked hard, swallowed. "This is stupid, Miranda. We can't do this." His voice sounded tortured, just like he felt. "I can't love you again. I can't love anyone. It's all been so hard, and I can't go through the heartache again. The truth is, I'm a coward."

"We're all afraid of something, Carter..."

"Not like I am. I won't let this happen between us."

"Mom! Where are you?"

Miranda jerked away from him, stared over his shoulder. "I'm here, Em. I'm coming." She stepped aside, looked one last time into Carter's eyes and left the shelter of the apple tree. "It's okay, Carter," she said. "I get it." Without looking back, she headed toward the house.

CHAPTER TWELVE

CARTER LEFT WITHOUT saying goodbye to anyone in the house. Her mind burdened with thoughts of what had happened, Miranda took Emily for a walk around the farm. Every step reminded her of the past, other walks and another hand in hers. Those days were not always sweet, but the same could not be said for the sights and smells she allowed herself to experience today. The meadow grass was fragrant and green. Homey, natural scents from the barn made her think of late evenings doing chores.

Miranda still loved him. She couldn't keep denying it. Had she come to that conclusion after only one kiss? No, she'd known it shortly after marrying Donny. She'd known it from the first moment she saw Carter at Dale's cabin on Liggett. She hadn't treated him fairly that day, but she'd been overwhelmed with feelings and memories and the agonizing joy of seeing him again and coming to terms with what she'd lost.

But Carter didn't want to love her. He called himself a coward. But how could he be otherwise? How was a man supposed to face the heartache the relationships in his life had brought him? He was content with his job, his cabin, this little town where he knew who he was and was respected and liked. How could Miranda upset the calm, peaceful passage of his days? How could she convince him that something was missing from his life when he didn't want to believe it?

"Mom, aren't the goats cute?"

Miranda turned toward her daughter, who was scratching the head of one very docile ruminate. "They are indeed," she said. "I know the Cahills still have a cow and a horse, if he's not out in the pasture. Why don't we go in the barn and check them out?"

They finished their tour with a trip around the barn where Cora's vegetable garden was flourishing. Already the fall gourds were trailing along the ground in all their warty splendor. Pumpkins were well on their way to becoming scary jack-o'-lanterns.

"Would you like to live on a farm, Em?" Miranda asked her daughter as they were headed back to the house.

"I might," Emily said. "But I don't know if I like my hands being this dirty."

"I'm sure Miss Cora has some soap in the kitchen." Miranda sighed. Perhaps it was just as well that Emily wasn't sold on a life on the outskirts of Holly River.

"I hope you had as fine a day as I did," Cora said when they were ready to leave. She handed them a sack of cookies and travel cups of cold iced tea. "Come back anytime." She hugged Emily and held Miranda back from following her daughter out the door. "She's a precious little thing," Cora said. "Please bring her to visit again. It can get lonely out here, and Emily is a ray of sunshine."

"Thanks for everything."

"I'm sorry Carter ran off like he did," Cora said. "He always has an emergency or someone that demands his attention."

Miranda nodded, unable to admit that

Carter had left because of her, because of that kiss.

They were almost back to the Hummingbird Inn when Miranda's cell phone rang. She checked her car's digital screen hoping to see Carter's name, but knowing he wouldn't call her. Like her, he was probably still reeling from the emotions that had overtaken both of them. Donny's number appeared. She connected, putting the phone on speaker.

"Hi, Donny. Everything okay?"

"I'm a little lonely," he said. "There isn't much to do at this charming bed-and-breakfast you're staying in."

"You're here?" Miranda's heart sank. He hadn't mentioned coming to Holly River when they'd talked earlier, and right now her mind was full to overflowing with Carter. What did Donny want? How long did he plan to stay? He didn't think he could move in the small cottage with the two of them?

"Just came for the afternoon," he said. "Had a few hours and thought I'd drive over from Durham to see my girls."

"Hi, Daddy," Emily said with her usual enthusiasm.

Miranda knew she couldn't spoil this surprise for her daughter. "We'll be at the inn in a few minutes," she said.

"Hope you don't have any plans," Donny said. "I remember this pond on Mr. McDougal's property that always had a lot of trout in it. Emily, how would you like to go fishing?"

"I'd like to, Daddy."

"No, we don't have plans for the rest of the day," Miranda said, figuring she could run the errands she'd planned for Lawton tomorrow. Now all she had to do was steel herself to spend an afternoon with Donny when all she really wanted was to sit in the garden and think about how she'd led her life, the mistakes she'd made and the future that would never be hers.

CARTER DID NOT want to go back to his cabin. He'd checked with Betsy, and he wasn't needed at the station. And with the rest of the day stretching ahead of him and the turmoil of unfamiliar thoughts going on in his mind, he knew he didn't want to be alone.

Why had he kissed her? He'd kept his emotions in check pretty well until she'd put her hands on his face and leaned into him. Then his instincts, his needs, took over and he had to feel her mouth under his. The kiss was more than he'd hoped for and more than he could handle. It was as wonderful as he remembered and as terrifying as he'd feared. Why did she have to come back? And with Donny Larson's child to mock his own losses?

With that unanswerable question burning in his brain, he pulled into the River Café parking lot. He'd go in for a late lunch even though eating was the last thing on his mind. He'd find a booth in a corner and nurse a cup of coffee and a ham and cheese sandwich until he felt like himself again. No matter how great Miranda's pull was, he wouldn't kiss her again. He was bigger than his temptations, stronger than his desires.

He was on his way to a back booth when he heard his name called. Oh, great. Sam McCall visiting his favorite waitress. He'd been dating Allie steadily for more than a week, and the waitress was beginning to look as smitten as Sam. The restaurant wasn't crowded since the lunch crowd had vacated, so Allie stood next to Sam's table, her hand on his shoulder. Love seemed to encompass them as she leaned down to whisper something in his ear.

"Have a seat, buddy," Sam said to Carter. "I just ordered the soup of the day—can't remember what it is now, but I'm sure it will be good."

Allie chuckled. "I'll leave you two alone. What'll you have, Chief?"

Carter placed his order, and Allie went into the kitchen.

"What's up with you?" Sam asked.

"Nothing. Why do you ask?"

"You look like your puppy just ran away. I'm going to guess that it has something to do with the beautiful Miranda."

"Then you'd be wrong," Carter lied. "If anything's bothering me, it's those hang-dog eyes you and Allie keep pinning on each other." He paused, then said, "Who's running the town right now?"

"Les and Phil. I'm back on duty in a half hour. And by the way, have you always been this anti-love, or are you just jealous?"

"Jealous? Heck no. I wouldn't be in your shoes for all the gems in the Bolton County tourist mines."

"I wouldn't give you my shoes, pal. I'm happy wearing them myself."

Carter managed a smile. "You've really got it bad, don't you?"

His face becoming serious, Sam nodded. "I'm crazy about her, Carter. She's sweet and funny, and even a jaded old bachelor like yourself has to admit she's pretty as all get-out."

"She's all that," Carter agreed. "So you see this relationship going somewhere?"

"If I have anything to say about it. I can see myself marrying this girl some day."

"You're going to break the hearts of every single girl in town," Carter said.

"I'm just worried about my own heart right now."

Carter turned his water, swiping at the moist ring underneath the glass. "Tell me about her," he said suddenly. "Where's this piece of womanly perfection from? Where does she live now? How long is she planning to stay?" Carter wished he'd backed off on the questions. He sounded too much like a cop, and this was the love of Sam's life. Carter smiled to himself. Once a cop...

"She's from around Wilmington," Sam

answered. "Ran away from an abusive relationship and is keeping a low profile these days." Sam frowned. "I swear, Carter, if that ex finds her, he'll answer to me."

Carter held up his hand. "Hold on, now, Sam. You can get into trouble making statements like that. Is this guy likely to find her?"

"I hope not. She's using a different name and she lives way out in the country on a road that doesn't even seem to have a name."

"She lives by herself?"

Sam seemed reluctant to answer. "No. She lives with an old family friend."

"Anyone I know?"

"You've mentioned her a time or two." A pause settled between them until Sam added, "Allie is staying, just temporarily, with Sheila Blount."

Carter took a moment to process the name. "You mean the Sheila who works at the Muddy Duck?"

Sam nodded.

"She's Dale Jefferson's girlfriend," Carter said.

"On-again, off-again girlfriend," Sam said. "And yes, I know, but Allie is nothing like Sheila. I mean, Sheila is a bartender. Allie works here at the café. Allie is sweet and nice. Sheila…well, you've met her. She says what she thinks and doesn't care who she insults. I can't say that a woman who would hang around Dale has the best moral character, and I'm not particularly happy that Allie is staying with her. But like I said, it's only temporary."

"Okay." Carter thought a moment. "Maybe Allie can get her own place soon. Are she and Sheila related by blood?"

"No, just friends." Sam stared long and hard at Carter while Allie brought his sandwich to the table. When she'd left, he said, "I don't want you to draw any conclusions about Allie based on what you know of Sheila."

"I wouldn't do that," Carter said. "By the way, has Allie mentioned anything about Dale?"

"No. Why would she?"

"I don't know. Maybe he's been out to Sheila's house."

"I don't think so. I doubt if Allie even knows him. And even if she does, that doesn't mean she approves of him. Look at your own situation. Because of Lawton, you're more involved with a Jefferson than anyone in town."

Carter took a steadying breath. "This conversation isn't about my relationship with Law. I'm only helping him because Miranda asked me to."

Sam smiled, easing what could have turned into a tense moment for the two friends. "I know. Women. And I'm defending Allie for basically the same reason. I'd say we've both been suckered in and neither one is complaining."

There was some truth to what Sam said. Carter couldn't say no to Miranda.

"And while we're on the subject," Sam said, "I should tell you that your involvement with Lawton has some townspeople riled up."

"Like who?"

"Well, Lenny Franklin for one. I saw him this morning, and he said you called him about interviewing Lawton for a job at his used car lot."

"So? Lawton knows about cars. He could turn out to be a valuable employee. And he has to leave the tree farm as soon as shearing is done. I also talked to the two mechanics in town." Carter waited a moment before saying, "So what's your point, Sam?"

"Only that you're not making friends over this association with a known criminal. Most people think Lawton didn't have any reason to come back here, and he should have picked someplace else to live." Sam took a spoonful of soup and swallowed. "Folks are talking, Carter, and they're not happy. I'm just telling you so you can guard that pristine reputation you've managed to achieve. Don't let Lawton bring you down."

"Nobody's going to bring me down," Carter snapped. "That's just crazy talk." He stood.

"Where are you going?" Sam asked. "Your sandwich is coming up."

"Somebody's got to fight crime around here," he said. "Tell Allie to cancel my order. I'm suddenly not hungry."

SAM WATCHED HIS friend walk out of the restaurant. Poor Carter, he thought and wished his boss could make amends with Miranda, or at least get her out of his mind. Carter was a good guy, the best. If true happiness couldn't come to Sam, he would hope it would happen for Carter. Right now Carter seemed to be wound as tight as a Swiss watch, and all because that woman had come back to town.

Sam shook his head and tried to concentrate on his meal. He'd been around. He knew what it was like to fall for the wrong person, and he didn't want that to happen to Carter. He smiled at Allie, certain that the feelings he had for her were genuine, the real thing.

He'd waited a long time to find a sweet woman like Allie, and he believed she was the one he could give his heart to because she would always take care of it. Maybe it was too soon to feel that level of trust in another person, but Sam did trust Allie, and it was a good feeling. He wanted the same for Carter, but mostly he was darned happy he'd found a perfect love for himself.

CHAPTER THIRTEEN

DRIVING INTO THE station on Saturday morning, Carter contemplated the changes in his regimented life. A little over two weeks ago, he was Chief of Police Carter Cahill, known, respected and, dare he say it, even admired. He'd suffered some loss in his time on earth, but he'd grounded himself with work and dedication and honest friendships. He'd come back to stand tall and steadfast in the town he'd always returned to.

Now he was mentoring a recent ex-con, one who, along with his brother, Dale, had made his job more difficult in this town. According to Sam, the townspeople were practically organizing a lynch mob. He was being accused of mistreating an innocent child over a dang cookie. He was battling pangs of jealousy for a guy who, like him, had known Miranda and lost her. And worst of all, he was fighting a reincarnation of feelings he'd struggled to bury with his past.

He shook his head as he pulled into the station. There was no denying it. There was something about Miranda. There always had been. He wasn't over her, but he could sure as heck learn to cope with her presence in his town. Pretty soon Lawton would be settled and Miranda could go back home to Durham with her pretty little daughter and her determination to make the world a better place. But until then Carter would have to depend on his fortitude to avoid getting trapped by those old feelings.

Betsy was hanging up the phone when he walked in. "Carter, you might want to handle this one yourself," she said.

Alarmed by her tone, Carter stopped. "What's happened? Who was on the phone?"

"Lucy Dillingham from the Hummingbird Inn."

The hairs on Carter's nape prickled. "Go on."

"There's been some vandalism over there. Nobody's hurt, but apparently property was damaged…"

He didn't hear the rest of what Betsy said.

The station door slammed behind him as he darted to his patrol car. Within five minutes he was racing up the drive of the Hummingbird Inn.

Miranda, Emily and Mrs. Dillingham were standing around Miranda's car. Miranda looked worried, and Mrs. D, wringing her hands, looked as if a blight from heaven had descended upon her. Emily was running around the car taking pictures. The closer Carter got, the more the reason for the commotion was obvious.

Miranda's car, the one she'd bragged was the first new car she'd ever owned, was covered in graffiti. On the sleek charcoal-gray exterior was painted the words "Go Home, Take Lawton with you, Down with the Jeffersons" and a few other noteworthy comments. And the poor victim was sinking into the ground on four flat tires.

The car may have taken the brunt of the vandals' creativity, but clearly Miranda was the victim here. She stared at her car and repeatedly shook her head. Carter got out of the patrol car and walked up to the women.

"Thank goodness you're here, Chief Cahill," Mrs. Dillingham said. "I feel so violated."

Carter tried to find some sympathy for the inn owner, whose late-model Cadillac was pristinely devoid of graffiti, but the feelings were hard to come by.

"I came as soon as you called, Mrs. Dillingham." Turning to Miranda, he said, "You okay?"

"Yes, I'm fine."

Only she wasn't. Her eyes were red, and streaks of moisture had dried on her cheeks.

"My beautiful car..." she said.

"I'm taking pictures," Emily said proudly. "Mommy says we'll need them for assurance."

Carter didn't bother correcting the girl.

"Mommy says we'll get the car painted, and it will be good as new."

"That's true," Carter said. "Maybe even better."

She darted around to the other side of the car and began snapping photos on a smartphone. Carter doubted an inch of that automobile hadn't been preserved for posterity in the memory of the phone.

"I'm going to send a picture to Daddy,"

she said. "The car didn't look like this when he was here yesterday."

Carter darted a look at Miranda. "Donny was here?"

"Yes, for a few hours."

"You don't think...?"

She frowned. "No. Donny wouldn't do this."

Not completely convinced, Carter stepped back and directed his next question at both ladies. "What happened here, other than the obvious? Did either of you see anything?"

"I thought I heard some noise in the middle of the night," Mrs. Dillingham said. "I'm a light sleeper, and well, you know, Carter, that my entire life savings is wrapped up in this house. I'm quite vigilant about protecting my property."

"What time was that?"

"I didn't look at the clock," she said. "I didn't see anyone outside, but I expect the criminals were wearing black. Isn't that the custom when crooks are sneaking around?" She sighed, glared at Miranda. "I suppose I'll have to invest in extra lighting now."

"I'm so sorry this happened," Miranda said. "I've already called a tow service to come for the car. Hopefully it will be gone before too many people notice."

"I'm sure it's too late for that," Mrs. Dillingham said. "This is a busy road and dozens of cars have gone by."

Carter cleared his throat, an attempt to get back to business. "I think we all should be grateful that just an automobile was the target of this vandalism. Do either of you have any idea who might have been responsible?"

Miranda shook her head.

"Oh, it could be anyone," the innkeeper said. "Ever since Mrs. Larson arrived, I've been hearing comments." She returned to her hand wringing. "This has always been such a quiet town, a place where the residents could feel safe, and now…"

Carter took his cell phone from his pocket. He called Betsy and requested that an officer be sent to the inn immediately with a full investigation kit. When he got off the phone, he said to Miranda, "We'll get samples of the paint. I figure it's your garden-variety spray paint, but maybe we'll get lucky and discover where it was purchased. We can dust the car for prints, but generally in a case like this…"

"I know what you're going to say," Miranda responded. "Whoever did this will probably get away with it." She raked her fingers through her loose hair. "I can't believe anyone in Holly River would do this. I'd heard that some folks weren't happy that I'd come here to help Lawton, but this is violence. It's one thing to have a difference of opinions, but this…"

Carter took Miranda's elbow and led her away from Lucy. "Look, Miranda, you've had more contact with Dale lately than I have. Do you think Dale could have done this?"

"Lawton's own brother? My cousin?" She shook her head. "I would hate to think so, Carter, but perhaps. Truthfully he seems to resent everything I'm trying to do for Lawton."

"Excuse me, Chief," Mrs. Dillingham interrupted. "Mrs. Larson, I'm afraid I'm going to have to ask you to find other accommodations. I just can't have this type of incident occur again."

"I think the vandals made their point, ma'am," Carter said. "My hunch is that this was a one-time only event."

"Still, I would be more comfortable…"

"I'll look for something else today," Miranda said. "I don't know if I'll find anything on such short notice. Besides, we're now in the middle of a busy weekend." She stared longingly at the comfy cottage she'd been sharing with Emily.

"Tell you what, ladies," Carter said. "Until Miranda finds something that will work for her and her daughter, I'll make sure this property is watched closely by the department. I can guarantee you, Mrs. Dillingham, that your inn will never be safer than it will be as long as Miranda is here."

"What do you intend to do?"

"I'll send a patrol by at scheduled times during the night. I'll make certain all my deputies know that this occurred."

"That is some comfort," the innkeeper said.

A second patrol car pulled into the inn, and Sam got out. After speaking to the people gathered, he walked around the car. "Wow, that's some fancy artwork."

"See if you can get me some evidence," Carter said. "We can't have this type of thing going on in Holly River. And you'd better hurry because a tow is coming for the car."

"I'm on it, Chief," Sam said, and opened the investigation case he'd brought from the trunk of his car.

"Can I help?" Emily said, staring with wide eyes at the assorted implements in the case.

"Oh, no, honey…" Miranda said. "The officer…"

"Of course you can," Sam said. "I can always use a good assistant to hand me stuff from the box."

Miranda gave Carter a sideways glance as if to say, *That's how you treat a child, Mr. Clueless.*

"Anything else any of you can think of?" Carter asked, getting back on familiar ground. "If not, I'm going back to the station to file a report on this."

"One thing, Carter," Miranda said. "Where can I rent a car? I'm sure the repairs on mine will take a couple of days."

"Call Ready Rent in Boone," he answered. "They will bring a car out to you."

"Great. I'm supposed to pick Lawton up this afternoon and take him for his driver's test. Then I was going to help him find a reasonably priced secondhand car. He's been saving his money from the farm job, and has enough for a good down payment."

Hoping to avoid frightening Emily or giving Mrs. Dillingham more ammunition to insist that Miranda move, Carter spoke in a low voice. "Miranda, do you think you should stick with your plan? I mean, this car incident is meant as a warning, but a warning for what is the thing that worries me. This level of vandalism is rare in Holly River, and I don't like that it's directed at you."

"I'm not leaving, Carter. I came here to do a job. The fact that I'm helping my cousin is incidental to my role as a social worker. I will see this through until I'm convinced Law will make it here in Holly River. And while I'm here—" she smiled "—I'll depend on the local law enforcement personnel to keep Em and me safe."

"We'll do our best." Before he returned to his car, he asked one more question that stuck in his mind. "How is Donny? It's been a long time."

"He's fine," Miranda said. "Funny, but he

often asks about you. Maybe you two should sit down over a beer some day and talk about your differences."

Knowing that wasn't likely to happen, Carter simply nodded. Too much had happened for him and Donny to make amends, though he wouldn't mind if Donny were here now as an extra measure of safety for Miranda. But he wasn't, and Carter figured Miranda wouldn't tell him about the damage to her car. It was up to Carter to protect Miranda and Emily. As he drove away from the inn, Carter decided just how he would do that.

LATE THAT AFTERNOON, near the end of his shift, Carter drove out of town to the Muddy Duck Tavern. The bar wasn't crowded, so he took a seat on a stool at the end of the worn wooden counter. He had a few minutes to talk to Sheila before the usual Saturday afternoon crowd came in for beers.

Sheila was wiping down the surface of the bar. He knew she'd seen him, but obviously wasn't in a big hurry to get him a drink. He was in uniform and wouldn't order anything that would ensure her a big tip anyway.

She looked tired, her face void of obvious makeup, her brown hair pulled back into a thin ponytail. She wore a pair of skin-tight jeans with a tan Muddy Duck T-shirt.

She sauntered down the bar to where Carter was sitting. "Afternoon, Chief Cahill," she said. "What'll you have?"

Her voice was husky. A cigarette smoldered in an ashtray next to where she'd been standing.

"Just a ginger ale," he said. "And some information."

She unscrewed the top from a soda and poured the contents over ice in a glass. "That part was easy," she said. "Now, what sort of information brings you all the way out here to the Duck?"

"I'm checking with several of our local businesses, Sheila. We've had some incidents lately, mostly thefts, and I thought you might be able to tell me something. I figure your clientele might have let something slip and you overheard."

She slapped a hand on her hip. "You think the guys that come to the Duck are criminal types, Chief? I'd have never taken you for a prejudiced person. Our drinkers are the salt of the earth."

Carter glanced around the bar, taking in the grease-stained walls and soiled upholstery on the chairs. "I'll bet they are," he said. "But just in case…"

"What's been stolen?" she asked.

"Sounds strange, I know, but gardening equipment. That leads me to believe that whoever took the things must be interested in putting in a crop of some kind."

"I wouldn't know anything about that," she said. "We don't get many farmers in here."

"I'm not saying the thief is a farmer," Carter said. "More than likely this is an amateur who's just trying his hand at growing something and stealing the tools rather than investing a lot of money."

"Can't help you, Chief. Conversations around here don't usually center on who's planting what." She walked away. "But good luck with the case."

"One more thing, Sheila." She stopped but didn't turn around. She polished a glass at the bar sink. "You would call me if you heard anything? I mean, even the slightest hint could be a big help. A couple of our local businesses have suffered considerable loss."

Putting the glass down and bracing herself with her hands against the bar, she stared at him. "You know I would. And since one favor deserves another, I have something to ask of you."

"What's that?"

She came back to his end of the bar. "You may know that one of your officers is seeing a good friend of mine, a gal named Allie who came from Wilmington to stay with me. She's a good kid, had her heart broken and is trying to rebuild her life."

"Holly River is a good place to do that," Carter said.

"Maybe. Maybe not. Like you said before, occasionally I hear things working the bar. And I've heard some things about Sam McCall. He's a rounder, Chief. You know that. Every single woman in town knows Sam, and he could probably have any of them. So I don't know why he's picked Allie."

"Maybe he likes her, simple as that," Carter said.

"I doubt it's that simple," she said. "Here's

the thing… I promised Allie's mama I'd look out for her, and I'm trying to do that. I'd much rather see her hook up with a nice stable guy, not a player like Sam. I just don't want her hurt, you know?"

"Why are you telling me this?" Carter asked. "I don't make a habit of getting involved in my officers' personal lives. If you don't want Allie seeing Sam, talk to her about it."

"Oh, I have. I've warned her about him, and I'm going to keep warning her. But she's only half listening. I thought if you talked to Sam…"

"I'm not going to do that, Sheila. Sam and Allie are adults. They make their own decisions as far as I'm concerned, and some of them might turn out to be mistakes. That's life, isn't it? We learn by living?"

Sheila shrugged. "I'm kind of surprised to hear the nicest cop in North Carolina say that. I figured you'd help me out with this."

"I guess people think I'm nice because I mind my own business."

Sheila frowned at him. "Just thought you should know how I feel."

"Okay. But this won't affect your letting

me know if you hear anything about the recent crimes in Holly River, will it? I can count on you?"

"Absolutely, Chief. I'm as good a citizen as anybody else."

"Thanks." He took three bills from his wallet and left them and his half-full glass on the bar. "Appreciate your time, Sheila. Have a good night."

SINCE THE DUCK was close to Hidden Creek Road, Carter took a detour past his mother's house. He'd left so abruptly yesterday that he hadn't really welcomed his sister home. Seeing Ava's car in the drive, he pulled in and found her in the vegetable garden. He'd almost forgotten how pretty she was, and today she looked like a teenager again, her dark hair tucked into a straw hat, her cheeks glowing with sunlight.

She wiped dirt from her hands onto her faded jeans and called to him, "Hey, little brother. No crimes to fight today?"

"Actually, yeah. Some vandalism at the Hummingbird Inn. Miranda's car was spray painted."

"Oh, no." She walked toward Carter. "Are Miranda and Emily okay?"

"They're fine. I think Miranda was kind of shook up. But the kid was taking pictures of the car like she was part of the paparazzi."

Ava smiled. "She's a spirited little thing, as well as being cute as a button. Don't you think so?"

Carter knew a setup when he heard one. Obviously his mother had complained to Ava about his indifference to Emily yesterday. He shrugged and said, "She's cute."

"We hardly got a chance to talk yesterday," Ava said. "I had just arrived and you left so quickly. And since I hate working in dirt anyway, why don't we go to the porch and catch up?"

"I just have a few minutes. Got a special detail I'm working on tonight. Wanted to see if everything was okay out here." He looked around the property. "Where's Mom?"

Ava stepped over some plants and stood at the border to the garden. "She loaded up her purse with coupons and drove twenty miles to a low-cost supermarket to stock up."

Carter didn't like the sound of that.

"Why'd she do that? We have two great supermarkets in town. It will cost her more in gas than she'll save with the coupons."

"Apparently she'd done a cost analysis and figured all that out."

"This is exactly what's been worrying me, Ava. What's going on with Mama? She's letting repairs go on the house, clipping coupons, canceling vacations with Aunt Dolly. Is she having money problems?"

"I don't know, but I've noticed the trend, too. She's tending this vegetable garden like she's going to depend on homegrown tomatoes to survive the winter."

"Have you asked her?"

"Sure. She says everything is okay and I'm not to worry. She said something about the wisdom of saving money whenever possible and then turned the whole discussion on me and told me I should take the lesson to heart. When I couldn't get a straight answer from Mama, I called Uncle Rudy and asked how the paper mill is doing since Daddy died. He said all is okay there."

Carter frowned. "I wish I trusted him completely, but I don't."

"I'm with you, brother."

"I guess Dad trusted him since he left controlling interest in the mill to Rudy."

"Not to mention making him executor of his will and sole owner of the factory."

"I figured you'd be executor, Ava," Carter said. "You being the favorite kid and all."

She smiled. "Didn't happen. But anyway, Dad made provisions for Mama. Generous ones. She got this house, whatever was in their joint bank accounts and monthly profit sharing checks, which she says Rudy has been sending regularly. At the time of Daddy's death, I thought that was a good arrangement. Mama wouldn't know what to do with the mill, and you boys had no interest in it."

Carter couldn't argue. "I guess as long as Uncle Rudy doesn't screw things up, Mom will be fine."

"I hope so." Ava looked worried. "But this pinching pennies has me concerned."

Carter thought a moment. Two of Cora's children had noticed the change in her. Only Jace, who stayed as emotionally detached from the family as he could, hadn't said anything. "How are your investigative skills, Ava?" he asked.

"As sharp as ever. I don't go through trash cans looking for notes from old boyfriends anymore, but I'm not above a bit of sleuthing."

"You know where Mama keeps her checkbook?"

"I assume it's in Dad's rolltop desk. All their records are there." She tapped her finger on her lower lip. "I know what you're suggesting, Carter, and it's absolutely an invasion of Mom's privacy."

His daredevil sister had obviously lost some of her mettle. She was right, of course. "Okay, forget it."

She smiled. "I didn't say I wouldn't do it."

Carter chuckled. "Call me if you find anything. Maybe we can get to the bottom of this."

"You got it, bro. I'll invade Mom's privacy tonight. Can I reach you on your cell later?"

"Sure. Call me as late as you want. I should be up most of the night on a stakeout."

Ava grinned at him in that sisterly way that meant she knew what was going on in

his head. "At the Hummingbird Inn, I'll bet,"
she said.

"None of your business. But maybe."

CHAPTER FOURTEEN

MIRANDA COULDN'T SLEEP. She'd tucked Emily in bed at nine, and had spent the last three hours reading on her Kindle. After all that time, she wasn't sure what she'd read. Last night's vandalism had left her wary of the same thing, or worse, happening again. It wasn't that she was afraid. After all, Carter said patrol cars would drive by the inn through the night. But nothing like that had ever occurred to her before. She was in the business of helping people, not stirring up bad feelings among citizens of a small town.

She looked out the kitchen window toward the main house. The windows were dark, with only soft illumination from nightlights Lucy must keep on for guests. Since this was Saturday night, the inn was fully occupied. Miranda said a silent prayer that nothing would happen while that No Vacancy sign was up. Lucy may not have shown a great deal of empathy for Miranda's problems, but she certainly didn't deserve to have vandalism occur on her property.

Finding all well at the house, Miranda went to the front door of the cottage and looked out that window. All was not quiet on the gentle slope from the inn to the main road. A car was parked on the shoulder, and a man stood next to it.

Her heart racing, Miranda squinted into the darkness. Had the vandals from last night returned? Were they just waiting for her to extinguish her reading light before attempting more damage? She considered calling the police but decided against it when she noticed something about the car. It appeared to have a light bar on top, regulation cop equipment.

She sighed with relief. Carter was better than his word. He'd obviously sent an officer to be on guard at the inn rather than just passing by during the night. She watched the officer circle the car, looking in all directions from his vantage point. And then she made a positive identification.

There was no mistaking that confident stride, the squared shoulders, the wisps of dark hair catching the breeze. Miranda smiled. Carter.

She brewed a pot of coffee, filled two mugs, checked on Emily and left the cottage. She'd taken only a few steps toward the car when Carter whirled around to stare at her. He immediately relaxed his stance, raked his fingers through his hair and leaned against the patrol car.

"Can't sleep?" he asked her when she got to the car.

"No, not really. I see I'm not the only one doing without eight hours tonight." She handed him a mug of coffee.

He took a sip. "Sleep is overrated. I do my best work on an overload of caffeine."

She tucked a strand of hair behind her ear, aware that he was watching her movement. "This is really nice of you, Carter. I had no idea you would come back here tonight. I thought you would just tell the officer on duty to drive by."

"I could have done that."

"Why didn't you?"

He set the mug of coffee on the trunk of his car and took a deep breath. "What do you want me to say, Miranda? That you used to mean a lot to me, and I personally want to see to your safety? That I'd never forgive myself if something happened to you or your kid?"

She smiled at him. "Either one would do just fine."

"Okay, then. The truth is, I *don't* want anything to happen to you. I don't know why you felt like you had to come here to make everything right for Lawton. He's a grown man after all. But you're here, and as long as you're in my town, I'm going to watch out for you."

She smiled. "You sound an awful lot like Donny right now. He didn't think I should come here either."

Carter scowled. "Who would believe it? Donny and I actually have two things in common, and both of them concern you."

"Don't go there, Carter," she warned. "It's nice that you're here, but I don't want you to feel like I'm your responsibility."

"Like you feel Lawton is yours?"

"Law is my responsibility, Carter, for two reasons. One, he was the best friend I ever had…until I met you." She watched his face for any sign that her confession meant something to him. His expression didn't change. "And two, helping released prisoners is my job."

"By the way, Miranda, did Law get his driver's license this afternoon?"

"He did. And we have a good lead on a car. He found one in the Boone Trader for only a thousand dollars. If I cosign for him, I think he can get a loan for half the amount."

"Would that car be an older-model Dodge Neon, and isn't Lawton familiar with the engine from when he worked on one in high school auto shop?"

"How did you know that?"

"I stopped and had a chat with Law this evening before I came out here."

"You did? I'm so glad."

Carter smiled. "I take my mentoring job seriously. Besides, I had some good news to tell him. I'm taking him for a job interview tomorrow in Pine Grove at a body shop. The owner is coming in on a Sunday to meet with us."

"Pine Grove? It's a good thing he's getting a car, then. That's at least ten miles away."

"It is, but I wasn't having much luck getting him hired in Holly River."

"Thanks, Carter. Now, if I can see Lawton settled in Holly River and even becoming part of the community, then I'd say my job is done."

Carter rubbed his chin.

"What?"

"Lawton has a way to go to be part of the Holly River community," Carter said. "I don't know if that's ever going to happen. At least not while his brother is around. Folks don't seem to be able to separate the two of them."

Miranda didn't argue. Carter was correct. People in Holly River seemed to think anyone with the name *Jefferson* was trouble. She'd been lucky as a teenager that she'd been able to live down that reputation through decent grades and cheerleading. She never experienced the kind of prejudice her cousins had. But then again, she'd never broken the law.

A cool breeze suddenly swept down from Sawtooth Mountain, and Miranda wrapped her sweater tightly around her shoulders. "It's going down into the fifties tonight," she said. "Why don't you come back to the cottage with me? I've got a fire going, and you can catch a few winks on the couch."

She wished she could read his mind. His eyes widened, his lips thinned. Did he want to accept her offer, or did he think a few hours in front of a fire with her could only lead to trouble? The chill she'd experienced a moment ago suddenly vanished, replaced with a warmth deep inside her that had everything to do with the image she'd just formed in her mind. All at once she couldn't think of anything nicer than sitting next to Carter...

"I'm fine out here," he said. "Got a jacket in the car. But thanks."

Disappointment washed over her. She looked down at the ground so he couldn't read her reaction to his words in her eyes. What did she expect? Carter hadn't shown any romantic interest in her since she'd returned except for that one spontaneous kiss yesterday. And he knew Donny was here when she returned from the Cahill farm and had probably drawn a false conclusion about that visit.

She raised her face and looked into his eyes. "I didn't invite Donny here," she said, surprised when the words burst from her lips. "He just showed up to see Emily."

Carter shifted from one foot to the other. "Ah, okay."

She'd gone this far… "Carter, we kissed in the apple orchard. I know that upset you. It was a spur-of-the-moment thing, but maybe we should talk about it. I think the kiss made you uncomfortable."

"Darn right it did," he said.

"You didn't like it? Not even a little? Because, well, I did. I could kiss you again right now, but I won't do it since I know how wrong it made you feel…"

He reached out and touched her hand. "You have no idea how it made me feel, but remember one thing. There was never a time in our lives that your kiss didn't make me feel pretty darn spectacular. And there's no reason for you to think anything different now."

Then, with gentle hands, he grasped the lapels of her sweater. She thought he was going to draw her close and give back the kiss she'd been thinking of since yesterday. Her breath caught. Blood pounded in her temples. He was so close. But instead he pulled the sweater close against her neck and rested his hands on her shoulders. "It's getting cold, Miranda. Go on back to the cottage. And get some sleep. I'll be here till sunrise."

"If you change your mind..." But she knew he wouldn't. The walk back to the cottage seemed to take forever, especially since she felt his gaze on her back warming her all the way to her heart. When she reached the door, she went in without looking down the hill. She knew he'd be there as he promised. And she knew she wouldn't sleep.

CARTER WENT TO the station when he left the Hummingbird Inn. Few officers were at their desks because of the early hour, but he did find Sam McCall filling out reports.

"Saw you at the inn, Chief," Sam said. "Everything okay there?"

"Yeah, I stayed the night just to be sure. Mrs. Dillingham wants Miranda out of there. She's afraid the trouble will hurt her business."

"She might be right. Feelings about the Jefferson boys don't seem to be calming down any. Where's Miranda going?"

Carter shrugged. "It's Sunday, Sam. You know that all the local places still have their No Vacancy signs up. And the Best Western is always full."

"Does that mean you're going to pull an all-nighter again tonight if need be?"

Carter rubbed the tired muscles at the back of his neck. "I was hoping you might offer."

"Have a date with Allie tonight. But when I drop her off, sure. I'll hang out at the inn."

"I appreciate it." Carter started for his office, but remembered his conversation with Sheila the day before. "You're seeing a lot of Allie, aren't you?" he asked Sam.

"Not as much as I'd like. Saw her last night, though. She said you grilled Sheila about the stolen property."

"I'd hardly call it a grilling, but yes, I asked her if she'd heard anything about the robberies." Anticipating Sam's next question, he said, "She hasn't."

Sam nodded. "Too bad. By the way, did she happen to mention me?"

Oh, boy. Carter dodged. "She did once, but I told her I didn't think you were responsible for those thefts."

Sam gave him an indulgent smile. "Funny, Carter. I mean did she mention me with regard to Allie?"

"Why would she do that?"

"I get the feeling she doesn't like me. Or maybe doesn't approve of me."

"Who you date is your business, Sam. I can assure you that I wouldn't encourage any conversation that included you and your women."

"Woman, Carter. Only one."

Carter patted Sam's back. "Oh, how the mighty have fallen." He continued into his office.

AFTER COMPLETING SOME REPORTS, Carter went home to grab a few hours' sleep before picking up Lawton for the job interview. When he got up, he checked his cell phone and discovered an urgent message from Ava, so he drove to Hidden Creek Road.

Cora was busy in the kitchen. Carter smelled a chicken roasting in the oven. Ava was shelling peas into a bowl. "Company for dinner?" he asked.

"You, if you'll stay," Cora said.

"Sorry. I need to put in some extra hours

tonight. I was on a special detail last night."
He didn't mention the errand he had planned
with Lawton. Maybe his mother and Ava felt
the same as Jace did about his involvement
with Miranda's cousin.

"Oh, I heard," his mother said. "You
stayed all night at the Hummingbird Inn
after Miranda's car was vandalized to make
sure nothing bad happened again." Cora
wiped her hand on her apron and patted
Carter's cheek. "You can be a sweet boy
when you want to be."

"I'm always a sweet boy, aren't I?"

"I can't imagine who would do such a
thing." Cora sighed. "You're going to miss
a good meal, Carter. I was at the supermarket yesterday."

Carter glanced at Ava. She gave him a
nod, indicating she had some news to share.

"I'll finish up in here, Mom," she said.
"You've been working all day. Why don't
you lie down for a while?"

"I just might do that." She took off her
apron and hung it on a hook by the back
door. "Call if you need me, Ava."

Once she'd left, Carter closed the door

to the kitchen and pulled out a chair for his sister. "What did you find out?"

"Plenty." Ava sat, crossed her hands on the tabletop. "I'm not sure what it means, but Mom has been writing checks to the same woman practically since Daddy died. Sizable checks, too."

"Really? For the same amount each time?"

"Yep. Seven hundred and fifty dollars every two weeks."

"Holy cow." Carter drummed his fingers on the table while he tried to make sense of the startling revelation. "What's the woman's name?"

"Gladys Kirshner. I found an address stuck in the checkbook. She lives over in Wilton Hollow."

"I've never heard of her," Carter said.

"I haven't either."

"What's the money for? And why so much?"

"Beats me," Ava said. "But with fifteen hundred dollars going out of Mom's checking account every month, I can understand why she's watching her pennies."

Was his mother being blackmailed? Was she paying off some debt? Was Cora involved with bad people? None of this made any sense. No one in Holly River was as respected as Cora Cahill. "I assume the checks are being cashed," he said.

"Almost immediately. From what I can determine from studying Mom's accounts, she's barely making ends meet. So far the money coming in from Uncle Rudy is more than the sum she's sending to this Gladys lady, but the money from the mill fluctuates, so Mom can never count on how much she'll get."

"No wonder she isn't keeping the house up."

"And I was surprised at the amount in the checking account she shared with Dad. It's down to less than a thousand dollars."

"Wow. It's no surprise she isn't taking a vacation with Aunt Dolly."

Carter took his cell phone from his pocket and called the station. "Betsy, put me on with Sam."

"What's up Carter?" Sam asked a moment later.

"Get me all the info you can on a woman named Gladys Kirshner in Wilton Hollow. Age, address, any priors, and while you're at it, any connections she might have had to the paper mill."

"I'm on it," Sam said. "Call you back when I have anything."

When he disconnected, he sat at the table and let all sorts of wild thoughts fill his brain.

"This worries me, Carter," Ava said. "I hope Mom's not in some kind of trouble."

"If she is, we'll get her out of it." He stood and headed to the kitchen door. Before he could open it, his mother came into the room.

"Mama? What happened to your nap?"

"I'll take it in a minute. But I had a thought."

"How long have you been outside?"

She chuckled. "I wasn't spying on you, Carter, if that's what you think. I just came down from my bedroom because I couldn't sleep. I can't help worrying about Miranda and that darling girl of hers."

Carter breathed a sigh of relief. His mother hadn't heard the conversation between him and Ava. "She'll be okay, Mama," he said. "Sam is going to stay out at the inn tonight."

"That's just not good enough, Carter," Cora said.

"Why not?"

"I wasn't going to say anything, but Lucy Dillingham called me today to see if I knew of any place Miranda could move to until she finishes her business with Lawton. As soon as my head hit the pillow upstairs, I realized that the old grouch must be intending to ask Miranda to leave. She won't find any place on a weekend, and nothing as nice as that cottage at the inn."

"Sam and I will watch the cottage," Carter said.

"No. I want those two to stay out here with Ava and me. You and Jace can come by and check on us, and Buster will bark up a storm if anyone comes on the property."

The Cahills' fourteen-year-old Labrador had gentled with age, but his vocal cords still worked fine. All the locals knew no one could sneak onto the Cahill farm.

"Are you sure about this, Mama?" Carter asked.

"Completely sure. You go on and tell Miranda to pack up her things and come out here." Cora smiled. "Maybe now you'll change your mind about showing up for dinner tonight."

"I couldn't possibly, Carter," Miranda said when he called her on her cell phone. "It's an imposition on your family. Ava's there now, and…"

"Look, Miranda," Carter cut off her list of objections to Cora's plan. "Either you agree to stay with Mama, or I'm going to take the heat for your refusal. She still hasn't forgiven me for the cookie incident, and she'll blame me if anything happens to you or Emily."

Miranda sighed into the phone. "I suppose there's enough room."

Carter smiled at the relief in her voice. "You bet there is. Ava is staying in her old bedroom, and you can take your pick of mine or Jace's room, or the guest room, for you and Emily."

His hands tightened on the steering wheel as he backed out of Cora's drive. Miranda sleeping in his room. Years ago they'd spent many hours in that room, listening to music, doing homework, lying on his bed thinking about the future. They'd been happy hours, and now his blood heated just thinking of Miranda on that old plaid bedspread.

"I'm so grateful," she said, and Carter had to shake his head to bring himself back to the present.

"You need any help?" he asked her.

"No. We just have a bit of food and two suitcases. I can pack us up in a few minutes, and we'll head out to Hidden Creek. Emily will be so excited. She enjoyed her day at the farm."

"Mama's the one who'll be delighted," Carter said. "She'll love having the two of you there."

"Thank you, Carter."

"Don't mention it. Maybe I'll see you later if I finish with Lawton in time for dinner. Mom had a chicken in the oven and it smelled pretty good."

There was a pause before Miranda took a deep breath.

"You okay?" he asked her.

"Yes, fine. I was just thinking how nice it would be if you made it to dinner."

He disconnected and turned onto Hidden Creek Road for the fifteen-minute drive to Liggett Mountain. What was she doing to him? Miranda had him thinking back to the happy times and even wondering what his life would have been like if she hadn't left Holly River. But she had left, and she'd broken his heart at the time.

"She's just being nice," he said aloud. "She's grateful. And one kiss. That's all it was. Certainly not worth risking your heart again to see if you and Miranda might make it this time."

He drove a little fast to Liggett Mountain, anxious to get with Lawton and force his mind away from thoughts of Miranda. Yet, all he could think about was that one mind-blowing kiss in the apple orchard, and the one he'd ached to give her last night.

CHAPTER FIFTEEN

"How did it go?" Carter had been waiting in the parking lot of Pine Grove Automotive Repair for thirty minutes while Lawton went inside for his job interview. Carter believed he had prepared Lawton well with tips on readying for a successful interview, but nothing was guaranteed. Once he went in the door of the auto repair place, Lawton was on his own.

Lawton settled into the passenger seat. The smile on his face was all the answer Carter needed.

"I start tomorrow," Lawton said.

Carter held up his hand for a high five. "I'm proud of you, Lawton. You did this by being yourself, and just like I told you, he hired you."

"You also told me what I needed to do to impress Mack, and it worked. I was upfront with him about my record as well as my skill with automobiles. I'll need some training on the diagnostic machines, but if anyone brings in a clunker older than ten years, I'm the guy to fix it."

This was good news, of course. Miranda would be happy to hear it. Carter had mixed emotions. Yes, Lawton would make enough to be on his own now, but Miranda's job would be done. She'd accomplished most of what she came to Holly River for. All that remained was for her to help Lawton adjust to the Holly River community and see that he had health insurance.

Carter didn't know how she would get folks to accept Lawton, but he'd seen first-hand that she could be persuasive.

"I'm going to call Miranda," Lawton said. "Mack said I could get health insurance through his business. I have to give a little out of my paycheck, but that's okay."

"She could be online with the bank right now," Carter said, remembering that Miranda said she was going to try to secure the loan for the car Lawton needed. "You'll have to carry liability on your car, too," he said. "Shouldn't be too much."

Lawton stared out the window at the passing scenery. "Things are really looking up for me, Carter. There's no way I can ever thank you and Miranda for what you've done for me. A car, a place to live, the tree farm and now a real job..."

"Hold on, Law." Carter had just thought of a way Lawton could repay him. "There actually is something you could do for me."

"Anything. Just ask."

"I need some help clearing a couple of theft reports off my desk," Carter said. "Mostly garden and cultivation equipment gone missing from the hardware store and the winery. I've been on this case for a while, even talked to you and Dale about it, and I haven't gotten any good leads."

Lawton's expression became guarded. "You don't suspect me of taking that stuff? I mean, didn't we clear that up when you came up to Liggett Mountain to question us?"

"I don't suspect you, Lawton, but I can't say the same about Dale. His Jeep places him near the hardware store the night of the robbery. And let's face it, he's gotten away with far more in this town, and has remained as slippery as an eel."

Lawton shook his head. "I can't help you, Carter. I don't know nothin' about that missing equipment."

Carter studied his face. The lines around his eyes, the vein working in his temple, the way he chewed his bottom lip. "I think maybe you know more than you're telling me, Lawton. I believe you didn't steal that stuff, but this happened when you were still living with Dale. You would tell me if you heard Dale say anything that might help me solve this case?"

Lawton threaded his hands in his lap. "Carter, you're putting me in a difficult place. I'm just so glad to be away from Dale. I don't want him to get in any trouble, but he's got a grudge against everyone in this town that just won't go away."

"I'm glad you're living away from him, too, Law, but I need you to tell me if Dale tried to get you involved in some of his dealings when you were with him."

A bitter chuckle escaped Lawton's lips. "He tried all right. He said this town owed us Jeffersons, that we've always been treated like dirt around here. He talked about you especially, Carter, saying that you threw the book at me just because I'm from Liggett Mountain."

"Do you believe that?"

"No. I was guilty. You did what you had to do."

Carter sensed he was beginning to tear down the wall of loyalty Lawton had built around him and his brother. "I hope you never listen to Dale again, Lawton. He'll only use you and let you take the blame when it's really him who should be in jail."

"Like he blamed you for me serving time," Lawton said. "Dale said you were just out to get us Jeffersons. He gets things all screwed up sometimes."

Carter waited a moment and then tapped his index finger on the steering wheel. "One last time, Lawton, and then I'll drop the subject. Do you know where that stolen property is? Do you suspect Dale of anything to do with these thefts?"

Lawton released a long and deep breath. "I wouldn't let him tell me anything, Carter, honest. I left the cabin whenever he tried to tell me about one of his cockamamie schemes. I knew I'd just get in trouble again if I listened to him."

"So you do suspect him?"

"You might want to check some property out-of-town way. Dale's girlfriend, Sheila, lives there. I've never been there, so I can't tell you where it is exactly, but the three of them—Dale, Sheila and this gal who's living with Sheila—might have answers for you." He paused before adding, "But I don't know anything for sure, and that's the truth." Carter grimaced. He wasn't surprised to learn that Dale was involved, but Sheila? And now Allie was implicated. He thought of Sam, his best friend, who was hoping to build a lasting relationship with Allie. This news, if true, would devastate him.

They'd reached the bottom of Liggett Mountain, and Carter drove the quarter mile to Lawton's cabin. When Law got out of the car, he said, "Dale's still my brother. Guess that's why I wouldn't let him tell me what he was planning. I don't feel right going against him, and I didn't want to lie for him."

"You've done the right thing, Law, telling me what little you know. You have a good evening, now."

Carter headed past the station and the Hummingbird Inn. He picked up his cell to call Sam and tell him not to worry about staking out the inn tonight. He could enjoy his date with Allie. If Lawton's instincts were correct, this might be the last one Sam would have with her for a while.

"I've got some info for you on Gladys Kirshner," Sam said when they'd connected.

"Go ahead."

"You were right. She worked at the paper mill as a secretary for a few months. I called Personnel out there, and the gal looked up the records and said Gladys quit after a short time, and never came back wanting her job."

"How long ago was that?" Carter asked.

"Long time ago. Thirteen years. She's still living in Wilton Hollow. According to the latest census, she shares a house with one other person, a male named Robert."

"Is it her husband? A boyfriend? What's his age?"

"He's off the radar, Carter. Don't know anything about him."

"Thanks, Sam. This information will help me."

Tomorrow morning was soon enough to check out Sheila's property. He'd find this out-of-the-way dirt road and by noon he hoped he'd put an end to the case of the missing garden equipment. And then he'd swing by the farm to pick up his sister and they'd head out to Wilton Hollow. Together they would discover whatever was going on with his mother. It promised to be a productive day for Carter, one he relished. As for tonight, he was going to the Cahill farm for a chicken dinner.

"THAT WAS DELICIOUS, Mom," Carter said, getting up from the table.

"Sit back down, Carter. We still have dessert."

"None for me, Mom. What I need is a good walk."

Cora looked from her son to Miranda, a cunning gleam in her eye. Miranda began clearing dishes.

"Never mind that, Miranda," Cora said. "Why don't you two go out on the porch or have that walk Carter seems to want so badly? It's a nice night to take the air."

"No way, Cora," Miranda said. "You and Ava cooked. I'm cleaning up."

Cora passed a suggestive look at her daughter, who quickly took the hint.

"Let the dishes go a few minutes, everyone. I'm thinking Emily and I would like some ice cream. If I know Mom, she has sprinkles around here somewhere."

Ava and Emily set about finding the sprinkles, while Cora remained at the table. "The dishes will wait. Now go on, you two."

"Miranda?" Carter waited for her to deposit a stack of plates on the counter.

"Sure. That sounds nice." Truthfully, Miranda couldn't think of anything she'd like better than walking the farm with Carter, even if Cora had been so obvious about setting it up.

Dusk had fallen when they went onto the porch, but enough light remained to see the trees in the distance. Miranda immediately thought of her time in the apple orchard with Carter. The kiss. The way she'd felt. She hadn't imagined that the last fourteen years would slip away so easily with just one kiss.

"Where would you like to walk?" he asked her.

"How about the barn?"

"Sounds good. I have to round up Jasper and give him some fresh oats and water."

"You still have that horse? He must be

getting old now. I didn't see him the other day when I was here with Emily."

"He was probably in the far pasture," Carter said with a smile. He was obviously remembering his youth with his beloved Morgan horse. Carter had gotten him when he was sixteen and the horse was two. Miranda did some quick math. Jasper was nearly twenty years old, quite a ripe age for an equine.

They stepped off the porch with Buster trotting behind them. "What happened to Buster's daddy?" Miranda asked, stopping to pet the soft yellow fur of the Labrador.

"Mom and Dad had to put him down five years ago. It was sad but we had Buster, and he's so much like his sire that we don't have a problem remembering Chief."

They reached the barn and walked through the structure to the other end, open to a paddock. The early moon shone down on the grassy enclosure where Jasper, his dark coat glistening in the waning day, was munching contentedly.

Carter whistled, and Jasper came to the gate. After slipping a cotton rope around Jasper's neck, Carter opened the paddock stile and led the horse inside to his stall. Jasper went to his cozy straw bed willingly, waited for Carter to pat his neck and close the door. "It's me today, boy," Carter said. "Mama told Tommy not to come over this evening to feed you since I was coming to dinner."

Miranda petted the animal's nose while Carter filled the feed bucket and hosed water into a trough inside the stall. "Who's Tommy?" she asked.

"He's a neighbor kid. Comes over twice a day unless Jace or I happen to be here. If I'm around I usually take Jasper out for a slow ride. When I'm not here, Tommy rides him." Carter smiled. "I think that's why old Jasper still looks like a young stud."

"I recall how much you enjoyed taking him out." *And the times I rode with you, my arms around your waist as we cantered across the meadow grass.*

Carter settled his elbow on the top of the stall door and watched Jasper chew his oats. "I had hoped to teach a child of mine to ride on this horse," he said. "Things change don't they?"

Miranda placed her hand on Carter's

back, feeling the soft flannel of a shirt he'd put on when he'd arrived for dinner, having changed from his uniform. "I'm so sorry for what happened to you," she said. "So much heartache. I should have reached out to you, but it seemed awkward. How horrible that time must have been."

He turned toward her. "It was rough. Sometimes I think losing three babies is a big reason I'm not great around kids."

She started to say something to make him feel better, but he held up his hand. "You and I both know I've had my moments with your daughter. I suppose I still have a fear of getting too close to anyone again. I mean… first there was you…" He stopped, took a breath. "I'm sorry. I didn't mean to bring that up again."

She reached over the stall door and grabbed his hand. As if a map of his palm was ingrained in her mind, she felt the familiar places—the calluses, the slight protrusions at the knuckles. She wanted to place that palm against her cheek and feel the caress she knew as a girl. Instead, she reached up and placed her hand on his face. Her thumb brushed the corner of his mouth.

He swallowed. "What are we doing here, Miranda?"

"I don't know," she said on a soft rush of air. "My work with Lawton is almost complete. I'll talk to my minister tomorrow about involving him in some activities. But beyond that, I don't think there is much more I can do for him." She moved her hand to the back of Carter's head, and down to his nape. His back stiffened.

"But the truth is," she said, "I don't really want to go. Not yet."

He blinked, cleared his throat. "You've made a good life in Durham, haven't you?"

She smiled up at him, losing herself in the mossy-green eyes that at one time threatened to swallow her whole. "Yes, I have a life in Durham, but somehow I don't believe my life should be in that city," she said. "I believe it's here. It always has been."

He drew in a ragged breath as his arms came around her. He hesitated for a moment, the longest moment of Miranda's life, and then he did what she'd been dreaming of. He pulled her close, tightened his arms at her waist. His chin rested on the top of her head.

"I don't think we can go back, Miranda. It's just not possible."

A slow ache began in the chest that felt so blessedly sweet against his. Here they were, as close as they'd once been, but it wasn't the same. He didn't even want to try. Tears gathered in her eyes.

And then he put a finger under her chin and lifted her face. "I don't know if I want to try."

Those words could have been the cruelest she'd ever heard, but they came from his mouth choked on emotion, as if he didn't believe what he was saying but needed to protect what was left of his heart.

Miranda wiped a drop of moisture from her cheek. How had she hurt him so badly? Why had she given up the most important relationship she'd ever had or ever would have?

"I understand what you're saying, Carter, and I don't blame you, but right now, for this minute, if you don't kiss me, I think I'm going to die, and I don't know how we'll explain that to those people in the house…"

His mouth descended to hers with a muffled cry in his throat. His lips crushed hers.

His tongue delved deeply between her lips. It was a kiss of hunger, passion, and most of all, relief, as if a simmering pot had just reached a boiling point.

She wrapped her arms around his neck and kissed him back, equaling the fierceness and demand in the press of his mouth on hers. And then, suddenly, the kiss gentled. His lips became soft and seeking. His hands on her back moved slowly, languorously. She pressed her chest even more thoroughly against his and moved her head, her mouth, her tongue in perfect harmony with his.

When the kiss ended, they were both breathless and clinging to each other. Miranda was certain there had never been a kiss like this one. And she believed with all her heart that what had existed for them at one time was still burning. Yet now the fires of their emotions could give them even more, a lifetime of perfectly blended lips and equaled passion.

"We should go in," he said hoarsely. "I've got a big day ahead of me." He stepped away from her, rubbed his nape briskly.

She was a mere two feet from him and

yet suddenly she'd never felt more alone. "Carter...?"

"Don't say anything, Miranda. Please. Let's go in."

He whistled for Buster, his mind and body adjusting much more quickly than hers to the lives they'd built apart. He waited for her and the dog to precede him out of the barn. Then he closed the door and followed her back to the house.

CHAPTER SIXTEEN

MIRANDA WENT DIRECTLY to the kitchen and began stacking Cora's dishwasher. Carter retrieved his uniform shirt, said a quick goodbye, which Miranda apparently pretended not to hear, and left the house. He felt like a heel. He'd been completely into the kisses in the barn, and he knew that Miranda darn well knew it. There was no way to hide that level of passion. And yet in moments, his old insecurities had turned that passion as cold as a March wind.

Driving to his own cabin, Carter contemplated his behavior. Self-preservation was the only excuse he could come up with. Did he care about Miranda? Every bit as much as he once had, maybe even more. Did he want to see where this new relationship might lead? That was the part that was driving him crazy. No, he didn't. He was over the heartache she'd caused him fourteen years ago. At least he told himself daily that he was, but then he'd kissed her like that in the barn, and all his arguments went up in the smoke of that kiss. But, no matter what he finally admitted to himself about his feelings for Miranda, he couldn't risk going through that kind of pain again.

He shouldn't have kissed her. With each nibble of her soft lips, each press of her body against his, he was reminded of what they once had. And it made him long for that kind of sweet bliss again.

He'd told himself on many occasions that he was a coward, and he believed it now more than ever. It's just who he was. He wouldn't test fate by hooking up with Miranda again. He wouldn't let himself get close to her little girl. Carter knew loss, more than most men, and another tragedy in his life might send him into a downward spiral from which he'd never recover. There were many kinds of cowards. Carter was an emotional one. He'd learned to live with that fact. He'd accepted it as true so he could move on.

Yet right now on this lonely dark road to a lonely dark cabin, he felt almost as miserable as he had during those tragic turning points of his life. But in a way, tonight was worse. Tonight his misery was doubled because of his cold treatment of Miranda. He'd seen the hurt in her eyes. He'd watched her body stiffen with his indifference. Did he want her to hate him? Maybe he did. Hating her was impossible, but if she hated him, he wouldn't have to risk hurting her again or setting himself up for another unbearable loss.

He pulled into his driveway, turned off his engine and sat in the patrol car for several minutes letting his mind adjust to the emptiness he'd find on the other side of his door. Thank goodness he had the trip to Wilton Hollow and an investigation to pursue tomorrow. His brain would be functioning on a professional level once more. Tonight, he'd drink some warm milk and read a couple of articles in the latest *Mountain Times Magazine*, and maybe…just maybe, he'd sleep.

CARTER WAS AT the station early Monday morning. He checked the schedule and discovered that Sam was on the roster for today. Sam was the best backup Carter could ask for, but Carter considered that this investigation might present some unpleasant truths to his rookie. But even if evidence was found on Sheila's land, that didn't mean that Allie was responsible. No. Considering what Allie meant to Sam, Carter couldn't conceive of her guilt in any of this mess.

Carter studied a local map of the area. The mountains were a web of short, mostly uninhabited roads, many of which bore the name of some distant settler who'd landed there and staked a claim. Recalling Sheila's last name, Sam uncovered one such rural track of dusty road called Blount Lane. Maybe Sheila hadn't lived there for decades, but obviously one of her ancestors had.

A closer study indicated a walking path around the back of Sheila's property that extended several hundred yards behind the plot of land where the county had identified a structure. Sheila's house, Carter figured. Even if Sheila were home, he and Sam could enter the property without being seen.

"Good morning, Chief."

Carter looked up from his spot behind his desk. "Sam, will you have a seat for a moment. I want to talk to you."

Sam pulled out a chair. "It's still early, Chief. Surely I'm not in trouble yet."

"No, you're not in trouble, but I'm investigating a lead on the hardware and winery thefts, and I'd like you to go with me."

"Sure. No problem."

"Actually, there may be a problem," Carter said. He wanted to be completely up-front with Sam so his rookie wouldn't feel blindsided when they reached Sheila's land.

Sam waited patiently for Carter to continue.

"The lead I got is a good one," Carter said. "I feel like it might pan out. But you need to know that we'll be heading out to a little-known road called Blount Lane."

"Don't think I ever heard that name," Sam said.

"Maybe not, but you know the place. It's Sheila's house, and more importantly, the place Allie is living."

Sam shook his head. "There's got to be some mistake, Carter. That stolen property couldn't be on Sheila's land. Granted, Dale is a suspect, but Allie would have told me…"

"Are you sure about that?"

"As sure as I can be about anything. Allie wouldn't be involved in anything criminal."

"I'm not saying she is," Carter assured him. "I don't know what we'll find when we get out there today, but you've got to be aware that anything is possible. If Allie is guilty of aiding Dale, then…"

"She isn't. She wouldn't."

"Okay." Carter sensed he was pushing too hard. Sam was crazy about Allie, and of course he would defend her. He just hoped Sam wasn't about to get his heart broken. "We'll leave in a few minutes." He picked up his desk phone. "Just have to call Judge White to see if he has my search warrant ready. Then you and I will head out."

"You don't have to worry about me, Carter," Sam said. "Whatever we find, I've got your back."

FOR MOST OF the trip out to Blount Lane, Sam was relaxed, even chatty. Only when they neared Sheila's land did he stiffen slightly in the passenger seat and stare alertly out the window. "We're getting close," he said.

Carter passed the narrow turnoff to Sheila's drive and took the next rutted lane. He stopped when the car couldn't go any farther. "We walk from here," he said. "If the tip I got is the real thing, then we might be walking right into the middle of that stolen property."

Sam darted a quick glance in Carter's direction. The muscles in his neck tensed.

"Are you sure you're ready for this?" Carter asked. "Who knows what we'll find."

"I'm ready. And I'd bet my last dollar that Allie didn't have anything to do with stealing that equipment."

"You're probably right. I hope you are, but I haven't heard you say the same thing about Sheila."

"No. Truth is, I've never been too pleased that Allie lives with that woman." As the sun crested the trees on the eastern horizon, the two men picked their way through an overgrown path toward the back of Sheila's property. They'd gone a few hundred yards when a woman's voice, demanding and sharp, drifted toward them.

Both men stopped. "Sounds like Sheila," Carter said.

"I've only heard her voice once, so I can't

be sure. Whoever it is, she's angry about something."

Carter made out a few of the words. "Put more fertilizer on those plants. Dale'll kill me if this isn't a good crop."

Carter stared at Sam.

"Something tells me we're not going to find rows of lettuce," Sam said.

SAM EXPERIENCED THE first twinges of anxiety. He still believed Allie was innocent of any wrongdoing, but they were on Sheila's property and the little conversation he'd heard didn't sound good. He and Carter continued toward the sound. Sheila's voice, recognizable now, became more strident. "Freakin' bugs!" she said. "How am I supposed to know how much insecticide to use?"

As Carter and Sam got closer, Sam stepped on a dry branch. Sheila's head snapped around to the direction from which they were approaching. "Someone's coming," she said in a loud whisper. "Cover this stuff up, and let's get back to the house."

Carter stepped into the clearing just ahead of Sam. "You're not going anywhere,

Sheila." Another woman, lost in the dawn shadows on the other side of a green field, tried to run, but Carter hollered a warning to her, as well. "Hold on!"

Sam gave chase, but stopped suddenly. No, it couldn't be. Unfortunately, that cute figure and those long, strong legs were a giveaway. "Allie," he said, fighting his mounting disbelief.

She halted, dropped her arms to her sides and turned to face him. Her features reflected her surprise, her shock and, worst of all, her guilt.

"What's going on, Allie?" Sam asked.

"I can explain, Sam…"

But Sam knew she couldn't. It was true that sometimes a picture was worth more than the cleverest explanation, and so far what he'd seen didn't paint a pretty picture. Clearly Allie had been trying to get away… from him.

Assorted cultivating equipment lay in the clearing, and Sheila was holding a drop cloth as if she were intending to cover the evidence. Carter and Sam stayed apart and took small, slow steps through the field, surveying the unmistakable crop. Sam had seen his share of marijuana and knew he was looking at a healthy sampling of product.

Carter's voice carried across the field. "I'm pretty sure we're dealing with the biggest cash crop to come out of the mountains in a long time," he said. "At least two acres of marijuana plants, in different stages of growth."

Since Dale's name had been mentioned earlier, Sam figured he was behind the endeavor. But, apparently, Sheila and Allie were helpers, willing or not.

Sam broke off a leaf and sniffed it. He shook his head as if he were trying to make some sense of what was so blatantly obvious.

Having kept his gaze on the women, Carter said, "Ladies, you want to come over here, so we can have a little chat?"

Sheila answered with a string of curse words effectively ordering Carter off her property. Allie moved slowly toward them. In spite of what Sam knew to be true, his heart still ached for her. She suddenly seemed so small and vulnerable. But he was a cop, and the facts mattered more than his emotions at this minute.

Carter handed Sheila the search warrant. After reading it, she closed her eyes and lowered her forehead into her hands. "Don't say anything, Allie," she warned. "We're gonna need a lawyer."

Carter walked in the direction of a hastily constructed lean-to against a tree. "If I look in there, am I going to find bigger equipment like tillers and other items from the winery in town?" He strode along a line of plants. "And this setup of hoses and sprinklers looks just like the items stolen from the hardware store."

Sheila answered with a hard stare, her lips clamped tight. A few feet away, Allie was pleading with Sam. "I wanted to tell you about this," she said. "None of it was my idea. I never wanted to go along with Sheila and Dale."

"But you didn't tell me, and you did go along with them," Sam responded, keeping his voice calm and impersonal.

"Shut up!" Sheila screamed at Allie. "What part of 'don't say anything' don't you understand?"

Sam felt like he'd been punched in the gut. All at once his words became hoarse, choked. "Allie, you're dating a cop." He paused. "More than dating I'd thought. How come you couldn't have found a way to tell me about this?"

"I wanted to, but I was scared."

"Scared my fat…" Sheila ground out until Carter silenced her with a look.

Allie flinched. "I *was* scared. I'm living in your house. I don't have any money." She spared a pitying glance at Sam. "I don't know what I would have done if I'd made Sheila and Dale angry."

Sam tried to ignore the pain in his gut. She could have come to him. He would have found her a place to live. Heck, she could have moved in with him.

"We're all going down to the station," Carter said. "It's a bit of a trek back to the patrol car, but it's a lovely day, so it shouldn't be too hard. Once we get there, you can call anyone you like, Sheila. Maybe a lawyer, maybe Dale. In fact, I'd kind of like you to give Dale a call. I have a few questions for him, too."

"Sorry, Chief," she said, her voice dripping with sarcasm. "He's out of town on business."

Sam realized that anything else he might hear from these two women would probably be lies. Until a few minutes ago, he'd have believed every word Allie said; that she was an angel brought to earth just for him. But, he had a job to do, and like other love-struck men before him, he would have to accept that an angel's wings could be tarnished.

Sam took Allie's arm, but this time it was not with affection. This time he was making sure she didn't escape. They marched side by side, not speaking. Sam figured there'd be plenty to say later.

SHEILA HAD REFUSED to answer any questions, which didn't surprise Carter. She'd sat at his desk drinking coffee and glaring at him as if sparks from her eyes might ignite the whole building. Allie, on the other hand, talked freely to both officers. Between tears and apologies, she gave them all the information Carter needed, including the fact that she'd been a willing participant in the scheme because of the promise of a share of big profits. When she was taken to a waiting cell for transport to the county jail, Carter felt certain he'd heard the truth.

Later that morning, Carter took Sam for a coffee.

"What do you think will happen to her?" Sam asked.

"Can't say for sure. Probably a year's sentence. If she doesn't have any priors, maybe a couple years' probation after that. She'll definitely serve some time. She knew about the crop. She was helping Dale and Sheila voluntarily, and she admitted her reason for getting involved." Carter sighed. "She was in pretty heavy, Sam. I'm sorry."

"She just wanted to get out of Sheila's house," Sam said. "And she wasn't making enough at the café to afford her own place." Sam waited for Carter to say something and finally added, "It's no excuse. I know that."

"You've got a decision to make, buddy. Are you going to stick by her through all this?" Carter figured it was probably too soon for Sam to know the answer.

But Sam surprised him. "No. No way. I trusted her. I thought she trusted me. I guess no man likes being played for a fool, but somehow I think it's worse when the guy is a cop." He took a long swallow of his beer.

"I can't forgive her for breaking the law right under my nose."

"I hear ya," Carter said. "Forgiveness can be like drinking a whole bottle of castor oil. Might help eventually, but it doesn't go down so well." He stood up, ready to continue with the second part of his trying day. "Put some space between the two of you, Sam. Things can change with the passage of time." *Yeah, like fourteen years...*

Carter left the café and tried to reach Lawton. Law hadn't answered any of Carter's phone calls, but he had to keep trying. This time, he picked up. "Hey, Carter."

"Hello, Lawton. Just wanted you to know that I found all that stuff taken from the hardware store and the winery. Couldn't have done it without your help."

"I didn't do anything," Lawton said, his voice quavering. "I never gave you any information about that stuff, Carter, remember?"

"Yeah, I know, Law. You didn't." It was okay with Carter if Lawton needed to keep his part in the investigation just between the two of them. "But in case you might feel more inclined to talk, can you tell me where Dale is now?"

"I don't know, Carter. Honest I don't."

"Okay. We'll find him. Oh, and Lawton…?"

"Yeah."

"Just watch your back, okay?"

CHAPTER SEVENTEEN

MIRANDA ENJOYED MORNINGS in Cora's house. She could wake slowly, letting bird sounds and the rustle of leaves on the trees bring her to complete alertness. But this particular morning, when she was fully awake, she remembered the heartache of the last night.

Today was Monday, and Miranda had to accept that she needed to get on with her life. Carter didn't want her. He hadn't called to apologize for his indifference the night before, and Miranda didn't blame him. She'd made a choice fourteen years ago that excluded him from her life. Would she do it differently now that she was older and wiser? Yes. If she could go back to that time again, she'd do anything to make it work.

She called her daughter in from the barn. "Come on, Em. We're going to see the minister this morning. I made an appointment to talk to him about Lawton."

Emily stood at the barn door with Buster close by. "Can't I stay here, Mom? Miss Cora will watch me, and I'll be here when you get back."

Miranda smiled at the tactics she'd used when she was Emily's age. "No, you cannot. Miss Cora has done enough for the two of us."

Emily headed toward the house. An hour later, at eleven thirty, both she and her daughter were respectably dressed and ready to go to the Methodist church. They went out to the porch just as a car pulled into Cora's drive. A familiar car. Carter's personal vehicle.

With her arm around Emily, Miranda continued down the steps. She wouldn't run back in the house and risk looking like a coward, or a fool.

"Hi, Carter!" Emily called. "We're going to church even though it's Monday."

"Good for you," he said. "You're looking mighty pretty this morning."

Emily beamed, basking in the rare attention.

"Good morning, Miranda," he said, his voice in perfect control. His eyes told a different story as he avoided looking directly at her.

"Have you seen Ava?" he asked. "I'm here to pick her up."

"I'm here!" Ava hollered from the front door. "I'm ready." She bounded down the stairs. "Don't you two look nice," she said to Miranda.

Miranda wanted to ask where brother and sister were going on a day that was a workday for Carter, but, of course, their plans weren't her concern. She merely said, "Thanks," and went to her car.

Miranda pulled out of the drive ahead of Carter. She tried not to think about how he looked this morning in faded jeans and a light green shirt that matched his eyes and molded to his broad chest. Or the fine lines in the corners of his eyes that indicated he might not have slept so well last night. In fact, he seemed tired, as if he'd already put in a full day's work, and it was only noon.

She put the radio on, but immediately turned it off. It was definitely time to go back to Durham. The words were out of her mouth before she had a chance to think about them. "We're leaving on Wednesday, Em., We're going home."

Emily sat forward and stared at her mother. "What? No, Mom, not yet. I'm not ready to go."

"We don't have a reason to stay, honey. Lawton is doing well, and I have other cases in Durham."

"How about fun?" Emily argued. "Isn't fun a good reason to stay? I like it at Miss Cora's. And Ava is really nice."

"Ava will be going back to Charlotte soon," Miranda pointed out."

"I know, but she's coming back. She's going to be ministerator of the home for children."

"That's administrator, Em, and yes, I know that. Ava is very happy to have gotten the job."

"I can make lots of friends with the kids in the home. Ava showed me pictures. It's really pretty there."

"Running the home will be Ava's job, Emily. She won't be able to entertain many visitors, no matter how well-intentioned they are."

"But what about Carter? He's starting to be nice now, too."

Yes, she thought, Carter had come a long way since he first met Emily.

"And Jace. I really like him," Emily said. "He's so funny."

Miranda took a deep breath. They probably could stay a few more days, but what would be the point? She'd attempted to revive Carter's emotions in the barn last night, and all she'd succeeded in doing was making him uncomfortable. What difference would a day or two make?

"No arguments, Em. We've got to go home. Our car will be ready tomorrow. And anyway, I'm sure Daddy misses you, and you miss him."

"Yeah, but he was just here. And besides, Miss Cora has a horse, and I bet Carter would teach me to ride."

"I wouldn't count on that, honey. He's a busy man with an important job. He doesn't have time."

Emily stomped her foot on the floor of the car. "Well, just darn it!"

Miranda gave her an indulgent smile. "I hope Reverend Babbitt has time to give you a short message about patience and understanding."

Miranda's mind was made up. She'd talk to the reverend this morning and see Lawton one more time tomorrow evening after he'd put in two days at his new job. There was nothing to keep her and Emily from returning to Durham. So early Wednesday morning, they'd be on the road, and Miranda didn't know when or if she'd ever come back to Holly River again. She'd expected to leave Holly River with a sense of accomplishment after helping Law. She hadn't expected to leave with this overwhelming sense of loss hanging over her.

"WHAT'S YOUR PROBLEM?" Ava didn't mince words. Nor did she hide her opinions behind a false smile.

Carter gave her a sideways glance as they pulled away from Cora's. He hoped Ava wasn't getting ready to give him one of her big-sis lectures. It was nearly an hour's drive to Wilton Hollow.

"I don't have a problem," he answered, trying not to sound too much like the petulant little brother.

"You barely acknowledged Miranda just now. What's going on?"

"Nothing's going on," he snapped. "What's going on with you all? I get yelled at if I'm not sweet as pie to Emily. So today I compliment her, and I'm getting yelled at for ignoring Miranda."

Ava narrowed her eyes at him. There was no mistaking her pre-lecture look of disapproval. "Is it really too much to ask for you to be nice to two people at the same time, Carter? Especially when one of them is the girl you swore you were going to marry one day."

"Ancient history, Ava. Let it go."

"You should give Miranda another chance."

Oh, heck no. Ava wasn't going to get away with playing with his emotions. "Not going to happen. Once was enough."

Ava tapped on the door handle while she planned her next attack. "Women know things, Carter. And I happen to believe… correct that, I happen to *know* that Miranda would like to give your relationship another try."

"How would you know that, Ava? Are you a mind reader now?"

"More or less. At least I'm not totally clueless like you are. Can't you read the signs? The way her eyes follow you? The way she smiles and her cheeks turn pink when you enter the room? Mama's noticed it, too."

"Oh, great," he said. "The Cahill coven twisting fate to suit themselves."

Ava sighed. "Are you actually expecting me to believe that you have no feelings for Miranda at all? Are you telling me you're not the least bit interested in a redo of your history?"

"I'm not asking you to believe anything, Ava. And as far as telling you what I might be thinking, you can forget it. Conversation closed."

She tsked, a habit she'd picked up from Cora. "It's not good to keep things bottled up, Carter."

He gave her a quick, hard stare before returning his gaze to the road. "Do I have to remind you what we're doing today, Ava? We're on our way to the home of a complete stranger. A woman neither of us has ever heard of before this week. A woman who, for the last year, has been cashing checks written by our mother to the tune of fifteen hundred a month."

"I haven't forgotten any of that," Ava said, with just a hint of haughtiness. "I just figured that since we're trapped in the same car, we might as well hash out some details of your life."

He held a frustrated breath before saying, "I can pull over anytime and let you out."

She sighed. "No. I'll stop. I just want you to be happy."

"Fine. Then why don't you leave my life up to me and make me happy by thinking about what we're going to say to Gladys Kirshner when we get to her house."

One of Ava's failings, and she didn't have many, was her inability to admit when she was losing an argument. Thankfully today she gave up rather graciously. "Okay, I said I'd drop it." After a few minutes she said, "Let me do the talking when we get to Wilton Hollow. I'll tell Gladys what we know. You might just bite her head off."

Carter rolled his eyes. True that.

WILTON HOLLOW WAS a small town even by small-town standards. Two intersecting roads met under a single traffic light with a half dozen or so side streets running off until apparently people had lost interest in building houses on them. Despite the seriousness of his mission today, Carter smiled as he surveyed one such road. *Well, looks like we have all the houses we need for this one*, he imagined a founding father saying.

Still, it was a pleasant enough town, mostly senior citizens, Carter figured. There was one gas station, a small convenience store and two churches. Dining out was apparently limited to a fast-food place in the middle of town. Wilton Hollow-ites were folks living out their lives on tiny little lots with small trim bushes in front of porches big enough for two chairs and a table.

"This is it," Ava said. "Turn right. That's Landsdown Street."

Carter did as instructed and pulled in front of the fourth house, a frame structure with faded window shutters and peeling paint on the walls. Evidently Gladys hadn't been using her fifteen hundred a month on home improvements. And she'd been keeping his own mother from using the money to keep her place up.

He and Ava got out of the car and walked up a short brick walkway to the front door. He pressed a push-button doorbell, and a rusty chime announced their presence.

"Remember," Ava said. "I'll do the talking."

"I got it, Ava. I'll let you begin, but I'm jumping in when I need to."

The front door was opened by a middle-aged woman whose brown hair was striped with gray. She had on tan baggy pants that Carter figured would have been appropriate for the senior women's golf tournament. The woman must have prized the pants since she covered them and a plain brown blouse with a full apron.

She stared at Carter and Ava. "Yes?"

"Are you Gladys Kirshner?" Ava asked.

"I am. State your business. I'm very busy."

Ava introduced herself using her and Carter's full names. She did not indicate that Carter was a police officer. Carter immediately noted that the woman's gray eyes widened when she heard the name *Cahill*.

"I have nothing to say to you," she snapped in a true High Mountain drawl. "Everything is legal. I have it in writing."

"We're not here to accuse you of anything, Mrs.... It is Mrs., isn't it?"

"It's Miss, as if you didn't know."

"May we come in and speak with you?" Ava asked, her voice low and pleasant. How could anyone not invite Ava, in her crisp blouse, tailored black pants, sensible shoes and hair swept into a tidy bun, into their home?

The woman pondered her options for a moment and then opened the door wider. "You might as well. I figured one of y'all would show up one day."

"Thank you." Ava stepped inside and Carter followed.

Gladys thumbed at a pair of chairs by an old fireplace. "You can sit if you want."

Ah. True Southern hospitality, Carter thought.

Ava chose a wicker chair and Carter settled on the floral sofa. Gladys sat in a rocker and set it going with one slippered foot. She waited until Ava spoke.

"Miss Kirshner, we've come here today because we are aware of money my mother, Cora Cahill, is sending you each month."

"What about it?" Gladys asked.

"We don't know what it's for," Ava said. "We'd like to know why she's sending you fifteen hundred dollars a month."

"Why don't you ask her?"

Ava darted a glance at Carter, who rubbed his chin. It was a darn good question. He and Ava had argued about being direct with their mother, but Ava had insisted that forthrightness would never work with Cora. She would only give them another of her mini lessons about appreciating the value of a dollar in their own lives.

"We didn't think she'd tell us," Carter answered honestly. "My mother can be secretive about things." Like she never once complained to her children about Raymond. And she never argued with him in the presence of her kids. But she protected them from Raymond's worst fits of temper with some kind of magic power that quieted her husband.

"That's right," Ava said. "All her life, our mother bore her burdens privately. If she had wanted us to know about this money, she would have told us. The fact that she didn't, and that the transactions were kept in a shoe box in the back of my father's desk, indicates to us that this is a private matter."

"She's been paying this money for over a year," Carter said. "Since my father died. That amounts to quite a sum. And we'd like to know why. We know that you worked for a short time at the paper mill, so you and my father are connected."

"Oh, we were connected all right…"

A loud crash came from the back of the house. Ava emitted a gasp, and Carter went into cop mode, though weaponless. He didn't know what he would do if there were real trouble, but he was alert. Gladys jumped up from the rocker and hurried toward a hallway. Before she'd exited the living room, a tortured wail followed the crash.

Carter quickly took an offensive position and followed her down the hall and into a small bedroom. The only furniture in the room was a bed with metal bars on the sides and a three-drawer dresser. One of the drawers had been pulled out and overturned, likely the source of the loud noise. The only light was an overhead fixture, currently turned off. Sunlight struggled to find a path through slightly opened blinds.

A boy sat cross-legged in front of the dresser. He rocked back and forth while uttering a repetitious sound that was a cross between a cry and a sob. He tore through the pile of clothes on the floor as if he were looking for something.

Having followed the other adults, Ava stopped at the threshold of the room. "What's going on?"

"Shush," Gladys ordered. "Can't you see you've upset my son enough? Robert's not used to visitors." She got down on her knees, put her hands on each side of the boy's face and spoke slowly and methodically.

"It's all right, Robert. I'll find it." She spotted a tiny stuffed tail among the clothing and pulled it out. "Here's your giraffe. He's fine, see?"

Robert grabbed the toy and clutched it to his chest.

"Everything's okay, Robert," she said, stroking the top of his head where his straight hair fell to his eyebrows. "Mama made everything all right again."

Robert stilled, looked up at his mother. A small upturn of his lips indicated he was content for now. He began counting the spots on the toy giraffe.

"He's okay now," Gladys said to Carter and Ava. "Sometimes he puts that giraffe in a drawer like he's putting it down for a nap. Then he can't remember exactly where he placed it." She stood, wiped her hands on her apron. "If I've looked for that giraffe once, I've looked for it a thousand times."

Ava stepped farther into the room. "Miss. Kirshner, what's happening with your son? Is he autistic?"

She nodded. "Worst case the doctors around here have ever seen. Can't do anything for him. When your daddy was alive, I took Robert to a whole slew of medical people. They tried all sorts of things, but in the end, Robert is just like he is."

Carter was puzzled. "Miss Kirshner, did our father help you with Robert's expenses?" he asked. Such generosity was uncommon for Raymond Cahill.

"You bet he did. He had to. Your daddy is Robert's father."

CHAPTER EIGHTEEN

CARTER RECOGNIZED THE same shock he was experiencing in Ava's eyes. "Maybe we should go back to the living room and discuss this further," he said. "Will Robert be all right?"

Gladys nodded. "Yes, he's okay now." She placed her hands on her son's face again, demanding his attention. "Mama's going in the other room now, Robert. I'll be right here if you need me. Can you play for a while so Mama can talk to these nice people?"

Robert did not give an answer, but he held the giraffe close to his chest and began crooning a song.

"How old is Robert?" Ava asked when the adults had taken seats in the living room again.

"Twelve."

"Has he always been like this?"

"I didn't notice anything was wrong until

after his second birthday," Gladys said. "Other babies were trying to talk and walk. Not Robert, so I knew something was up. And then it was one doctor after another."

"And our father knew his connection to Robert?" Carter asked.

"He knew from the time I first found out I was pregnant. He made me quit my job. I worked in an auto parts factory until the baby came, and then I had to get your daddy to pay for child care. After a while, Robert being like he is, I couldn't work at all."

"Did our father go with you to the doctor's appointments?" Carter asked, trying to determine the extent of Raymond's involvement with the child and perhaps discover a shred of decency in the man.

"A few times, but he made it clear to me from the start that he had a business to run and a family to go home to every night. *A real family*," she added bitterly.

"Did Robert have a relationship with our father?"

"You couldn't call it a relationship," Gladys explained. "Ray was here enough so that Robert finally stopped reacting to him with fits and temper tantrums. Raymond stopped coming at all two years before he died, and honestly, Robert didn't seem to notice the difference. For the last three years it's just been Robert and me, and a few aid workers sent by the county."

Ava sat forward, a look of relief on her face. "Does he go to a school designed for children with his challenges?"

"He went for a while to the Blackthorn School in Ridley two mornings a week. The public school system paid for it."

"Did he quit going?" Ava asked.

"Yes. Robert would become so upset that I'd just have to go get him. He couldn't seem to adjust. Now I let him stay home with me. I can't work, obviously, but thanks to your father's money every month, I've managed."

Carter was forming a clear picture of how the money chain started, and how it progressed. Either his father truly felt an obligation to this child or he was simply paying hush money to his mother. "When did my mother first hear of Raymond's support of Robert?"

"I went to see her two days after the funeral. It was a bad time for your mama, but I couldn't wait. Your daddy's payment was late, and I had to pay the electric bill. Plus the town was about to shut off my water."

"Is this also the first time my mother learned of Robert's existence?"

"It was. Truthfully she wasn't as surprised as I thought she'd be." Gladys folded her hands in her lap. "She's a good woman, your mama. She never questioned that it was her responsibility to keep up Raymond's payments."

Carter felt a need to clarify the misconception. "Miss Kirshner, I don't think my mother…"

"She agreed," Gladys stated emphatically. "Didn't even object when I asked her to sign papers saying she would continue."

Oh, Mama, why didn't you come to us when this happened? Carter cleared his throat. "And my mother's continued the payments all this time?"

"It may not seem right to you, Mr. Cahill, but I didn't have any choice."

"Frankly, Miss Kirshner, I'm not sure how I feel about this," Carter said. "I know my mama wouldn't want you and your son to be homeless."

Gladys nodded. "Robert's here. He's healthy as a horse in most respects. And I love him. When he gets to be an adult, I don't know what will happen to him. Maybe he'll have to go into a care facility. I'm not going to live forever. But right now he has to be with me full time. That's the way I want it."

Carter stood. "Thank you, Miss Kirshner, for providing this information. Ava, I guess we heard what we came for," he said. "Might as well head back to Holly River."

Ava followed him to the door. "Thank you for your time, Miss Kirshner."

"You're not planning to stop the payments, are you?" she asked. "I don't think your mama'd like that, and I'd hate for this to get messy with lawyers and all."

"No, ma'am, we wouldn't want this to get messy," Carter said, though he didn't know what the family was going to do about this situation. His and Ava's lives had changed in the last hour. And Jace's would, as well. The Cahill children had a half sibling whose existence had been hidden for years. Their father had not been the sterling leader in the community he'd professed to be. And Cora Cahill was sacrificing every day to make up for her husband's infidelity. This was already a messy situation.

"We won't need to involve any lawyers, ma'am," he said as he followed Ava out the door. "I'll keep you informed as things progress."

"I just can't believe this," Ava said when they were in the car. "Daddy cheated on Mama. That overly righteous, narrow-minded, son of…"

"I know, Ava. I know. But what's done is done."

"I wonder if Mama ever had a DNA test performed to prove that Dad is Robert's father."

"We'll ask her, but knowing Mama, she might have accepted the woman's story as gospel."

Ava nodded. "It's not going to be easy to confront her about this, but we have to. Should we talk to her today?"

"Do you see any reason to wait?"

"No. And we have to let Jace know what's going on. Let's clear the air and hopefully one of us will figure out what to do."

MIRANDA HAD ASKED Lawton to meet her at church on his lunch hour. If he'd been working on cars, he didn't look it. He had on a clean shirt.

He smiled when she greeted him and checked his watch. "Just have a few minutes, Miranda. Don't want to take advantage on the first day of my new job."

"I understand." She knocked on Reverend Babbitt's office door, and he indicated they could come in.

Lawton's smile faded. "I'm guessing this meeting has something to do with me."

"Absolutely."

He shook his head. "I should tell you, Miranda, this is my first time at church since I've been back. I went to services a few times in prison, but I'd hardly call myself a practicing Christian." He wrung his hands. "And nobody in town would either. I don't want anyone to pressure me to pick any church."

"This isn't about you going to church regularly, Law," she said. "This is about you meeting people and taking a first step in becoming part of the community."

"What do you mean? The folks in this town aren't anxious to have me be part of the community. I can tell you that."

"Only because they don't know you, the way you are now at least. I'm hoping to change that. And the best way to do that is to have you talk to the reverend with me."

The minister stood behind his desk as they entered his office. Reverend Babbitt was a kind man. Miranda had listened to his sermons through her growing years. She hoped, and prayed a bit, that his kindness would extend to her cousin this morning.

Dressed in cotton pants and casual shirt, without his robe, his glasses perched on his nose, the reverend seemed approachable. Miranda noticed that Lawton seemed to relax.

She explained everything she'd done to help Lawton acclimate to life outside prison. "So you can see how well Law is doing, Reverend. He started a new job today. And before that, he'd been helping Jace Cahill at the tree farm. He has his driver's license and a decent place to live."

"I understand our police chief has been helping you, Law. Is that right?"

"That's right, Reverend. Carter has been great. He's helped me a lot."

"I certainly respect Carter," Babbitt said,

folding his hands on the top of his desk. "I'd like to help, but I don't see what you think I can do for you."

Miranda cleared her throat. "You may know, Reverend, that I am a social worker for the state of North Carolina."

He nodded.

"I've worked with other inmates once they've been released. I understand what they need to lead productive lives and not fall into the cycle of returning to prison. I've pretty much done all I can for Law. The only part of his rehabilitation still lacking is his contact with other people. I was hoping you could help with that."

Babbitt nodded slowly. "Well, Miranda, church folks are supposed to be forgiving. And they're supposed to believe in second chances. Attending church for an hour on Sunday is a start for Lawton, but I don't know that it will make a whole lot of difference until people get to know him personally."

"I agree," Miranda said. "That's why I'd like you to suggest a community project, perhaps one associated with the church… or not, that Law could participate in. He's strong and a good worker. And you have your weekends free, right, Law?"

Lawton indicated that he did.

Babbitt reached for a pencil and tapped it lightly on his desk. After a moment he said, "I have something in mind. The town council is looking for volunteers to improve the equipment at Vanover Park. Some of the swings are worn out, and the slide needs to be replaced. We don't want any of our young'uns to hurt themselves."

"No, of course not," Miranda said. "That sounds perfect for Lawton." She glanced at her cousin and was grateful to see his nod of approval.

"And there's another advantage. It's mostly the young men in town, fathers of young kids and even a couple of young professors from the college, who are heading up the team to modernize the park. Lawton would be among people his own age. I can't guarantee that this idea will be a success. That's up to Lawton and the guys he'll be working with. But it's a beginning, a way back into the town's good graces. If you give me the go-ahead, Lawton, I'll speak to Craig Jones and tell him we have a new volunteer.

Then you show up on Saturday at the park, and he'll put you to work."

"That'd be fine, Reverend," Lawton said. "I'll be there."

Miranda shook the pastor's hand. "I appreciate this," she said.

"No problem, Miranda. But do me a favor. Don't encourage your other cousin, Dale, to come around the park while Lawton's there. I don't want any trouble, and trouble seems to follow him wherever he goes."

"I doubt this is something Dale would be interested in," Miranda said. "Lawton hardly sees Dale anymore anyway. Isn't that right, Law?"

"Haven't seen him since I moved into the McNulty place," Lawton said. "And I like it that way."

As they walked to the church parking lot, Miranda said, "Is that true, Lawton? You haven't seen Dale for days?"

"It's true. He's in real trouble. I'm not sure of all the details, but Carter told me they'd found stolen goods, and he believes Dale has something to do with it."

For once Miranda didn't think Carter was jumping to the wrong conclusion. She'd seen enough of her cousin Dale on this visit to suspect he was capable of anything. "You stay away from him, Lawton," she said. "You know Dale. He'll try everything to get you involved. And if he is guilty, he'll try to get you to take the blame."

Emily, who'd sat quietly in the minister's office while the adults talked, left her mother's side and skipped around to slip her hand into Lawton's. "Yeah, Law," she said. "Stay away from Dale. You're really nice now, and he's not."

Lawton smiled down at her. "Thank you, Emily. I'm gonna try to keep it that way."

"Why didn't you tell cousin Lawton about us leaving, Mom?" Emily asked when she and Miranda were in the car. "Have you changed your mind?"

"No, honey. We're still going on Wednesday. You and I will stop by Lawton's cabin tomorrow night to tell him goodbye. I didn't want him to feel that we were abandoning him right after he started a new job. But he'll be fine after we go. And now that Reverend Babbitt has a project for Law to work on, my job here really is done." She reached over and patted Emily's knee. "We have to go back, sweetheart."

Emily sighed. "I kind of thought…"

"What, honey? What did you think?"

"Well, I thought that maybe since you found out that Carter wasn't a ghost, that maybe he would be your boyfriend. You've spent lots of time with him. And he's always smiling." She gave her mother an earnest look. "You can have a boyfriend now that you're not married, you know."

"Yes, I know, but as much as I like Carter, it won't be him. He lives here in Holly River, and we live in Durham."

"It's not so far. Daddy came over and visited us, remember?"

"Yes, I remember. But please, Em, don't count on us coming back here anytime soon, okay?"

Emily nodded. "I'm just kind of sad about it, that's all."

"So am I, honey," Miranda said softly. Whether it's now or fourteen years ago, leaving is always hard.

CARTER AND AVA arrived back at Cora's a little after three that afternoon. Carter immediately noticed that Miranda's car was not parked in front. They entered a house fragrant with roasting pork. Cora had always been famous for her slow-cooked barbecue.

"Where have you two been?" she asked when they came in the kitchen to find her.

"We had an errand to run," Ava said, sniffing the air. "That smells delicious, Mom."

Cora stared at Carter. "I thought I'd fix something special today since Miranda will be leaving soon."

Carter stood stock-still in the middle of the room. "What are you talking about? When is she leaving?"

"Wednesday. Just told me this morning. She didn't tell you?"

He pretended an indifference he didn't feel. He'd just seen Miranda a few hours ago when he'd come to pick up Ava, and she hadn't said a word about leaving. Apparently Ava didn't know either. His mother's words had struck him. "No, she didn't mention that," he said. Shaking off his stunned reaction he added, "I knew she was about done helping Lawton, but I didn't know she was going so soon."

Ava gave him a slight punch to his shoulder. "See? You happy now?"

"Maybe you should have asked her," Cora snapped at him.

"Asked her what?"

"To stay maybe."

"I can't suggest what Miranda does with her life."

Cora released a long, deep sigh. "I don't know what's going on with you two, but it's obvious that whatever you had years ago could be fanned back to life with a little effort."

Carter pulled out a chair and sat heavily. "We aren't interested in renewing what we had."

Ava responded with a bitter-sounding chuckle.

"Speak for yourself, Carter," Cora said. "I can tell when a lady is interested in a man. And, child, Miranda is interested in you. Why, she can't take her eyes off you. Don't be a prideful fool and let her go without a fight this time."

This situation was getting out of hand, and Carter wasn't going to just sit here and take an all-out assault from both women.

"Mom, I didn't *let her go* last time. She made her decision and I was forced to live with it." He glared at his mother. What had happened here? He and Ava were prepared to talk to their mother about her involvement with Gladys Kirshner, and all of a sudden he was the target and Cora was acting like a ballistic missile. "Don't rewrite history, Mom. It is what it is."

Cora harrumphed and took a cooked potato from a pot in the sink. "I've got to make potato salad," she said. "Now, tell me, what sort of errand took half the day?"

Ava shot a look at Carter, and he returned it with a let's-get-this-over-with hunch of his shoulders. At least they would be changing the subject.

Ava pulled out two more chairs. "Come and sit, Mama. This could take a while."

Cora put her peeling knife on the counter, wiped her hands on her apron and came to the table. "What's going on?"

Carter indicated a chair and she sat. "We went to Wilton Hollow today, Mama."

Her eyes widened, but she made no sound. Her lips thinned as she crossed her arms tightly over her chest.

"I guess you know why we went there," Carter said.

"I have a lot of questions, but I'm figuring you interfered in business that's none of your concern," she said.

"Mama, how can you say that?" Ava leaned over the table. "You are sacrificing every month for this woman and her son. Meanwhile your house, your lifestyle, everything you deserve at this time of your life is being put on a back burner."

"It's my decision," Cora said. "Has been all along. If you think somebody forced me into helping Gladys, you're wrong."

Carter drummed his fingers on the table. "Mom, you should have told us. We would have helped you. You were going through a difficult time. Daddy died. You had to deal with discovering his infidelity. You took this woman's word that Robert is Daddy's son."

"You must think I'm three times a fool," Cora said. "I didn't take anyone's word for anything. I wasn't married to Raymond Cahill all those years without learning a thing or two about trusting people. I had a DNA test done." She snorted. "Robert, that poor soul, is your daddy's offspring. No doubt about it."

"Mama, don't be angry with us," Ava said. "We just want to know how you were coerced into paying Gladys every month."

"I wasn't coerced," Cora said. "Your father had been paying that amount to Gladys for years. He couldn't deny that Robert was his responsibility, so he paid for the support. Lord knows, Gladys can't go out and get a job like most folks. Who'd take care of her son then?"

"But Robert was Dad's responsibility," Carter pointed out. "I understand that you're just trying to be decent about this, but I think we can adjust the money you're giving her…"

"Stop it, Carter. I'm doing the right thing," Cora said. "I was married to Raymond for thirty-five years. My debt was his, and his were mine." Her gray eyes sparked with determination. "Don't you remember a couple of years back when the tree farm had a bug infestation? Your daddy covered the loss even though his name wasn't on the deed to that property. That's what married people do.

"I'm not saying your daddy and I had a perfect marriage, far from it, but he was doing right by Gladys and her boy, and I'm not about to leave them without means of support now just because I'm signing the checks instead of Raymond."

"But how long can you go on like this?" Ava asked.

"Until the well runs dry, I suppose."

"But Mama, you're giving up everything, letting the house go…"

"It's just a house, Ava. Timber and bricks. It'll stand a long time yet even if it doesn't look so pretty. That woman needs help now."

Ava placed her hands over her face and expelled a long breath into her palms. "Mama, when I start my new position with the children's home, maybe I can suggest an answer to this problem. There are files and references there about places that might be able to help Robert. Maybe we can find a resource to take the financial burden off you."

"I've already looked into it, Ava. Gladys gets help two mornings a week from a county worker who knows how to treat Robert. And any attempt to put Robert into a public school has been met with nothing but disaster." She shook her head. "He's your father's son and your half brother. We owe for that. Gladys loves the boy. She knows she's the best one to care for him." Cora straightened her spine. "I admire her for that. There may come a day, later, when Robert will have to go into some kind of care facility. When that happens, when he's of age, my responsibility will end. But for now..."

Carter knew his mother, and he wondered if she would ever believe that her responsibility to Robert was over.

"If you don't mind my asking," Ava said, "where's the money coming from that you're giving Gladys? It's fifteen hundred a month."

Cora's expression remained obstinate, and Carter thought she might not answer the question.

"I take it out of my profit shares from the paper mill. As long as Rudy keeps the plant running, I'll be okay. And just so you know, I've got a little put away for my own old age. And soon I'll get your daddy's Social Security money. Things will ease up then."

Ava rubbed her forehead with her fingertips. "Mama, it seems to me that you should be getting more than fifteen hundred a month from the mill."

"I get what I get," Cora said. "Things at the plant haven't been so great since your daddy died."

Ava's eyes clouded with concern, or perhaps it was suspicion. At any rate, Carter figured that she wasn't going to accept that explanation without checking further.

Cora stood. "I've got potato salad to make, so this conversation is over…"

"Hi, Miss Cora!" Emily raced into the kitchen. She stopped long enough to greet Carter and Ava, and then related all the news of her afternoon. "We went to church and talked to the minister. Law was there, and he's going to fix the playground equipment. And Mom says her work is done." Emily's smile faded. "I don't like that part."

"Where is your mother?" Carter asked.

"She went up to our room. She needs an aspirin or something."

Carter left the kitchen and headed for the stairs. His day was far from over.

CHAPTER NINETEEN

CARTER DIDN'T EVEN KNOCK. He ignored the little voice in his head that told him to calm down, take a breath. He opened the door to the room Miranda and Emily were using—his room—and walked inside. Miranda stood next to the window. She still wore the clothes she'd had on for the church visit this morning—a long skirt and a soft white cotton blouse. The sunlight streaming through the window created golden halos of her hair. When she turned to look at him, she took his breath away.

"What's wrong?" she said. "Is it Emily?"

"Emily's fine. And you know darn well what's wrong." He regretted his tone immediately. Miranda's eyes were moist. She'd been crying.

"No, Carter, I don't," she said.

How was he to tell her what was wrong when he couldn't explain it to himself? *I'm a coward. I'm afraid of losing you again. I'm afraid of my life falling apart for a third time. I want you to stay, but yet, I don't. I know you should go.* Of all the emotions warring inside him, he finally took a deep breath and said, "You were going to leave without saying goodbye."

She clenched her hands at her waist. "I would have said goodbye if I'd run into you. At the very least I would have called to thank you again for all you've done for Lawton. And for me."

Great. She would have called him. *Well, so long, Carter. Thanks again.*

She blinked hard. "The truth is, I just decided this morning that it was time for Em and me to go."

He didn't say anything. Just stood there mute and let her words wash over him. A stupid phone call maybe… The past and the present became one to Carter for a heart-stopping moment. *I never meant to hurt you. I have to go…* She was his Miranda. But she'd broken his heart fourteen years ago and was about to do it again. She was leaving…again. But he hadn't given her a reason to stay.

She took a step closer to him. "Are you all right? You look pale."

And you can't even see the pain deep inside, the part of me that is hidden well below my skin. "Stay a while longer, Miranda," he said. "Don't go on Wednesday. What difference will a few days make?" They were his words. He'd said them, and his mouth felt desert dry. If he said anything else, he was certain the words would crack coming from his lips and fall like dust to the floor. What was he offering her? A few more days of back-and-forth? Loving her and yet being afraid enough to let her go?

"That's just it," she said. "A few days won't make much difference, Carter. I will still be the girl who left you, the girl who married Donny. And nothing will change. I'll still be a package deal. Me and Em, and Donny is her father. And to tell the truth, Carter, every time you look at her you see Donny."

"That could change. I'm starting to get over it."

She smiled. "Maybe a bit, but it's not good enough. Emily deserves the best from you, and I know you have it to give. You're a good man, Carter, but maybe you'd have to be a saint to forget how messed up our history is. You don't want me. You don't trust me. And I can't offer you any guarantees. Life happens, and if I stayed a few days or a few years, there are no guarantees that happiness will follow us into the future."

She sighed, ran her fingers through her loose hair. "I admit there were times in the last few weeks that I thought… I hoped… But you were right not to encourage me. And now that I'm seeing everything more clearly, I'm right to take my daughter and go."

He walked to her and cradled her hands in his. "I've been a fool not to admit what your coming here has meant to me, Miranda. But I can't let my fear determine my life. I want to give this a chance. Stay a while. Just a while." His thumbs lightly caressed her knuckles. "It's too soon for us to give up. Let's see if this could work."

She stared at their joined hands. "Maybe now I'm the one who can't risk a broken heart, Carter. And the only way to do that is to leave."

He raised his hands and settled them on

each side of her face. He kissed her, a soft, gentle press of his lips. "I will always care about you, Miranda. I've never stopped."

She smiled again, and he tried to trap the memory of her beautiful face in his heart. "I…" she paused. "I care for you, too. But that's not enough, is it?"

He kissed her forehead before returning to her soft lips and kissing her with all the frustration and desire warring in his soul. Why couldn't he take her in his arms and just admit he loved her?

"Mama's making dinner," he said. "If this is the way it's going to be, then it's best that I don't stay."

He left the bedroom, closing the door quietly behind him. He didn't know when he would be able to enter that room again without thinking of what he'd lost.

"DOES LAWTON KNOW we're coming, Mom?" Emily watched out the window on Tuesday evening as Miranda turned onto Liggett Mountain Road.

"Yes. I called his cell phone and told him we wanted to stop by tonight."

"Did you tell him we're leaving tomorrow?"

"No. I'll wait until we're there to tell him that." Miranda paused to see if Emily would once again express her regret at leaving. She merely sighed. "I want to thank you for all your help packing today, Em," Miranda said. "All that's left now is to throw in our jammies and jump in the car."

"You're welcome." The words had the same enthusiasm as if Emily had said, "I'm ready to go to the gallows now."

Miranda pulled into the gravel space that marked Mr. McNulty's cabin. Lawton's old Dodge sat in the narrow one-car lot, so Miranda drove around to the side of the cabin and parked. Emily got out and ran to the front door.

"Hey there, pretty girl," Lawton said from his door.

"Mom brought chicken wings, Lawton," Emily said. "And french fries."

"That sounds mighty good," Law said, waving at Miranda, who approached with a restaurant carry-out bag. "You didn't have to do that, peanut," he said. "I could have offered y'all salami sandwiches."

"Want me to throw out these wings, then?" she teased.

"Not on your life." He moved aside so the ladies could come in. He had on a nice pair of jeans and a plaid shirt that made him look as respectable as any citizen of Holly River. He'd gained weight, and working in the outdoors at the tree farm had brought color to his cheeks. His journey back was almost complete.

Miranda hadn't been in the cabin since she'd added a few cozy touches to it. She was pleased to see that the living room was tidy, the floors free of dust. Each time she witnessed Lawton taking pride in himself was like a salve to her heart.

"What brings you out here?" Lawton asked. "Not that I'm complaining, you understand. Haven't had any visitors yet."

"I'm hoping that will change, Law." Miranda sat on the sofa. "I hope you'll make friends with the volunteers at the playground this Saturday."

"That would be a welcome change around here," he said.

"As for why we've come tonight, Emily and I are here to tell you goodbye."

"What? You're not leaving?"

"You know our stay was only temporary," Miranda explained. "You're doing well now. I'm so proud of you. You've come a long way since that first day I saw you up the mountain when you were living with Dale."

Lawton nodded. "Still I hate to see you go, 'Randa. I feel almost as close to you as when we were kids. You've seen me through every step. Wish there was some way I could thank you."

"You'll thank me every day you move forward in your journey, Law. That's all the thanks I'll ever need."

"When are you going?"

Miranda swallowed. "Tomorrow. Em and I are driving back to Durham in the morning. But I'll call you, every week or more often if you need to talk to me. And you can come to Durham and visit."

"I'd like that."

"I don't want to go," Emily said from a rocking chair where she'd settled.

Lawton smiled. "You kind of like the mountains now, eh?"

"I do. Mom doesn't even know when we'll

come back again. Maybe when I'm older I can come and visit you, Lawton."

"That'd be fine with me," Lawton said. "Would you gals like some lemonade?"

Emily jumped up from the rocker. "I'll get it!" She darted into the kitchen just as the sound of a car engine interrupted the peace of the evening.

"Who could that be?" Lawton went to the window and looked out. "It's Dale," he said, his shoulders stiffening and his voice dropping.

Inside Miranda's head an alarm warned her of danger. She reached her hand inside her purse and found her cell phone. "Did you know he was coming?"

"No. I know he's been hiding out somewhere, avoiding the cops. He slipped through Carter's fingers since Sheila and Allie were arrested. But my cabin is the last place I figured he'd come. He's never been here before, but I expect he knows he's in a heap of trouble, now that the stolen goods have been found."

Miranda took her phone out and palmed it. "You mean the garden equipment Carter has been tracking down?"

"Yeah. He found it yesterday."

She squeezed the phone more tightly in her hand. "Did you have anything to do with Carter finding that stuff, Law?"

He gave her a hard stare and hunched his shoulders.

"Oh, I see." She backed up to the kitchen door, opened it a crack and tossed the phone inside to Emily, just as Dale rushed into the cabin. "Run to the woods, Em," she said in a whisper. "Call Carter." One glance showed her that Emily hadn't moved. "Go now!" Emily picked up the phone and darted out the back.

"Well, well," Dale said, eyeing his brother and cousin. Miranda couldn't take her eyes off the pistol cradled in the palm of his hand.

"If it isn't the ex-con and the do-gooder," Dale said with contempt. "I'd only expected to find one of you, but it looks like I got a bonus."

"What are you doing with the gun, Dale?" Lawton said. "Put it down."

Dale flexed his hand on the butt of the pistol. Miranda noted that his white T-shirt was covered in grass stains above his hip-hugging jeans. His ball cap was backward on his head, barely keeping long strands of hair from obstructing his vision. She decided Lawton was right. Dale had been hiding out in the brush where Carter couldn't find him.

"I thought I might do some hunting, little brother," Dale said "And lucky for me I found just what I was looking for. I might need a little help from you, though, in the next couple days."

"You're not gonna shoot me, Dale," Lawton said.

"You think not? It'd be what you deserve, Lawton," Dale answered. "But first we're going to have a little talk." He waved the pistol at Miranda. "You sit down, cousin, and have a listen, because I have a hunch you deserve a big portion of the blame in this deal. Everything would have worked out just fine if you hadn't showed up."

"That's not true, Dale," she said. "Lawton is a different man from the kid brother you influenced all your life. He wouldn't have helped you in any of your get-rich-quick schemes."

Dale stared at her until she was forced to close her eyes for a moment to block his menacing expression. "I believe I told you to sit, Miranda."

She went to the sofa and clasped her hands to keep them from shaking. She glanced at the kitchen door and prayed that Emily had run far and fast.

BETSY HAD STAYED at the station an hour later than usual to finish up with some filing. She grabbed her purse and sweater and was just about to turn the phones over to the night service when a call came through.

"Holly River Police," she answered.

"This is county dispatch. I've got someone on the line who called 911 with an emergency. Sounds like a child. She insists on speaking to Chief Cahill."

"He's out on patrol," Betsy said. "You don't think this is a crank call, do you?"

"Sounds serious to me," the dispatcher said.

"I'll put you through to the chief." A moment later, Betsy said, "Hold, Carter, for a 911 call. Person only wants to talk to you."

Betsy put her things back in her drawer and settled in for a while. She had to know what was going on and if she could be of any assistance. "Hope nothing's wrong with a young'un," she said and straightened her desk.

CARTER CONNECTED HIS radio to the incoming call. "This is Chief Cahill."

"Carter, it's…" The small voice began to crack. "It's me, Emily."

Carter felt the blood rush from his head. He gripped the radio. "What's wrong, Emily? Where are you?"

"We're at cousin Lawton's, but there's trouble…" She took a deep breath and tried to talk through her sobs.

"I'm headed there right now," Carter said, estimating his travel time at about ten minutes. "Keep talking to me, honey. Tell me what you can."

"Dale is here. He's inside with Mom and Lawton. I'm outside, but I heard him through the back door. I heard…" She coughed, sputtered out the rest. "I heard Lawton say he has a gun."

Carter stepped on the accelerator and turned on his bar lights. The countryside flashed by his window in a blur of green.

"Where are you now, Emily? Tell me as exactly as you can."

"Mom told me to run into the woods, and that's where I am now. But I can still see the cabin."

"Okay. That's good." Carter wondered if Emily could hear his words over the pounding in his chest. "Here's what I want you to do, honey. Go farther into the woods and find the biggest tree you can. Hide behind it, and don't look back at the cabin. You understand? Look straight into the woods only. I'll find you."

"O…okay. I see a really big one."

"Crouch down now, Em. Stay as low to the ground as you can. Just keep talking to me. I'll be there in a few minutes. Everything's going to be okay."

Carter felt his face twist into an agony of uncertainty. How many times had rescue workers said that same thing to people in danger? And how many times had they unintentionally lied? *Please, God*, he prayed, *don't let this be one of those times*.

NONE OF MIRANDA'S training had prepared her for this situation. *Stay calm*, she kept admonishing herself. *Do not give Dale a reason to raise that pistol.* Except for one attempt to persuade Dale that Lawton had changed, she'd remained quiet, letting him vent his anger on Lawton. Maybe the blood connection would keep Lawton safe. Maybe Dale would realize that he didn't want to harm either of them, and that Lawton couldn't help him out of this latest jam. They were family after all.

"How many times did I tell you, Lawton, that the people of this town don't care about you or me or any of the Jeffersons?" Dale said, turning to Miranda. "I hear someone targeted your fancy new car, 'Randa. Guess you're not excluded from us Jeffersons just because you moved. Everybody here has been out to get us from day one."

"Nobody's out to get us, Dale," Lawton said. "We just have to prove ourselves to the people of this town and everything will be all right."

"You live in a dream world, Lawton. Always have." He raised his voice to an annoyingly high pitch. "Sweet little Lawton and his do-gooder cousin, trying to make us Jeffersons fit in. Well, it didn't work, did it?

And now you turn on the only kin you've got left on this godforsaken mountain."

"I didn't turn on you, Dale," Lawton said. "I don't know what you're talking about."

"You can lie to 'Randa, brother. You can lie to the whole dang town, but I know better. Carter would've never found that plot behind Sheila's if you hadn't clued him in."

Dale's voice lowered, almost in regret. "I would have cut you in, you dang fool. You could have had more money than you ever dreamed of without giving me up to Carter and others who think they're so high and mighty compared to us."

Lawton took a step closer to Dale. Dale raised the pistol, aimed it at his brother. "Put the gun down, Dale," Lawton said, stopping in his tracks. "You're mad. I get that, but nobody is trying to hurt you, least of all, me."

Dale shifted his hand to the barrel of the weapon, stroking the metal almost lovingly. "How'd you find out about the field, Law? How'd you know that Sheila and I were fixing to grow a fine crop of marijuana?"

"I didn't know anything about that," Lawton said. "And if I had, I wouldn't have turned you in. You know that. We're brothers."

Dale took a deep, shuddering breath. "I never thought I'd see the day when you would lie to my face." He shifted his attention to Miranda. "I suppose this holier-than-thou cousin changed you when you got out of prison. She poisoned you against me."

"You're wrong, Dale," Miranda said at last. She would try one last attempt at reasoning with Dale. "My visit was only about helping Lawton, not turning him against you. You're every bit my cousin as much as Lawton is. Put the gun down before it's too late."

Dale chuckled. "You'd like that, wouldn't you, 'Randa? Too bad, but I've got this sorted." He held the gun up, showing the complete profile of the piston. "Recognize this, Law? This here is your pistol, the one our daddy taught you to shoot with." He ran his finger over the pearlized butt. "See your initials right here? You carved them yourself. I kept this gun for you, Law, knowing you'd want it again someday. But now it's too late. You went against me, Lawton. You made your choice. Now I'm making mine. If you don't agree to get me out of town, you'll be sorry Daddy ever gave you this pistol."

Miranda knew that if Dale shot his brother, there was no way she would walk out of this cabin alive. Maybe Dale hadn't expected to find her here, but now that he had, he couldn't let her go. She thought of Emily and prayed she would be safe. She thought of Donny and said a prayer that he would take care of their little girl. She thought of her mother, Carter… The people she loved presented a kaleidoscope of emotion in her mind. She didn't want to leave them.

"Now that Miranda's here, I have to change my plans. I'm going to make it look like you killed our cousin and then ran from this cabin. No one will doubt it. You've been down on your luck since prison, working for the Cahills at that tree farm and now just a grease monkey at a garage over in Pine Grove.

"You've let Miranda decide your future. It's true, isn't it, Law? You could have been so much more if you'd stuck with me. Easy money, clean hands. That's what I could have offered you. But now…" He tapped the barrel of the gun against his palm. "Anything you'd like to say, Miranda?"

She swallowed, shook her head, felt tears sting her eyes. She couldn't have spoken if she'd found the words. A sob tore from her throat, the only sound breaking the awful silence in the cabin. Dale toyed with them both, like a panther with his prey. Two phrases echoed in her mind. *I love you, Em. I love you, Carter.* She closed her eyes against the coming blast, the one that would tear into her heart.

WHEN HE GOT close to Liggett Mountain, Carter cut his siren and lights and parked on the road in front of the McNulty place so his engine wouldn't be heard. He walked carefully to the cabin, mindful of every branch in his path. As he made his way to the front door, he saw Dale's Jeep blocking Lawton's car in the one parking space. He looked left and right, hoping he wouldn't see Emily. Thank God it appeared she'd done what he asked her.

Sam was on his way, but he might not make it in time. Carter might be the only person standing between life and death for the people in the cabin. He drew his weapon, a Glock 19 with fifteen rounds. He'd never aimed it at a human being, the targets at the driving range being the only practice he'd had in shooting at human anatomy. He'd always hoped it wouldn't come to this in Holly River, a quiet, peaceful little town.

He heard Dale's voice when he stepped onto the porch. He was threatening Miranda, ordering her onto the floor. Carter's blood turned to ice at the same time his instincts spurred him to act. Through the window in the door he watched as Dale raised his firearm and aimed it at Miranda's chest. She clutched her arms over her breasts, squeezed her eyes shut.

Carter burst through the door, aimed his Glock at Dale's back and hollered four words. "Police. Drop the weapon."

The events of the next seconds were a blur. Yet each of the three people in the room would tell it the same way. Lawton stretched out his arms and leaped in front of Miranda. She screamed. Lawton moaned as a bullet from Dale's pistol pierced his shoulder. Carter fired, hitting Dale in the spine. He dropped, writhing in agony.

Carter kicked Dale's gun across the room before ensuring that Dale was incapacitated. His eyes had rolled back in his head, but he was breathing. Lawton sat in the middle of the room, his hand over his wound, blood spilling down his arm. Miranda had crumpled to the floor, but she hadn't been hit.

Carter holstered his weapon and used his radio to call for two ambulances. He then went to Lawton. "I'm okay," he said. "See to Miranda."

Carter went down on his knees and pulled Miranda to his chest. He felt her sobs all the way to his heart. "It's okay, baby. You're okay. It's over." He smoothed her hair, her cheeks, and wiped tears from under her eyes.

Miranda hiccupped and gained enough control to whisper, "Emily."

"She's okay," Carter said. "She's a smart kid. She called 911 and asked to speak to me. When we connected, she did exactly what I told her."

Miranda seemed to melt in his arms.

Sam bounded up the porch steps and into the house. "Wow…" he breathed. "What happened here?"

Carter jerked his thumb toward the back entrance to the cabin. "Emily's out there in the woods," he said. "Find her, Sam. She'll be by one of the large trees. Bring her to your car. Tell her that her mom is okay, but don't let her come inside."

Miranda trembled violently, and Carter feared she might be going into shock. He pulled a blanket from the sofa, wrapped her in it and rocked her back and forth. "Thank God, honey, you're okay. I don't know what I would have done if something had happened to you."

She dragged a finger under her nose and sniffed. "You know what I was thinking when that gun was aimed at me?" she said.

He shook his head, laid her damp cheek against his neck. He couldn't get her close enough.

"I was thinking that I love you," she said. "Maybe now's not the time to say it, but you should know."

He whispered against the top of her head. "I'm thinking I love you, too, baby."

She disentangled herself from his arms enough to look into his face. "Got to see about Lawton," she breathed. "He saved my life."

Carter let her go. She crawled over to her cousin, bent and kissed his forehead. "Thank you, Law," she said. "All those years as I was growing up, you protected me and kept me safe, and you're doing it still."

He smiled through his pain, raised his good arm to her shoulder. "Didn't I tell you I wanted to find a way to thank you?"

"You did that in fine style," she said. "Now all I want is for you to live your life and be happy because you made sure I had a chance to live mine today."

She glanced back at Carter. The look of love she gave him was as sweet and special as the love she gave him fourteen years ago, but now they had another chance. He hoped the love in his own eyes found a way straight to her heart because this time they would make it work.

CHAPTER TWENTY

AT NEARLY MIDNIGHT at Mainland Hospital in Holly River, Miranda sat in a stiff armchair by Lawton's bed, where she'd been since he came up from surgery two hours ago. Cora had come to take Emily back to the house. Miranda thanked her but explained she couldn't let her go just yet. So Emily slept in a recliner a few feet from her mother, and Miranda watched both people who meant so much to her.

Lawton stirred, moaned softly. Miranda soothed him by gently rubbing her hand down his arm below the heavy bandage on his shoulder.

"Miranda?" he said.

"It's me, Law. You're in the hospital. I don't know if you remember coming here. You sort of took a nap for a while."

He tried to move his arm, winced in pain. "What...? What did the doctors do?"

"Stitched you up once they removed the bullet. You're going to be fine. In fact, they may let you go home tomorrow unless you're having too much pain."

He raised his elbow slightly, but gave up and dropped his head back to the pillow. Miranda positioned an IV control so it was closer to his strong arm. "You have a button here that eases the pain when you press it. But don't overdue."

His brow furrowed. "My job, 'Randa. I just got that job."

"Don't worry," she said. "Your boss, Mack Benjamin, was in to see you tonight. As a matter of fact, you've had a few visitors. Seems like word of your heroism spread pretty fast in Holly River."

"What did Max say?"

"He said you should rest up. Your job will be waiting for you when you feel up to it."

Lawton ran his tongue over his lips. "You said I had a few visitors?"

"Yeah. You know how a small town works. Once one person hears about something, it's part of the grapevine. The head of that volunteer group you signed up for with

Reverend Babbitt brought you flowers, great big sunflowers."

"Flowers? For me?"

"Absolutely. And Cora Cahill was here. She brought cookies. But you can't have any tonight."

Lawton pressed the morphine button, and a smile settled on his face. "That's better already."

Miranda lifted a glass to his mouth so he could sip water through a straw.

"What about Dale?" he said after a few minutes.

"He's currently in surgery in Boone. They didn't want to attempt such a spinal operation in Holly River, so they had him airlifted to the regional hospital. He'll probably recover."

Lawton sighed. "Okay. Good."

Miranda couldn't help marveling at the loyalty among brothers. Not that Dale would have shown such compassion for Lawton, but Law was just a different type of person from Dale.

"What will happen to him then?" Law asked.

"I expect he's going to prison for a long

time," Miranda said. "He was conscious when they put him in the ambulance, and in his dazed state he admitted to more than just attempting to kill us. He said he was the one who vandalized my car, and, of course, he was responsible for the robberies in town."

"It's a good thing Carter came when he did," Lawton said.

"Yes, it was a good thing." She kept her gaze on Lawton as his eyelids fluttered.

She knew Carter had entered the hospital room even before his hand settled on the back of her neck. She turned to see his face, reached up and covered his hand with hers.

Carter smiled at Emily in the recliner. "All the thanks go to that little girl over there."

Lawton opened his eyes, and cleared his throat. "Folks around here say that you've never fired your weapon, Carter. Is that true?"

"Not anymore," he said. "It's one thing to be nice to folks while you're trying to live down a bad reputation left over from your daddy. It's another to be able to use force when necessary to protect the people who depend on you. Especially…" His voice fell silent and his hand tightened on Miranda's nape. "I'm just glad I was there."

Miranda smoothed the covers on Lawton's bed. "You sleep now, Law. The rest will do wonders for you. You'll feel much better in the morning." She beamed. "I love you, cousin."

His eyes fluttered and closed, but she heard his mumbled response. "Love you more, peanut."

Carter took her elbow and helped her rise from the chair. "You should go home and get some sleep yourself. I'll drive you…"

"I guess you'll have to. My car is still at Law's. Will you carry Em to your car?"

"It would be an honor," he said.

Miranda didn't think her heart could swell with emotion any more than it had in the cabin. But the caring in Carter's eyes almost did her in. She let her tired body sink against his. He put his arm tightly around her.

"You okay?" he asked.

"I'm better than okay," she said, standing straight. His support had made her strong.

Carter lifted Emily and cradled her against his chest as if she were a baby. When they reached his car, he put Em in the backseat and helped Miranda slide into the front. They drove the dark road to Cora's in silence, each lost in their own thoughts. When they reached the turn to Hidden Creek Road, Carter coughed into his hand. "I lied to you yesterday, Miranda."

She shrugged and smiled. "You did? What did you lie about, Carter?"

"I said I wanted you to stay in Holly River for a while."

She studied his strong profile. "You mean you don't want me to stay?"

"Oh, I do," he said. "But not for a while. I want you to stay forever—you and that little girl back there. I want you to be a part of my life. I want you to live in my house and chase away the shadows that fill my nights whenever I walk in the door. I'll even make up with Donny. I want you to be my wife just like we always thought would happen."

Miranda stroked his arm as he drove. "Nothing can be like it was when we were kids, Carter. You've had a past. I've had a past. What we dreamed about back then won't be our reality now. We're different people."

He glanced over at her, his eyes moist.

She'd never seen him cry. This was a day of firsts for Carter Cahill, maybe the day when he finally could admit to the world that he was nothing like his cold, contemptuous father.

"My dream was only to have you by my side," he said. "I'll take that dream now and know that I'm the luckiest man alive. Everything else will fall into place." He squeezed her thigh. "Take the journey with me, Miranda."

She raised his hand to her lips and softly kissed his fingers. "To the bank of Holly River or the ends of the earth, I will, I promise."

EPILOGUE

CARTER ADJUSTED JACE'S TIE. "That's better."

"Good thing you're dressing the best man instead of the other way around," Jace quipped. "You'd end up looking like a hobo who just jumped off a freight train. I can't remember the last time I wore a tie."

"Have I told you I'm proud of you, little brother?" Carter said. "You're holding up pretty well considering this has been a month of revelations for you."

"You're not kidding. You back with Miranda Jefferson. I never thought that would happen."

"And you're okay with it," Carter added.

"Of course. I never had anything against Miranda until she left you with your bleeding heart messing up the entire house. In fact, I always thought she was good for you. And that Emily…" Jace chuckled. "She's about the cutest thing I've ever seen."

"Was that confirmed bachelor Jace Cahill who just said that?"

"I can be a confirmed bachelor and a favorite uncle at the same time," he said.

Carter smiled. "And I'll bet she'll be a great older sister someday."

"You've got some important plans, brother," Jace said. "I'd better brush up on my uncle-ing."

"Yeah, and it's a change for me. Two months ago, I wandered through my life without a thought as to what the next day might bring. I just figured it would be the same as today. Now I'll soon have a wife, a stepchild…"

"Don't forget a half brother," Jace added.

Carter recalled the day he'd told Jace about their father's infidelity. Jace had taken the news almost as if he'd expected such behavior from the man he'd grown up avoiding. "The man just lit fires and left the charred remains in his wake his whole life," Jace had said.

Jace's reaction to learning of Robert Kirshner had been unexpected. Jace had vowed the day he heard about the autistic boy that he wanted to meet Robert, establish a relationship with him if the boy wanted. Carter had seen a new side to his brother in that spark of family compassion that he'd always believed Jace avoided. Jace would probably still lead his life with no strings attached, but maybe their half brother would open Jace's eyes to that old saying that no man is an island.

"I suppose you and Ava haven't talked Mama into letting us help her out with some of her expenses," Jace said.

Carter grinned. "I'd have just as much luck trying to talk a hurricane out of hitting the coast. We just have to believe that Mama will be fine, and as long as she's got the three of us, she will be."

"Aren't you dudes ready to go yet?"

Carter and Jace turned toward the voice of Sam McCall, the one and only groomsman at the intimate wedding.

"Woo-hoo, will you look at Sam McCall," Jace said. "It's not as if all the women in this town didn't chase after you already. Now you're making me look like the pathetic best man."

Sam stood in front of a mirror and slicked his copper hair back with the palm of his hand. "I do look darn sharp, if I do say so myself."

Sam talked a good game, but Carter knew he hadn't recovered yet from discovering that Allie was involved with Dale Jefferson's illegal pot field. Sam had said he wouldn't trust her again, and that was just as well. Sheila and Allie had made bail thanks to Allie's mother, and despite Carter's claim that they were flight risks, both women had immediately run off. Carter had chased them across the state line, but by now they were probably so far away from North Carolina that they were dipping their toes in the Pacific Ocean. Maybe Sheila was bartending. Maybe Allie was a waitress in another café. Or maybe they were both hoping to hook up with another man who didn't mind being on the wrong side of the law. Sam would be okay in time. As Carter knew, a broken heart took a long while to heal.

"Let's get this done," Carter said, hooking his arms over the shoulders of his closest companions.

Jace laughed. "We don't want you changing your mind, bro."

"Not a chance."

They walked into the sanctuary, taking their places in front of the altar. Reverend Babbitt stood with the wedding service book in his hands. Lawton Jefferson, his arm now fully recovered, walked Cora to her place in the front pew before going back for Miranda's mother.

Carter looked at the friends gathered. People he'd known his whole life, people he'd tried to treat fairly, people he'd helped along the way. Carter had always set his sights on being a good cop, and today he thought maybe he'd achieved that. And so much more.

Donny Larson was there. Carter and he had shared a beer the night before, and Carter was glad Donny had come to the service today. Holding a grudge wasn't the way to lead a decent life.

And then Ava appeared, her dark hair piled in a cascade of curls shining in the candlelight. She was stunning in an ice-blue knee-length dress that showed off her beautiful eyes. Ava would soon be joining the rest of the family in Holly River.

Next was Emily, blonde and pretty and sweet as a spring breeze. Her matching blue dress reached the floor. She carried her head high and a bouquet of purple tulips at her waist. She smiled at Carter, and his breath quaked with love.

And finally the wedding march signaled the beginning of Carter's new life. Miranda's hand was tucked into her cousin's elbow as she walked slowly toward her husband-to-be. Lawton looked proud. Miranda looked angelic in a cloud of white with an ice-blue sash at her waist. There would be pictures later, but Carter wanted to remember this moment in time forever, just as he was living it now.

Miranda reached the altar. Carter took her hand and turned toward the reverend. But his eyes saw only the beauty of the face of the woman he'd always loved.

* * * * *

Get 2 Free Books,
Plus 2 Free Gifts—
just for trying the Reader Service!

Get 2 Free Books,
Plus 2 Free Gifts—
just for trying the
Reader Service!

HOME on the RANCH

YES! Please send me the **Home on the Ranch Collection** in Larger Print. This collection begins with 3 FREE books and 2 FREE gifts in the first shipment. Along with my 3 free books, I'll also get the next 4 books from the Home on the Ranch Collection, in LARGER PRINT, which I may either return and owe nothing, or keep for the low price of $5.24 U.S./ $5.89 CDN each plus $2.99 for shipping and handling per shipment*. If I decide to continue, about once a month for 8 months I will get 6 or 7 more books, but will only need to pay for 4. That means 2 or 3 books in every shipment will be FREE! If I decide to keep the entire collection, I'll have paid for only 32 books because 19 books are FREE! I understand that accepting the 3 free books and gifts places me under no obligation to buy anything. I can always return a shipment and cancel at any time. My free books and gifts are mine to keep no matter what I decide.

268 HCN 3760 468 HCN 3760

Name	(PLEASE PRINT)	
Address		Apt. #
City	State/Prov.	Zip/Postal Code

Signature (if under 18, a parent or guardian must sign)

Mail to the **Reader Service**:

IN U.S.A.: P.O. Box 1867, Buffalo, NY. 14240-1867
IN CANADA: P.O. Box 609, Fort Erie, Ontario L2A 5X3

* Terms and prices subject to change without notice. Prices do not include applicable taxes. Sales tax applicable in NY. Canadian residents will be charged applicable taxes. This offer is limited to one order per household. All orders subject to approval. Credit or debit balances in a customer's account(s) may be offset by any other outstanding balance owed by or to the customer. Please allow 3 to 4 weeks for delivery. Offer available while quantities last. Offer not available to Quebec residents.

HRCBPA18

Get 2 Free Books,
Plus 2 Free Gifts—
just for trying the Reader Service!

READERSERVICE.COM

Manage your account online!

- Review your order history
- Manage your payments
- Update your address

> *We've designed the*
> *Reader Service website*
> *just for you.*

Enjoy all the features!

- Discover new series available to you, and read excerpts from any series.
- Respond to mailings and special monthly offers.
- Browse the Bonus Bucks catalog and online-only exclusives.
- Share your feedback.

Visit us at:
ReaderService.com